THE LEGEND OF SKYCO

SPIRIT QUEST

Jennifer Frick-Ruppert
Amberjack Publishing
New York, New York

Amberjack Publishing
228 Park Avenue S #89611
New York, NY 10003-1502
http://amberjackpublishing.com

The characters and events portrayed in this book, while based in history, are used fictitiously. Apart from well-known historical figures and events, any similarity to real persons, living or dead, is purely coincidental and not intended by the author.

Publisher's Cataloging-in-Publication data
Names: Frick-Ruppert, Jennifer, author.
Title: The Legend of Skyco : spirit quest / by Jennifer Frick-Ruppert.
Description: New York, NY: Amberjack Publishing, 2016.
Identifiers: ISBN 978-1-944995-11-9 (hardcover.) | 978-1-944995-17-1 (ebook) | LCCN 2016951831
Summary: Skyco, an Algonquin boy, must learn how to hunt, fish, start a fire, and communicate with the spirits before he can take his place as the tribe's chief.
Subjects: LCSH Algonquin Indians--Juvenile fiction. | Algonquian Indians--Juvenile fiction. | Indians of North America--Juvenile fiction. | Spirits--Fiction. | Wilderness survival--Fiction. | BISAC JUVENILE FICTION / People & Places / United States / Native American.
Classification: LCC PZ7.F89582 Le 2016 | DDC [Fic]--dc23

Cover Design: Red Couch Creative
Artwork & Illustrations: Lorna Murphy
Historical sketches ©The Trustees of the British Museum. All rights reserved.

Note to Readers

Spirit Quest is a work of fiction, and while it is inspired by real historical events, many aspects of this book are products of the author's mind.

The Raid

THWACK! THE ARROW struck the tree directly behind me. I ducked involuntarily even though it was too late. The arrow was already vibrating in the tree, just above my left shoulder. A few inches more to the right and it would have hit me.

The narrow miss wasn't the worst of it, however. As I withdrew into the bushes, trying to hide from whoever had just shot at me, a powerful hand reached out and grabbed my ankle, jerking me to the ground. I struggled and kicked, but felt a heavy, muscular body fall on top of me, pinning me flat. It was no use screaming, even though I wanted to. We were on a war raid and a scream could only bring more enemies.

As silently as I could, I tried to twist out from underneath but could hardly move under the smothering weight. Tree roots ground into my back, and I could barely draw a breath because the man's entire mass rested directly on my chest. I squeezed my eyes shut, thinking I should try one big effort to buck him off me, but then I heard a familiar voice whisper into my ear, "Be still, Skyco. It is I, Roncommock."

I quieted instantly at the sound of his voice. When I stilled and relaxed my body, he released me, rising up off my chest, rocking back, and settling into a crouch. I rolled over quietly and imitated his stealthy moves, although a little less gracefully. A branch of musclewood, as tough as its name implied, scratched my shoulder while another poked me in the ribs.

"Now follow me, quietly. Keep your head low. We must make our escape before the enemy warrior arrives. He will surely come after us."

We wiggled through narrow breaks in the rough, bushy scrub of musclewood, arrowwood, persimmon, and blueberries. Soon, we emerged into a meadow of longleaf pines and tall grasses. The small bushes disappeared.

Roncommock darted among the majestic trees, pausing briefly to scan for the enemy warrior before dashing to the next big trunk. The tall trees, as straight as an Algonquin's back, were so wide that two warriors could not encircle one with their outstretched arms, and they concealed Roncommock completely. The grasses were so high, and we crouched down so low, that I would never have seen him running between the trees if I hadn't already been following his movements. We made our way quickly from tree to tree, protecting ourselves behind the dark trunks or dashing through the pale grass, always heading back toward our territory but alert for the enemy warrior we presumed was tracking us. Once out of this longleaf pine meadow, we would be much safer.

This meadow was the no-man's land between our tribe and the Mangoaks. We were Algonquin and shared the same language, called Algonquian, with most of the other nearby tribes. The Mangoaks, however, were different. They spoke another tongue and were fearsome warriors. Since their speech just sounded like hissing to us, and they were as mean as snakes, we called them the rattlesnake people.

The meadow was also a land of reptiles. As we neared the edge of the meadow and I dropped my guard a little, thinking we were almost home free, I nearly stepped on a huge snake, which, thankfully, was not one of the deadly rattlesnakes. It was a strange half-colored snake, its front-end nearly black and back-end much lighter, almost white. It was skinny and long, longer than I was tall, and it raised its head off the ground until it was looking in my eye. I was so startled that I let out a little yelp, jumping backwards and straightening up from my half-crouch.

As I jerked back from the menacing snake, I heard the *thwack* of another arrow, quivering now from its impact in the tree beside me. Once again, the arrow was barely off target, a little too far to the left. It had to be the same warrior, drawing his shots to the left like that. I saw Roncommock break from cover, waving me onward while drawing attention to himself like a grouse protecting its young. I needed no encouragement, but broke into a hard run straight for the forest edge where it gave way to a dense *pocosin,* full of dark shrubs and vines, which marked our nation's boundary. If I could reach it safely, I just might survive this day.

I heard another arrow whiz over my head, but from the opposite direction. Roncommock was defending me, shooting back toward the pursuing enemy. I thought I heard a groan from somewhere behind me, but wasn't sure, and didn't dare slow down or turn my head to look back. My heart was beating so fast that its sound deafened me to much else.

I dove into the *pocosin* at Roncommock's feet.

"You are safe now, little one. I struck the one who was tracking you. He will not be missing to the left anymore," Roncommock chuckled confidently. "You are lucky that he was not with the main war party. That is probably because the only thing he can hit is a tree. Always pulling to the left!"

I stood up, relaxing now that I was safe, and had to agree that I was lucky. Roncommock, however, wasn't finished teasing me.

"I am surprised you didn't whack your head on an overhanging branch back there. I have never seen anyone leap straight up off the ground the way you did when you saw that snake! It would make a good move for our next dance. Do you think you could teach the others? The snake jump?"

He chuckled again and my face felt a little warm from embarrassment. "Now, snake dancer, have you learned your lessons well enough to lead us back to our village?"

"Yes, I think I can," I replied. "This *pocosin* marks the western edge of our boundary. We should head east back to the village." I pursed my lips and took my bearings by looking at the sun's position in the sky. "*That* way," I indicated with my hand. "The sun has not yet reached its zenith. It lies in the direction we must travel."

"Well done, Skyco. That is why you have come on this raid, to learn our territory and its boundaries." Roncommock clucked like a mother bird indulging a feisty chick. "Lead on!"

Rather than cutting through the dense bush of the *pocosin,* which is a wet swampy area surrounded by thick shrubs and tangled vines, we skirted along its edge. I recognized that many vines were grape vines, which would soon bear the sweet, dark grapes that my mother liked to pick and squeeze into juice for us to drink. More common, though, were the green-briers, with thorns as long as one of my fingernails. They wrapped among the shrubs of musclewood and arrowwood like green snakes, binding them all together. Trying to push through that *pocosin* would be unpleasant. It was an effective barrier. I'd even heard stories about men getting trapped by the green-briers, entangled by the vines and impaled by the thorns until they could no longer move. Looking at the thick, tangled mess of vines and branches, I could believe the stories.

As we walked along, unwinding now that we were

back on our own territory, I felt the tension draining out of my body as my muscles relaxed. My first war raid was over, but I had nearly been shot! Considering my predicament, I began to worry about returning to the village. My mother would not be pleased, and I felt sure that her brother, Chief Menatonon, would hear of it as soon as we returned.

I was daydreaming about the recent past and worrying about the future, when I heard a snorting, snuffling sound that yanked me back to reality. I stopped dead in my tracks and extended my hand down and out to the side to signal Roncommock to stop as well. There was hardly any breeze, but our scent might be drifting out ahead of us, especially since we were sweaty from the raid and our close escape.

Roncommock quietly eased up beside me, shoulder-to-shoulder. Without speaking, I gestured to where I'd heard the sound and made the signal for "bear," but hesitantly. I wasn't certain. It was just a soft sound of exhaled breath, not like the sharp grunt of exhalation that I have sometimes heard from a startled deer. I'd never heard a bear sound before, but it had been described by some of the hunters when I was listening to them around the campfire.

Roncommock nocked an arrow in his bow and was creeping slowly around the *pocosin's* edge, when suddenly a huge black shape hurtled out at him. One moment there was nothing there, the next, a great bear was abreast of him, black and furred, rearing upright on its massive hind legs to tower over him while aggressively clacking its teeth. Before Roncommock could even take a shot, the bear swatted him with its colossal paw and claws, knocking him flat. A big gust of air forced its way out as he hit the ground, lifting a puff of dirt and dead leaves into the air.

This menacing giant must be the wily old bear that the hunters spoke of, the one rumored to live in the borderland between different tribes, where, fearing attack from hostile warriors, few men dared to hunt. He was enormous and as black as a moonless night.

In the terror of the moment, I realized that I had nothing in my hands, not even a rock to throw, so I did the only thing I could think of. I stood up on my tiptoes, raised my arms above my head, took a deep breath, and roared. Rather than continue mauling

Roncommock with his huge paws and claws, the bear turned his great, shaggy head toward me. *Now what?*

Not knowing what else to do, I took a giant step toward the bear and roared again, as deeply and loudly as if my life depended on it, which, of course, it did. The bear froze in apparent astonishment. He seemed to consider me a new and threatening life form, or perhaps was just confused that such a small and skinny human could make such an unexpected noise. As he stood on all fours and gazed at me, a large drop of saliva dripped from the corner of his mouth and fell to the ground.

Everything was moving in slow motion, but all the details were incredibly clear. I could see that one of his upper canines was broken, and the lip there was pulled up into a scar. Tufts of hair around his face were missing too, probably from other scars, and a fresh, pink welt curved in an angry line across the bridge of his nose. His nostrils quivered as he smelled me. A notch was torn in one ear, causing it to flop down slightly at its tip. He must be old to carry so many scars. I could smell him, a musty but sharp odor, like men smell after they have fought and sweated hard.

All of this went through my mind as the two of us stood there staring at each other, Roncommock on the ground between us, not moving, drawn up into a fetal position in an attempt to protect his head and throat.

A standoff with a bear. What was I thinking? I blinked and realized I had to do something else to break the link between us. It worked before, so I tried again. I took another step toward the bear, emitting another great roar, and this time I vigorously flapped my arms up high and then sharply back down to my sides. The bear was so surprised that he jumped a little, then turned and melted back into the thick brush.

Although my heart was thumping wildly, I turned to Roncommock, still on the ground, and gently rolled him from his side to his back to see how badly he was injured.

"Teacher, can you walk? I don't know how long the surprise will last. The bear might return. He will smell the blood."

Roncommock gritted his teeth and reached up to my shoulder. "Yes, I think I can walk, but I will need your help."

Blood was oozing from Roncommock's shoulder and thigh, where the bear had raked him with his claws and knocked him down. It was the thigh that looked the worst, with three parallel cuts so deep that they pulled apart at the edges. I could have stuck my finger in them without touching the torn flesh on either side.

We had to get moving, but if he walked far on his heavily injured leg, he would pump out too much blood. We needed something quickly. I took off my loincloth and wrapped it tightly around his leg, applying some pressure with my hand to staunch the flow of blood.

"Let's get moving. If we find some moss, we can make a packing for the wound." I knew that we needed to get the bleeding stopped, but we also needed to get away from the bear. The smell of blood would enrage him as soon as the shock of my actions wore off.

We started walking east, Roncommock leaning on me, one arm around my shoulder and the other holding tightly to the wrapping on his leg. After putting some distance between us and the bear, we paused, Roncommock leaning against a tree for support. He looked pale.

While he rested, I searched for moss growing at the base of a tree and found a nice clump of it large enough to treat his leg wound. Moss was the best packing for a wound, absorbing blood but also lessening a later infection. I was also very lucky and found a brown puffball still full of spores. After unwrapping his leg, I dusted the powder from the puffball into the gaping wound, which slowed the bleeding almost immediately. I dusted what was left onto his shoulder wound. Then I made a big wad of the moss and bound it up again with my loincloth, this time carefully wrapping my belt tightly around the package to apply more pressure and slow the bleeding even further. We should make it now, but because the exhilarating adrenaline rush of the bear attack was wearing off, pain and fatigue were beginning to overwhelm Roncommock.

I was tiring, too. He was a grown man, and I was still a boy. Supporting him was not an easy task, and we had a long way to go. Why weren't other warriors from our village here with us? Surely they would come along any minute? No, I realized. We'd kept the raiding party very small, only a handful of warriors plus me. I'd been positioned on the far side of the skirmish, presumably out of harm's way. The idea was that I was along to learn the route and to see how a raid was set up and executed, but I was not to fight, not even to get close to the enemy village. All was going well until that arrow struck near me. It must have been fired by a rogue scout, out away from the central part of the enemy village where our warriors launched their raid. Our warriors would have made a direct return to Chowanook, whereas we'd been diverted first by being positioned well to the south of their strike, and then by the unexpected chase by the left-biased scout. No, Roncommock and I were on our own.

As slowly as we were moving, Roncommock leaning heavily on me, I realized that we would be unlikely to return to Chowanook before dark. We were hungry, having eaten nothing at all that day, and very little the day before as we prepared for the raid. We had slept the night before in the longleaf meadow to be ready for the raid at dawn.

The sun was now well past its zenith and we still had some distance to go. Roncommock needed food, water, and rest in addition to attention to his wounds. Remaining in the forest overnight would be dangerous, for the smell of blood might attract the cougar or wolves with whom we shared the forest. I had heard a cougar's scream the previous evening, when we camped in the meadow before the raid, and I shivered to recall its eerie wail.

"I am going to run ahead to our village for help. You lost a great deal of blood. That bear was powerful and we need the medicine man's healing abilities to help restore your spirit while it fights that of the bear."

"Can you find your way?"

"Yes, teacher. I know where we are. We are near one of the sacred groves you showed me."

"Good, Skyco. Remember these sacred places and treat them accordingly. Do not enter them when you are bloodied and impure."

I helped him to lean back against a tree, leaving him a gourd—which my tribe called a *macócqwer*— that held a few mouthfuls of water. I placed it, along with his bow that I had been carrying, next to him. He still wore a reed pouch of arrows slung across his back, and I helped him to remove it. I checked his wrapping, replacing the soaked, bloody moss with a fresh handful, and I added some elderberry leaves that I saw nearby, for they were good at stopping bleeding. He had my loincloth and belt as a wrapping for his wound and still wore his own.

Oh well, I thought. *It will be faster to travel naked. Nothing to hinder me!*

I began to trot in the energy-conserving way I had learned, much faster than walking, but not a full-out run that would exhaust me. I could maintain this pace for a long time if I needed to, but today the distance was not that great. The sun would be low in the sky, but not all the way to the horizon when

I reached Chowanook. The forest, with its large trees spaced far apart, was relatively open and easy to move through. I skirted the occasional *pocosin*, but kept moving in the same general direction.

As I predicted, I arrived in the village just as the sun touched the branches of the big live oak on the village's eastern side, on the bank of the Chowan River. I stepped out of the forest, passed the crop fields, and entered the large, open clearing that was our village. Running to the central group of wigwams, I quickly located Chief Menatonon, who was in council with the returned warriors, and I related my story as succinctly as possible, which was easy since I was already winded.

"Roncommock is injured. I left him near the sacred grove and need help to retrieve him. Two strong men can carry him, but I doubt that he can walk any farther. We were attacked by a big boar bear at the *pocosin* in no-man's land. The bear spilled his blood and weakened him."

"Inform Eracano, the medicine man," the chief said. "Tell him what has happened so that he is prepared to treat Roncommock." He pointed to a man, who immediately left the wigwam. Signaling to two others, he said, "You two are appointed to retrieve Roncommock. Go with Skyco." The other two men were at my side before the chief had even ceased speaking; when the chief spoke thus, there was no hesitation to obey. We left quickly, without so much as an acknowledgment that I was even there.

We found Roncommock without difficulty, but

his spirit was busy fighting that of the bear. He just groaned when the men picked him up from the base of the tree where I had left him. When they saw he would remain unconscious and unable to walk, one cut a supple vine with a piece of sharp quartz he carried, and the other found two downed limbs that were still strong enough to bear his weight. In a short time, they created a sling by wrapping the two stout limbs with the vine, and then they carefully eased Roncommock and his gear onto it.

With the sling riding between them, the two men were able to trot back to the village through the forest, carrying Roncommock along as if he were a slain deer or bear. Well, he was in a little better shape than that, but not by much! And, because of my small size and exhaustion, I was little help.

Arriving at the village, they took Roncommock straight to the wigwam of the medicine man. It seemed that everyone from the village was there. My sister was standing off to one side, and as soon as she saw me, she turned and left, no doubt to inform our mother. Roncommock's wife was also waiting, but dared not enter Eracano's wigwam, for women were not supposed to interfere when a wounded man was fighting in the spirit world. It was too distracting and might cause his spirit to lose the fight if he sensed his wife nearby.

Other than the two men carrying Roncommock, I was the only one to enter the wigwam of the medicine man. First Eracano removed the bandage I had applied.

"You did this?" he asked in what I interpreted as a rather displeased tone. I felt concerned that maybe I had done a poor job, but answered honestly.

"Yes, I found a puffball and some moss, packed the wound, wrapped it with my loincloth, and then bound the whole package with my belt to make it tight."

"This is a good job. How did you know to do this?" he asked as he worked, cleaning the wound now with water in which several herbs, including blue wild indigo, were steeping. I realized now that he was concentrating, his gruff tone a function of his focus rather than an evaluation of my work.

"My mother showed me these healing herbs. Puffballs are good for stopping blood flow if sprinkled directly into the wound. So are spiderwebs, but I did not find those. Instead I used elderberry, whose leaves not only slow bleeding, but help in healing. I did not have a rock mortar to grind them, so I chewed them a little to break them up and release their healing power before I put them next to the wound. Then I packed in some moss to absorb the blood."

"Yes, your mother is a good healer, almost as good as I am! Without a doubt, she is the best at assisting with childbirth. We are lucky to have her in our village." He briefly looked me over, and I could see the questions in his eyes. "I am surprised that you have been watching her and have learned some of what she knows. Most boys would be too busy hunting or playing at war games with their friends." I did not respond.

He worked for a long time without speaking. I was amazed to see that he actually pulled together the torn flesh, using a fish bone and some dried opossum-gut fiber to pierce the flesh and hold the worst of the torn sections together.

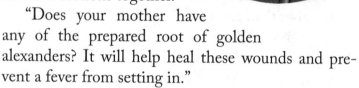

"Does your mother have any of the prepared root of golden alexanders? It will help heal these wounds and prevent a fever from setting in."

"I will go ask her."

"And bring me some more elderberry leaves. I am pleased with how they have worked in your preparation. I want fresh leaves to pack around the wound. Along with the spiderwebs I have gathered, they should slow the bleeding to a stop."

When I emerged from the wigwam, I saw Ascopo squatting on the ground, clearly waiting for me. Ascopo was my best friend, who I'd known for as long as I could remember. We were both born during a cold winter season, when ice formed on the creeks and snow lay on the ground, but neither of us had seen snow since. Every winter we hoped to actually see the white flakes fall from the sky, but so far we had been disappointed.

"Skyco!" he said. "What's going on? I heard that Roncommock was injured. Someone said he was shot, but then Tetepano said it was a bear!"

"Come on. We don't have time to talk. Help me gather some elderberry leaves. I will tell you while we pick the leaves."

We ran to the riverbank, where I knew elderberry grew. It was nearly dark, but the moon was up and provided enough light. We located the plants readily, and Ascopo helped me pick several handfuls of leaves. While we were picking, I told him about the bear, how it appeared from out of the dense brush with no warning and attacked Roncommock. Ascopo's eyes were wide open and white in the moonlight.

"A bear? Wow! How did you get away?"

That part was too embarrassing to tell. Yelling at a bear? Not too smart. Instead, I said, "We aren't finished gathering yet. Come along with me to my mother's wigwam. She has some herbs that Eracano needs."

While I entered my mother's wigwam, Ascopo waited by the doorway. My mother was inside and had already pulled out her baskets of dried herbs. She suggested that I take some dried geranium root along with the golden alexanders root I asked for. Before I left, she hugged me close and said, "I am glad you are safe, my son. Come back and tell me what happened to you as soon as you can."

Ascopo and I hurried back to Eracano's wigwam, but Eracano would not allow Ascopo to enter. A skin was hanging in the doorway and Eracano barely pushed it aside as he pulled me in. As Ascopo turned to leave, he hung his head and said, "See you in the morning, Skyco. I want to hear the rest of the story soon."

Eracano used all the herbs I brought him to prepare the poultices for the wounds. As he packed a poultice first around the leg wound and then around Roncommock's damaged shoulder, he sang to the spirits of the world that surround us all. He asked them to protect Roncommock and return him to us as he bound up the wounds with fresh new bandages. Instead of skins, he used cloth made from the inner bark of mulberry trees. I began to grow sleepy from his droning voice. Firelight flickered on the walls of the wigwam and seemed to make the spirit animals that were painted on the walls come alive.

"We are finished now, Skyco. It is up to Roncommock to return to us from the world of the spirits. The bear spirit is powerful. Only the rattlesnake is more dangerous to fight in the spirit world. You have done well to help him and we must hope that our care is enough to prevent his injured body from distracting his spirit. Go and rest yourself."

I returned to my mother's wigwam, where both she and my sister, Mamankanois, awaited me. Their fire was burning low, but they had set aside some food for me. I was grateful, but I could hardly eat because they asked so many questions.

"Yes, the raid was successful. At least I think so. I didn't actually see the raid because we were positioned to the south, as you well know, Mother. I think you must be the reason that I was not allowed to go along with the main war party. Why wouldn't you let me go?"

"Now, Skyco, you know that you are too young to be on war raid. You haven't yet been through the *husquenaugh*. And you are too important to this village. I didn't want you in harm's way and my brother, chief Menatonon, agreed."

"But we heard you were shot at anyway!" Mamankanois piped up and I could have swatted her as our mother's face reddened into an angry hue.

I tried my best to downplay the drama.

"It was nothing, really. One rogue scout found us, but Roncommock took care of him." This statement calmed my mother considerably, I was glad to see. My sister was just trying to get me into trouble.

"Yeah, but then a bear attacked him. How did that happen? Wasn't he supposed to be watching out for you?" Once again, I could have smacked Mamankanois for insinuating that I was in danger. She smirked as we both noticed the color rising again in Mother's face.

However, Mother turned to her and said, "Mamankanois, it is not your place to question another's duty or loyalty. Roncommock is Skyco's teacher and protector and our village's chief shaman. Not another word from you!" Now it was my turn to smirk.

She turned to me and asked, "Did Eracano use the herbs I sent with you? What is his prognosis for Roncommock?"

I told her what the medicine man told me—that we had done what we could do and now awaited the return of Roncommock from the spirit world. With my stomach finally full, I became incredibly sleepy. I lay down on my sleeping mat and fell asleep immediately. I did not even remember dreaming, waking only after the sunlight struck my face the next morning.

Mother was awake, but Mamankanois was already gone.

"Ascopo awaits you, but before you go with him to check on Roncommock, please stop to see Jackáwanjes. She too wants to hear of her husband's progress. It will ease her mind to speak with you."

Ascopo was bursting with questions.

"Is it true that you frightened off the bear without a knife, a bow, or even a spear? That is what the men are saying! I can't believe it, Skyco. How did you do it?"

"What do you mean, Ascopo? You seem to have the entire story memorized and I only told you a little bit last night." The last thing I wanted was for Ascopo to exaggerate what I'd done. I didn't have too many friends other than Ascopo, and even he seemed a little jealous of me.

"I've been outside Eracano's wigwam, same as everyone, waiting to hear if Roncommock is okay and listening to the men talking. They say that Roncommock was protecting you from the bear when it turned on him, but that you scared it away somehow. You didn't tell me that last night. Why not?"

Luckily we'd arrived at Jackáwanjes' wigwam and I ignored Ascopo's questions. When she saw me walking up to her doorway, Jackáwanjes smiled in appreciation. She had short vertical lines tattooed under her eyes and they crinkled when she smiled, accentuating her emotion. "I am on my way to see Roncommock and will return as soon as I learn his condition," I said to her.

On reaching Eracano's wigwam, Ascopo waited outside again. As I entered, I was relieved to see that Roncommock's eyes were open. He had returned! He won the fight with the bear in the spirit world, and I was glad to see him alive and awake, if rather pale.

"Teacher, can you talk with me?" I asked hesitantly, worried that he might be too weak.

"Yes, Skyco. What is on your mind?"

"Why did the bear attack you in the first place? You are a shaman, not a hunter or warrior. Didn't the bear recognize you?"

"Skyco, the bear was protecting you because his spirit told him to do so. The bear knew you had been attacked by an enemy warrior and felt your alarm. When I passed him, he thought I was that enemy and the threat on your life. Remember, I wore a warrior's loincloth and carried a bow and arrows rather than wearing my shaman's cloak and medicine pouch. The bear attacked me to protect you. After the physical fight, I slipped into the spirit world, where I continued the struggle with the bear spirit. When the bear stripped me of my physical being and searched my spirit in the spirit world, he realized that I was your protector. That is the reason I was released. That, and the fact that he recognized you when you spoke to him."

Roncommock paused, and I realized that he was preparing to tell me something serious.

"You must remember this, Skyco. The bear is your guardian spirit. He chooses few men to protect. He is the strongest of animals, but wise enough to know when to fight and when to retreat into brush. He does not fight every time he is provoked, but only when it is appropriate to do so, and then his great strength comes to his aid."

Wow! The bear was my guardian spirit! I felt pride that he had chosen me, but also awe. It was a lot to live up to—that of the bear spirit—and I hoped I was up to the task. I was rather small and puny to be a bear.

"When I am healed, Skyco, it will be time to turn to your training in the spirit world. It is very unusual that the bear recognized you so early, even before your spirit quest. The spirits are ready for you now, and we will oblige them by beginning with learning the way of the spirits before you learn the ways of the warrior or the hunter. You must enter upon the sacred quest as soon as the spirits decree it, even before you enter the *husquenaugh*. Your training will differ from that of the other boys who will also undergo the next *husquenaugh* as you pass from childhood to adult. You have more to learn." He sat back against the soft skins. "But now I need to rest. Please tell my wife that I am no longer in danger."

The *husquenaugh*! I was too young for that, wasn't I?

As I emerged from the wigwam, my mind reeling with new ideas, Ascopo interrupted, "Your mother was just here. She said that you must go to her wigwam directly. While you are there, she will visit with Jackáwanjes about Roncommock."

"How does she know what to tell her? How can she possibly know that he is recovered?"

Ascopo just shrugged and said, "She seemed to know. She was smiling."

I was relieved that Ascopo was no longer pestering me with questions. He walked beside me, deep in thought, and I was surprised when he stopped at his family's wigwam and said, "See you later, Skyco."

"Aren't you coming with me?"

Ascopo shook his head, but didn't say anything. That seemed strange. He always asked questions.

When I reached my mother's wigwam and entered it, I found Chief Menatonon waiting for me instead of my mother. I was surprised, but managed to appear calm even though he was fantastically outfitted. Resplendent in a mantle of iridescent green feathers collected from the heads of ducks and sewn onto a skin that rested across his shoulders, Chief Menatonon sat proudly on a beautiful mat woven from reeds dyed in yellow, red, and dark brown. The rectangular copper gorget identifying him as chief lay against his bare chest on a necklace composed of smooth, carved shells. He was an old man, and, unusually for a chief, his limbs were crippled. The tattoos encircling his once strong biceps sagged slightly under the weight of his aging skin. He is, however, a very wise and thoughtful leader.

He looked at me, not unkindly, and said, "Sit, Skyco," motioning to a mat directly in front of his. It too was a finely woven reed mat, dyed with colors of red, yellow, and brown. As I sat down, I carefully folded my legs so that each foot was underneath a thigh and rested my hands atop my knees, palms down, adopting the position I was taught. The chief smiled reassuringly.

He motioned to a new loincloth that was lying on a reed mat between us.

"This new loincloth, with its band of red, is for you. We have heard that you used proper medicines to treat Roncommock's wound and had the knowledge of binding it as well. You traveled a long way and returned safely to the village on your own, then led the warriors back to rescue Roncommock. You have done well. Congratulations, Skyco. I am proud to call you my heir. I know that you will succeed in the *husquenaugh*."

I stopped to admire the beautiful loincloth before I put it on. I could hardly believe it was mine. It was fringed along both the upper and lower edges rather than having the typical straight, simple edges. Instead of the normal brown color, it was white because it was made from the belly skin rather than the back skin of a deer, but the upper fringe and a band along the lower edge were dyed red.

I tied a new, soft-leather belt around my waist

and tucked in the front of the loincloth, allowing a short flap to overlap and hide the belt. The loincloth was cut in a circle so that once tucked in under the belt, it left the sides of my hips uncovered. The upper red fringe folded neatly over the belt, and I adjusted the loincloth to make the fringe hang down about the length of my fingers from the belt. The entire loincloth swung almost halfway down my thighs, the lower fringe ending just above my kneecaps. But, wait, did he just say *husquenaugh*?

Two of his most trusted men, Cossine and Tetepano, entered the wigwam, helped Chief Menatonon to his feet, and stood behind him to help if needed. He grasped my shoulder as he stepped outside, granting me special recognition with his touch and guiding me through the door. My heart was thumping with pride, but also with anxiety.

When I emerged, most of the village was there, and Chief Menatonon raised his hands and said in his booming voice, "You see before you my kin and recognized heir. I submit Skyco for the next *husquenaugh*. If he succeeds and becomes a man, he will be your next chief." He released my shoulder and the other members of my village inclined their heads in agreement.

I lay awake long into the night. On the one hand, I was proud of myself for scaring off the bear and returning my teacher to the village. But could I really be the next chief? And the greatest of all trials, the *husquenaugh*, loomed ahead. It is a grueling ritual, testing us in both body and mind to determine

The Black Drink

Ascopo was waiting for me the next morning, on the trail to the back side of the midden, the place at the village's edge where we relieve ourselves and discard any leftovers from harvest and hunting.

"Your uncle has really done it now!"

I sighed.

"Yeah. I can't believe I've got to go through the *husquenaugh* so early. I thought I had a few more seasons left to prepare myself."

"Well, don't worry, Skyco. As soon as my mother heard the news she made my uncle submit my name too. Now both of us must face it, and I have you to thank for that!"

I felt terrible.

"I'm really sorry, Ascopo. I don't know what else to say."

Ascopo glowered at me for a minute, but when I

added, "I'm glad I'll have you with me," he broke into a lopsided grin.

"Listen, what if we take off right now, leave the village, and avoid this whole, scary scenario? You and I can go somewhere on our own. We're almost old enough and I'm sure that if we stayed together we'd be fine," he replied.

"Wait," I said, "I have another idea. Roncommock told me that I have to start my study with him immediately. I am sure I can drag it out so that it gets too late in the season for the *husquenaugh*."

Ascopo rolled his eyes and snorted, "You know that will never work. Come on; let's get out of here right now!"

We took off down the trail, heading anywhere except back to the village. We were laughing at our escape, giggling about what we would do, when we turned a corner around a big tree and nearly ran smack into Roncommock standing there.

I stammered, "Roncommock! Shouldn't you be resting? What are you doing way out here?"

"Skyco, I was visited by the spirits again. Your bear guardian is particularly interested in you. It is time that you move in with me, away from your mother's wigwam. We will be busy. I have much to teach you, and you have much to learn. The spirits have decreed that you undergo the black drink ritual as a preparation for the spirit quest."

Uh-oh. I had heard about the black drink ritual. It was unpleasant, second only to the *husquenaugh*. I'd never heard of anyone dying from it, only that they wished they were dead, which might be worse. Ascopo's mouth dropped open.

"He's doing that *now*?" he asked with astonishment.

Roncommock turned to him and said, "Yes, and so are you, Ascopo. Memeo is waiting for you at his wigwam. You will be his apprentice. Go to him. He does not like to be kept waiting."

Roncommock paused to watch Ascopo leave, and then turned to see my reaction, which was probably written all over my face.

"This first day will be uncomfortable, Skyco, as you prepare your body to accept your new role. You will drink the black drink today for the first time. It will purge your body. When your body is clean and empty, together we will refill it with wholesome food and knowledge. I, too, will undergo the ritual to prepare myself as your guide in the spirit world. It would be best if you removed your new loincloth so that it is not soiled during the ritual."

"You mean *now*?" I stammered. "*Here*?" Roncommock just nodded, so I pulled the loincloth from under my belt, folded it carefully, and set it down. This was it. The fateful moment had arrived. From his cloak he pulled a *macócqwer* that was full of dark fluid and we both drank swiftly from the gourd, choking down the bitter liquid. Almost immediately I felt strong contractions of my stomach and bowels and soon purged the entire contents of my body. Everything came out at once. The cramps hurt and my mouth tasted bad.

"Once more," Roncommock said as he again handed me the *macócqwer*. "All at once is the best way," he said as I paused and stared at the *macócqwer*. Did I really want to do this? I looked up at him and he nodded, sensing my indecision. I took a breath, then almost gagged as I gulped down the potent drink, just hoping to get it over with and survive the experience. This time there was hardly any waiting and the purging came quickly. Just as quickly, however, the cramps subsided. I felt weak and empty, but no longer hurting from the cramps. Considering the effect, I was glad that Roncommock had told me to remove my new loincloth.

"Now that our inner bodies are empty, we go to the river to cleanse our outer bodies." We walked down the path, through the forest to the washing place. Roncommock carried the stem of a yucca plant, from which he'd trimmed the large, spiked leaves and tough outer skin.

We both waded into the water and picked up handfuls of sand from the bottom, scrubbing our bodies vigorously. It felt good to wash out my mouth and clean my sweaty, stinky body. Then we used the piece of yucca to scrub ourselves all over again, which left little soapy bubbles in our hair. The river's slight current swept it all downstream. Each of us scrubbed the other's back so that every bit of skin had been scrubbed clean. My skin tingled from the unaccustomed scouring. Once we rinsed off the sand and soap we were positively shiny, and I felt much better. Perhaps this black drink ritual was not so bad after all.

We returned to his wigwam and anointed ourselves with bear grease, which left my skin smooth,
soft, and a little darker than its natural color. Our
bodies were clean and purified both outside and
inside, and I felt ready for anything. When I donned
my fancy loincloth, I felt almost like a new person.

Looking over at Roncommock as he tied up his
shaman's cloak, I was reminded how much his hair
and clothing differed from the typical warriors of the
village because of his status as a shaman—a keeper
of our people's history. He lacked the thin, dark lines
and circles that were common tattoos among the
other men and women. He wore a short cloak year-
round that was made of rabbit skins. It tied up over
each shoulder to leave his arms free and came down
to just below his buttocks. Children often wore rabbit skins because they were so soft, but the loincloths
and cloaks of the warriors were made from the skin
of deer—noble animals and our most important
source of food. Only on the war raid did he wear a
deer-skin loincloth like the other men.

As was our custom, his head was shaved on each
side, leaving a ridge of hair down the middle and a
fringe across the front above his eyes. Most of the
warriors only shaved their head on one side, the side
of the hand they used to draw the bow, thus preventing their hair from tangling with the string when
they shot, but left the other side long so that they
could decorate it with feathers or other adornments.
My hair was long, down to my shoulders on both

sides since I was still a child.

Even as I was thinking this, he said, "It is time to cut your hair. You will learn to draw the bow as part of your training." I sat on a reed mat and he took a sharp shell, carefully cutting back the hair on my right side from my ear up to the crown of my head. He also trimmed the length on the other side, shortening it to less than a finger-length. It was a little uncomfortable, the way he pulled a section of hair out straight and then sawed through it with the shell. He had a jar of bear grease thickened with clay and dyed slightly red in color, and as the final touch to our cleansing ritual, he rubbed the stiff, colored grease through his hair and mine, making it stand up on our heads. I brushed my hand over the top of my head and could feel the short hair along the crown standing straight up while the rest of the hair on the left side flopped over; the right side was bare.

"You look like a small warrior now!" Roncommock said, and I puffed out my chest with pride. "You could be a little cocky redbird—a *meesquouns*—with that red crest of yours!"

When I moved my head, I felt the stiff ridge of hair move too, and the half of my scalp that lacked hair was cool. I kept touching my bare scalp and short hair because it felt so strange. I also felt hunger, but appreciated the feeling as I never had before. Now it was part of my training and preparation.

Roncommock said, "We will rest until sunset. Your body is clean and prepared. Now try to clear your mind so that the spirits will come to you."

I laid on a reed mat and rested. In fact, I may have fallen asleep, because I don't remember what I was doing until Roncommock touched my shoulder and said, "It is time."

While I sat on the reed mat, Roncommock added dried powder from the medicine pouch he wore around his waist to a small fire he had built while I was resting. *Uppówoc,* or tobacco, is sacred to us and used to contact the spirits. Only the elders who have the approval of the spirits can carry the small pouches of the dried leaves, which they add to fires or put into special pipes.

"Lean toward the fire and breathe in the smoke. It will tickle your nose until you get used to it, but it will stimulate your mind and open it to the spirits."

When I first breathed in the smoke from the fire, I nearly choked, but managed to stay calm and respectful even as my eyes watered. Roncommock said, "This is the sacred smoke that we use to contact the spirits. Now close your eyes and open your mind. Maybe the spirits will come. You are young and still must learn the proper way to contact them, so all you are likely to notice is peacefulness. Relax."

Relax? I was nervous. How could I relax when we were trying to contact the spirit world? The spirits controlled everything. They could strike a man dead or, worse yet, ignore him completely. If I failed at this, my training to be chief might cease as quickly as it had begun.

Relax. I could do that, just as Mother taught me. I began with my feet, imagining my muscles as I walked, willing them to relax. Next, my ankles, imagined them flexing, and feeling the muscles unwind. Calves, knees, thighs, buttocks—all were easy to soften. My stomach muscles and chest muscles were harder to relax, as were the muscles of my back since I was sitting up and using those muscles instead of lying down completely at rest, but I could imagine those different groups of muscles, remembering how they felt contracted and then relaxed. My shoulders, I realized, as I thought about them, were clenched. I unclenched those, then my arms, my elbows, my forearms. My arms now rested limply in my lap. Hands were tricky—so many small muscles everywhere—but I concentrated finger by finger as my mother had taught me.

Face muscles next—chin, lips, cheeks, eyes, eyebrows, ears, and forehead. When I reached my forehead, it felt as if some benevolent touch magically released all the tension within me. I experienced the sensation of being suspended in time, so that even my breathing ceased as I floated light and free as an autumn leaf drifting gracefully in space. I was as peaceful as a baby. I could even see my mother's gentle face beaming at me and feel her comforting arms holding me snugly against her chest. I could see her fingers approaching my cheek and felt the lightest caress. She touched me, and then directed my attention along her finger toward something just out of my view.

I opened my eyes, startled.

"Your spirit is strong, Skyco," Roncommock said to me when he saw my eyes open. "You have not yet learned how to call the spirits from the spirit world, but they came to you anyway. I could feel the peace that they bring flowing from you. And I could sense that they pointed you toward your quest."

I looked at him uncertainly.

"But I didn't see any spirits. All I felt was my mother, as if I were a baby in her arms. She pointed, but I couldn't see what she was directing me toward."

"That is good," Roncommock said, "very good. The spirits have recognized you. They are ready to receive you and to teach you. You are like that new-born babe to them. They have indicated the quest even if they have not yet revealed it. We will build your ability to contact them and will practice entering into animal minds other than that of the great bear. Eventually, you will be able to enter the spirit world, to see as they see, to understand what they know. I sense that you have a strong natural connection and will be able to strengthen it as you grow and learn."

"I will try my best, teacher." I was relieved. The spirits recognized me after all.

Roncommock continued, "But now sunset is near and it is time for food. The ritual is nearly complete."

We left his wigwam for the central fire, where the people of our village usually gathered together for the evening meal. I was proud of my new haircut and loincloth, and looking forward to seeing my mother, my sister, and Ascopo. My sister, Mamankanois, is older than I and likes to boss me around because of it. She will have to give me a little more respect now. At least I hope she will. And I wonder if Ascopo received a haircut today, too.

I felt oddly different as I walked through the village, noticing it as I never had before. Details stood out, reminding me of the experience when I saw all the scars and other features of the bear's face on the day that Roncommock was attacked.

The fragrance of fresh grass drifted over the village as it seeped from the doorways of the wigwams we passed, newly broken onto their floors to keep them clean and smelling sweet. Equally pleasant, the strong, smoky odor of deer meat grilling over the central fire mingled with that of the clean wigwams. I could even detect the rather pungent odor of the

THE LEGEND OF SKYCO

midden. Through it all floated the tiniest whiff of ammonia, the slightest indication of the river, full of fish and mud.

Looking at a new, as yet uncompleted wigwam that stood right next to an older, finished one, I realized how much the completed structure resembles the smoothly rounded back of a deer. Our wigwams are half-cylinders, built from a series of strong but supple saplings that are anchored in the ground. Wooden strips are woven in lengthwise to join the saplings together and provide stability. The sides and roof are covered with long pieces of bark and mats woven of reeds, tied down against the wooden structure. To let in light and vent out smoke, we roll up the mats. As I examined the site with my altered senses, the wigwams blurred in the smoke and seemed to move just like deer, but then something startled me and the sensation passed.

Although Menatonon's wigwam was not built differently from the others, it was centrally located. The dirt around it was pounded hard by the many feet that had walked to his door. The mats were open, and inside his wife tended their children, one of whom was still a baby, replacing the soiled moss in its wrap with a fresh bundle. As we passed, she smiled at me, her long dark hair sweeping across the dots and dashes tattooed decoratively on her forehead.

Next to Menatonon's wigwam stood my mother's, its bark siding a pale grey in the evening light. It was easy for anyone to identify, for outside the door grew a beautiful red paintbrush flower. Each small yellow flower tip was surrounded by a scarlet red sheath that changed into green lower down. It reminded me of the thorns used in tattooing, with the pointed yellow tip and the red blood. It was uncommon for anyone to plant a flower from the forest inside the village. We planted crops, of course, but only those we use for food. The medicine men gathered their herbs from the forest, never cultivating them in the village.

Mother planted it because the paintbrush plant was her spirit guide. Men always had animal spirits to guide them, but on rare occasions, women received a plant guide from the spirit world. No other woman in our village was guided by a plant, a sign of my mother's importance and her understanding of the ways of plants. She used the paintbrush plant either as a love tonic or as a poison, depending on the dose and her preferred application. It represented her knowledge of plants and their uses, her skill in administering medicine. It was both beautiful and deadly. It was a powerful plant, but one that needed her tending. It lived only a single year, and she gathered the seed and planted it each year in order to keep the flower nearby. It was a rare find in the open meadows of the flatlands, but grew happily in the bright light and cleared ground of our village.

My mother's wigwam stood near that of the chief because she was the head woman of the village. Menatonon was her brother—my uncle—and although men are chiefs, we trace our family line through that of our mothers. Menatonon was chief because his mother was head woman; I will be chief because my mother was head woman. Unless, of course, I fail the upcoming challenges. Then someone else will be selected from elsewhere in the tribe and my whole family line will be disgraced. For now, I am Menatonon's recognized heir, but if I fail the *husquenaugh*, he will choose another. He will have to, because I will be dead.

My father was killed when I was a baby, and I have only vague memories of him. Because of her status as the head woman of the village, Mother chose not to have another man as husband. It is unusual for her to remain alone, without a man to share her wigwam, but it is her choice. She is an unusual woman.

Once past my mother's wigwam and that of Menatonon, we reached the central fire, around which many villagers were gathered. Menatonon was already seated and my mother sat next to him. Ascopo was there, too, seated with his family, and he stared owl-eyed at me as he looked at my new haircut. His hair was still long. I smiled as I caught Mother's eye and moved to join her. She said, "I recognize the change in you. We must acknowledge your acceptance by the spirits. You have much to learn from them, and I am pleased with your progress. It is time for you to join the household of your teacher." How does she always know that something important has occurred before I tell her?

She offered me a bowl of water freshened with sassafras, or *winauk*, to wash my hands and face. Sassafras is unusual because its leaves come in three different shapes on each tree, instead of just one. It is the only tree that has such differently shaped leaves, which gives it power and makes it important in spiritual ceremonies. Luckily, its roots also taste good. I sucked a little water into my mouth and swished it around to cleanse my mouth and the words I would utter, and then carefully spat it on the ground. "I thank you, mother, and others of my family line. I gratefully acknowledge all that you have given me." I bowed low to her and she smiled. I sucked up another mouthful of water, spat it on the same place where the first mouthful soaked into the dry soil, turned to Roncommock and said, "I wish to join your household, Roncommock, my teacher. Thank you for accepting me as your apprentice." The words were spoken. The black drink ritual was now complete. My training to become the next chief had begun.

THE DAY I BECAME AN ANT

Now THAT I was officially apprenticed to Roncommock, my training in communication with animal spirits was ready to begin. I was excited, thinking
about all the spirits I might contact. Would we start
with the bear since he was my guardian?

I was surprised when Roncommock said, "Come
with me to the crop field, where the ground has been
cleared and the sun shines upon it. There we will find
an animal with a keen sense of community. You will
learn from this creature what it means to bond with
others of the village, to fight in support of your home,
to work together to harvest food, and you will appreciate the world better after having seen it from a different viewpoint."

Not a bear then. Maybe a cougar or a wolf? But
that didn't sound right either. Did birds live in a village? Redbirds hopped around the edges of the crop

field and sang and whistled to me from the trees when I was there. They were friendly birds, often found in the clearing, and the bright red males with their rakish crests were beautiful. Maybe I would study them, but redbirds didn't seem especially exciting, so what else might we find in the crop field?

"Here we are, Skyco." Roncommock delivered me from my musing. He slowly eased himself to the ground, his fresh scars tugging against tender new skin as he crossed his legs, folded his feet under his thighs, and placed his hands on his knees in the appropriate position of respect, but I saw no animals around us, none at all.

"Here," he said, motioning for me to sit facing him. I stepped toward him in preparation for sitting down.

"Wait!" he shouted. "Stop before you step on them!" His command startled me so much that I nearly leapt to the sky in another imitation of the snake dance.

He pointed to the earth, and there I saw an anthill. An *ant*? What was I going to learn from a tiny ant? The idea seemed preposterous.

I swallowed thickly, but moved as he indicated, hoping I had not offended my teacher or the spirits. I seated myself across from Roncommock, with the anthill between us.

"Here?" I asked tentatively.

"Yes," he replied, handing me a *macócqwer* full of water.

"Now you will learn the ritual of contacting the

animal spirits. First, cleanse your mouth with this herb water, spitting over your left shoulder. Wipe a little more water over your eyes, nose, and ears so that they are purified, too."

The water gave off the delicate fragrance of *winauk* and another herb I did not recognize. I followed his instructions, completed the ritual, and felt refreshed.

"Now, drink this, all at once," he said as he handed me yet another *macócqwer* full of a different liquid.

"It is bitter, but do not spit it out. It is sacred water and will help you contact the spirits." I drank the concoction and was glad he'd warned me about the bitterness. Still, it was an effort not to spew it all back out.

Next, Roncommock opened his medicine pouch, pinching a small amount of powdered *uppówoc* between his index finger and thumb, and scattered it over the ant mound. The ants went crazy, running frantically around and picking up the offering.

"Focus now on the ant mound. Watch their comings and goings. See the ant that just exited the hole? Watch it. Try to reach it with your mind. See its tiny head? Make it your head. See its six legs? They are yours. Feel how lightly the ant scuttles along."

As I opened my mind to meet the ant spirit, my teacher's voice became a low drone. Instead of his words I felt only a throbbing, or vibration, of the air. I also sensed something else, something that smelled really good, and I twitched my antennae as I raced along to follow the enticing scent.

I'd done it! I was an ant! But as soon as I thought it, I was a boy again. I looked up in surprise at Roncommock.

"It is okay, Skyco. You did well, but startled yourself when you made contact with the spirits and entered the mind of the ant. We started with these simple animals so that you might easily connect with them, but you were jarred back into your own self by the ant's radical differences in size, form, and sensation. Try again. See how much there is to learn from these industrious and largely unappreciated creatures. Choose another ant and merge yourself with it."

This time was easier, and I quickly slipped into another ant mind. I felt light and fast as I began to run along with six legs working together instead of just two, but the intensity and variety of odors suddenly struck me. I smelled many different things, but one powerful and pleasant odor was so dominant that I was compelled to follow it. Along the way to the source of this delightful aroma, I ran excitedly until I bumped into another ant. He promptly turned back toward me and dabbed his antennae over me like soft drumbeats and I returned the favor. And then I realized that it was *he* that smelled so good! He was from *my* ant village, my ant mound. The odor of my home was the sweet scent—the recognition of my own people, my own village.

I followed this sweetly-scented ant because he smelled so good. It seemed to be the right thing to do. We traveled a long way, clambering over tree trunks, dashing through fields of tall cane. The mind of the ant ahead of me reached back to probe mine, and I realized that Roncommock was in the other ant.

"Skyco, you do not realize that these creatures are all women. You keep thinking of us as 'he' rather than 'she.' In ant villages, the women are the workers—food gatherers and child carriers, as well as warriors. Here, among the ants, the queen is chief. Do not insult the ants by referring to us as men, for here the males are needed by the queen solely for reproduction. They do nothing else, except eat. Males and new queens are made only in the time of need, and then are fed and cared for until it is their time to swarm. When they swarm, they fly high into the air, mate, and leave the village. When they settle back down to earth, they find a new location and start another ant village somewhere else."

The speech from Roncommock-the-ant astonished me, but I promptly assumed my new gender and adopted the correct pronoun. Having settled myself, I soon smelled another odor that I recognized as food. Good. I was hungry. Where was this food?

I looked around and saw that I was high above the ground, having run up the stalk of a plant without even realizing it. I had not noticed the ascent because running upward felt no different than running along the ground, neither more difficult nor more tiring. I also realized that what I imagined to be tree trunks or fields of tall cane were just sticks and grasses of the field. My perception of them was different because I was a tiny ant instead of a small— but by comparison, gigantic—boy.

The Roncommock-ant approached a green bug, swollen like a fat round pumpkin, and I was astonished to see her stroke the bug with her antennae. The bug's head was anchored down to the plant stem, but it lifted up its free tail end and squirted out a droplet of liquid. The ant sucked up the droplet and patted another bug that then obligingly squirted out another droplet.

These swollen bugs were aphids, I realized. The ant was collecting their honeydew, the sugary sap extracted from the plant and excreted by the aphid. To an ant, an aphid was a *macócqwer* filled with honey. As a human boy, my mother had pointed out the aphids on our crop plants. Often they were guarded by ants, and my mother told me that the aphids offered honeydew to the ants in exchange for their protection. The ants fiercely guarded the aphids against other insects, or even humans, that brushed against the plant on which the aphids fed. Apparently, the ants must stroke the aphids to release the honeydew, so I decided to try it too.

The first aphid I patted with my antennae didn't respond. I watched Roncommock-the-ant with more care and tried to emulate the way she sensitively stroked the aphid with her antennae, encouraging it to release the honeydew. I tried again, more carefully and gently this time. Sure enough, my little, fat bug rose up and produced a droplet that I drank. It was delicious! Sweet and good, just what I wanted for food. Unlike human food, swallowing this ant food did not make me thirsty, for the honeydew was liquid and it provided all the water that I needed. We continued stroking aphids and swallowing honeydew until my stomach felt uncomfortably full and tight. Several other ants joined us. Before long, their abdomens were as swollen and nearly transparent from the golden liquid as my own.

No longer hungry, my comrades and I turned and followed the ever-present home scent back toward the mound. I kept my abdomen a little elevated so that it didn't drag on the ground as I ran along. Soon I could see our home mound ahead of us. As we entered, it turned dark, but I immediately discovered that I didn't need to see where I was going with my eyes. I followed the scent and my antennae touched the roof of the tunnel, guiding me like hands. Every time we passed another ant, we touched antennae and I smelled a strong whiff of the powerful, satisfying home scent.

Within the mound, other ants awaited us in a

deep chamber. Their abdomens were much larger than ours and they stood immobile, patiently waiting as each incoming ant stepped up and regurgitated the liquid from its stomach into the waiting ant's mouth. The sole function of these big ants, like living cisterns, was to store the liquid we brought back.

Task completed, we turned back toward the surface. It was clear that different ants had different tasks. There were cistern ants, soldier ants, the queen, the male drones, and workers like me, doing all sorts of different jobs. Among the workers, some cared for the larvae, some gathered food, some fought, some cleaned, but all looked identical. I couldn't distinguish the individual ants traveling with me. Which one was Roncommock?

As we approached the entrance, I smelled a strange and unpleasant odor. It made me uncomfortable and agitated. My companions began to hurry and so did I. When we reached the surface, there was chaos.

A huge ant, terrible in its snapping jaws and bulging eyes, grabbed the ant beside me and lifted her high, suddenly snapping her directly in half. The giant was a soldier from another tribe. I was stunned, but even more surprised when the half composed of my companion's head, thorax and two legs, but missing her abdomen and remaining legs, grabbed the big ant's back leg and heroically ripped it from the intruder's body. The leg amputation caused the soldier to swing around and, once again using those oversized jaws, clip off her head from her half-body. The severed head of my unfortunate companion, however, remained valiantly gripped onto the leg of the massive soldier, which was now under attack by two more of our workers. They too pulled off legs until the giant began to topple.

I stared at the small head affixed to the giant's leg and tried to probe her mind. "Roncommock?" I ventured hesitatingly.

"Behind you. Keep fighting!" he answered back, and I paused briefly in relief but soon redoubled my efforts.

Bodies were clashing together everywhere. Big enemy soldiers were lifting up our smaller workers and dashing them in pieces to the ground, but other small workers were successfully ripping legs off the huge enemies who then stumbled and fell like giant trees crashing to the forest floor. We were fighting ferociously, but there were just too many enemies. Every enemy soldier occupied several smaller workers, and a line of the big ants was pushing toward our entrance burrow. They were going to charge into the burrow and defeat our village! If they succeeded, we would all be taken as slaves by the enemy ants.

Just then, a phalanx of soldiers from our own village came spilling out of the entrance and turned the tide of battle in our favor. They went head-to-head with the invaders, chomping their way through enemies large and small. As our own soldiers began to overwhelm those from the other tribe, I could see that we were starting to push them back, clearing a zone in front of our entrance. I smelled victory, and then realized that was exactly right: my victorious side was releasing a triumphal scent that announced we had won. The invaders that still had legs hobbled away.

The battlefield covered a large area in front of the entrance to our mound. It was strewn with bodies and parts of bodies, detached legs most commonly. Whole legs, partial legs, broken antennae, and the claws from innumerable feet intermingled with the occasional oblong head, section of square thorax, or perfectly spherical abdomen.

Before all the invaders even left the scene, our clean-up of the carnage began. Other workers like me began picking up bits and pieces, invaders and comrades alike, and carrying them off to the midden, or trash pile. We formed a line of cleaners, hauling parts of carcasses back and forth. Our big soldiers just turned back and reentered the nest as soon as they smelled the victory signal, but all the smaller workers joined in the clean-up. With such a large number of workers, it did not take us long to clear the battlefield of all the refuse.

After the battle and the clean-up were over, I descended into the mound where I was greeted by another group of workers. They were pale and younger than those who were fighting, and they had never left the nest. They smelled only of the nest scent, whereas all of us who'd been involved in the fight smelled of ourselves, another nest, and of victory. The interior workers brought us food and checked us over for damage. I had some frass wedged into a joint on my back that I couldn't reach. One of the young workers cleaned it out for me and carefully groomed the rest of my body, checking for any other damage.

While the worker cleaned me, I smelled an odor that my ant-self recognized, but my human mind could not identify. It was wafting up from deeper in the mound and it filled me with concern. "Roncommock, are you here?"

"Yes," was the reply. "I am with you, Skyco."

"What is that new odor?"

"Be patient. You know what it is, but your human mind is interfering. Just be an ant and don't worry about me. I will stay nearby."

I tried to block out the part of me that kept intruding, tried to give up the idea of the human "I" and connect instead to the community spirit of the ants. The odor provided important information about the village, supplying instructions for the next task essential for the village's welfare. What was it?

At last, understanding arose out of confusion. As new workers emerged from their pupal cases, the queen laid more eggs in the newly empty chambers. The odors recruited workers to their next duty. Some of the pale, young workers were scurrying down deeper into the nest to assist the emergence, while others moved off to the royal chamber to take the eggs the queen produced and move them into the chamber of eggs. The different odors told us where we were needed, what the next task would be. All the communication was through scent instead of verbal commands.

The ant queen is responsible for producing the number of workers she needs to maintain the size and health of the ant tribe. This includes replacement of individuals lost to warfare and old age, just as in our human tribe. Our village of Chowanook held about a hundred people, but all the villages under Menatonon's care, eighteen in total, held around two thousand people, together forming the tribe of the Chowanoacs. There were about that many ants in this single nest.

Even though we'd just won a great battle, the ant colony did not sit back and enjoy it, recounting stories and celebrating around a fire as we did in a human village. Instead, we went back to work. As an ant, I sensed no sadness for the loss of comrades and no reluctance to join in the fighting when the time came. My colony mates were totally devoted to the defense of their village. They harbored no fear, no sadness, nor any joy at their victory. They just did what was needed when it was needed. These ants were true to their nature, without guile or regret, which seemed to me to be an admirable trait.

Some workers had found a good food source. I immediately recognized their call, a scent, for help to gather it. Other workers inside the nest were also recruited to be field scouts like me. I followed the scent trail from the entrance, along a path worn down by tiny feet, to the edge of the field where it gave way to forest. There, workers were picking up the seeds from a violet's seed pod. Several of the seed pods had split open, and the brown, shiny seeds each had a soft, white handle—the elaiosome—that was easy to grab. I bit into it to get a good grip and then slung it up over my back, still gripped in my jaws. The elaiosome smelled and tasted strongly of good food, but instead of the sweetness of the honeydew, it tasted more of oils and fats, like the roasted bear meat I ate as a human.

I followed the home scent back to the village and handed over the seed at the entrance. Pale workers knew exactly what to do with the food. They clipped off the soft, moist, elaiosome and hauled it below to the food chamber while other workers took the hard, brown seed to the midden. I made the trip from the violet to the nest and back again several times, running along a trail well-marked by our village scent. Soon our task was completed and all the seeds were delivered to our nest.

I felt sluggish and realized that the sun was no longer high overhead, heating up the sand surrounding the mound. Other workers were coming in from all directions, converging on the entrance. I could smell strange scents on all of them. Some odors were clearly different types of food, and the workers who stayed inside to collect the food approached these newcomers to touch and taste them with their antennae.

A column of wounded and undamaged soldiers marched back from the direction of the lowering sun. They'd been in another skirmish, this one clearly a raid by our own troops on another mound. Based on the scents they were releasing, they'd raided another village ambitious to extend its reach into our territory and had successfully repulsed the enemy. Our soldiers smelled of the foreigners, an unpleasant, sharp odor like sweaty men who'd been in battle. They returned home lumbering and limping, eagerly lining up to be examined and cleaned by the small workers.

In addition to our own workers, captured workers from the defeated village scurried alongside. They'd been sprayed with our village odor, and, although their foreign scent was still apparent, our village scent overwhelmed it. These captured enemies would soon lose their strange scent and be incorporated into our village, just as sometimes happened in my human village when we defeated another village and returned with captured enemies. Men were usually killed during battle, but if the whole village was captured, its women and children were adopted as members of the victorious tribe.

One of our returning soldiers hobbled up to the entrance of the mound, missing three of her six legs. Luckily, the remaining legs were distributed on each side, and her lurching gait carried her awkwardly along. The workers swarmed around her, cleaning her up before sending her down below. She could not grow new legs, but she could fight a while longer and would be used in another battle.

Another soldier walked up, weaving drunkenly along the path as she collided occasionally with other returning soldiers and workers. She had all six legs, but clearly something was wrong. I couldn't see any damage, and was stunned to see one of the workers grip her and drag her away from the mound, refusing to allow her to enter. She was being taken to the midden with the other rubbish! The disoriented soldier did not balk, but just allowed herself to be dragged passively by the small worker. Then I saw what was wrong. Both of her antennae were damaged. One was just a stump; the other was about half gone. Without antennae, she could no longer smell anything. She had lost her primary sense and would be unable to respond, unable even to return to the nest unless guided by another. She was helpless, and she knew and accepted it. She was walking dead.

One of the workers, acting as a cleaner, dashed over toward me and started frantically palpating my body with its antennae. She couldn't find the home scent on me because I had been outside the nest so long. I was in trouble unless I could tell her that I was friend instead of foe. I tried to tell her, but couldn't figure out how to talk. I just kept opening my mouth and snapping it shut. No sounds came out. My mouth opened and closed, opened and closed again, the only sound a loud click.

The cleaner-ant was getting agitated, about to call

me out as an enemy trying to sneak into our nest, and I couldn't figure out how to talk to her. Odors! I needed to make an odor! The only thing I could think of was to raise my abdomen and give a little squeeze. An odor came out of my back end, and the cleaner-ant backed away from me, but it seemed to work. She calmed down and left me alone.

A different worker approached me, running and excited, wafting odors of food from her antennae and recruiting other workers to help. Her excitement and frenetic activity indicated that we needed to hurry. I rushed after her, following along with several other ants—Roncommock no doubt among them—and we darted off down a scent trail that was identical to the odor the ant had been carrying.

We soon arrived at the scene of a fierce struggle. Two ants were clinging onto a dark, striped caterpillar covered in rows of stiff hairs. Another ant leapt up onto its back, trying to bite its head, but slid off when the stiff hairs prevented her from grabbing hold of the skin. The caterpillar was already bleeding green blood from several wounds. It whipped its head back and forth, bucking its whole body up and down, trying to dislodge the two ants on its back, but all to no avail. When another worker jumped aboard, successfully this time, I could see it was over for the caterpillar. Its thrashing began to subside and more workers moved in for the kill. I realized that it had fallen from a black cherry tree overhead, dislodged from its feeding when one of my sister-ants encountered it on a leaf and bit through its silken suspension line. The caterpillar failed to make it back to its protective tent, where it would have been safe from marauding ants underneath a sheet of tightly woven silk.

Once it was dead, all of us gathered under the carcass to lift it up and carry it back to the village. With several of us working together, we were able to lift the giant beast and haul it along the uneven trail back to the mound. It was as if a few men had picked up a dead bison and carried it back to the village. The caterpillar was at least ten times the size of any one of us, but by working together, we could carry it.

As we approached the village, a few of the most excited workers rushed out to meet us, then darted back with the news after they'd absorbed some of the caterpillar's scent. The rest of the village was abuzz when we arrived, and the interior workers set to work carving up the beast just as humans might carve up a bison. Small pieces of food were distributed to all the ants that were hungry. I was offered a morsel, but did not feel the need for it and merely shook my head at the worker, who gave it to the next ant in line. I felt tired and ready for rest after all the activity I had seen and participated in.

Now I had a problem. I was ready to leave this ant world, but didn't know how. Was I to be trapped here forever? Roncommock hadn't told me how to leave! Where was he? I began to panic as I realized my predicament. I was a tiny ant on the edge of our crop field! One of our own men, even one of the children of the village, might step on me, putting an end to my tiny life. How was I going to escape this dilemma? I looked frantically for Roncommock, but of course could not distinguish him from the other ants.

I slowed down and thought about it. How did I become the ant? I stared at the ant, I put myself into its mind and body, and Roncommock helped me to contact the ant's spirit. Now I needed to ask the ant spirit to release me. Perhaps I just needed to still my mind, to concentrate, and to ask.

My ant eyes could not close because they had no lids, nor could my antennae stop processing scents. Both inputs were distracting. So I shut my mind instead, which was much harder. As I focused my thoughts, I felt my body relax. As it turned out, I didn't need to ask for anything. I felt myself slipping back into my human form, a soft body, closed eyes, lungs filling slowly with air. Just before I left the ant consciousness, I squeaked out a "thank you" and I felt the answering sigh of appreciation from my ant host. The spirits were pleased that I remembered to thank the ant who hosted my visit.

As I came back into myself and opened my eyes, I saw that I was sitting just as I'd left. Roncommock was next to me, also in human form. He smiled at me, asked how I felt, and all I told him in reply was that we needed to thank the spirits. He chuckled and we walked to Chowanook's central sacred fire— which was always kept burning—and there we gave our thanks to the spirits. My mind was still reeling with everything I had seen and experienced. I needed time to reflect, time to calm down.

Roncommock and I sat by the fire, but he never said anything. He watched the flames just as I did, their orange curls licking around the dark wood and sending up pale grey plumes of smoke. Occasionally, a little spark glowed more brightly than the rest as it flew skyward. He waited until I was ready to talk. Finally, after clearing my mind, relaxing my body, and once again sending thanks to the spirits, I felt the peacefulness of their presence restore me. I was ready to tell him about my experience now.

"I learned so much from those tiny ants!" were the first words out of my mouth. "I am astonished at their lives. They lack emotions, yet are strongly drawn to their village and will protect it at all costs. They work together, each relying on the other. Some are specialized for different tasks. With the exception of the queen, none rank higher than others, but all are valued for their accomplishments. Whether they are soldiers or they are tenders of the egg chamber, all have jobs to do and all do their jobs to the best of their ability." I paused briefly, then added in a rush, "And, they are all female! Women can do everything in that village, even fight. Their world is so different from ours."

"Is their world really so different, Skyco? The women of our village raise crops, care for children, and tend the village itself. We trace our descent from our mothers and each clan within our village is related through the female line. The whole time you were with the ants, you never left the crop field of our human village. You were in the same world, so how was it different?"

"Perhaps because of the way I experienced it. I smelled everything. I could tell what had happened elsewhere because of the scents that were released and conveyed. As a human, it seemed strange that I lacked hands but could still carry, I had eyes but hardly used them, and I had antennae which turned out to be the most important organ of them all. One ant returned from a battle, completely whole except for her antennae—both were damaged. She was thrown on the midden to die. Yet an ant that had only three legs kept going and fought the next battle." As almost an afterthought, I added, "And in our world, the men do the fighting and the hunting. We at least contribute something to our village."

"I saw those ants, too. You appreciate the differences and their importance. This was a good introduction to the spirit world, Skyco. You will have more experiences, but later. For now, you need to rest, recover, and reflect on what you have learned from an ant."

It was true. I had learned an incredible amount in a short time. The village life of the ants was different from our human village, but like us, they worked together to make the village prosper. Each ant did its job, contributing to the village's success, and every ant was needed by the community. On the other hand, the ants lacked all emotions, and the life of an individual was completely subsumed by its tribe. On the whole, I would not like to be there forever. I was pleased to have such a powerful experience, and one from which I learned so much, but I was glad to be human.

"Is it okay if I tell Ascopo about what we did today, teacher? He is my best friend and I know that he will be curious about what we have done together."

"Friendships are important, Skyco, but you must remember that none of the other boys are undergoing this training in the spirit world. They will not understand."

Instead of heading to the river bank, where Ascopo and I often met, I went straight back with Roncommock to his wigwam.

To Build a Canoe

"IT IS TIME to learn one of the great skills of our people, Skyco," Roncommock said to me one morning. I was glad to hear that we were changing the routine. For days, Roncommock had been grilling me on the names of all the chiefs of the local villages. I was also learning the proper way to address the chiefs and introduce myself to them. He was teaching me diplomacy, a skill I needed, but I was ready for some action instead of just memorizing people and their relationships. I wished Ascopo were around, but Roncommock had kept me so busy that I hadn't seen him in days.

"Old Memeo has said that he is ready to build another canoe. He has already selected the tree," Roncommock told me as we walked into deeper forest farther from the village, where the trees grew larger. "It is tall and wide, an old master cypress tree.

A canoe built from it could last forever."

Ascopo stepped out from behind the tree along the trail, grinning widely.

"How do you like my hair?" he asked, and I clapped in appreciation. He too, had been initiated into his apprenticeship by having his hair trimmed like mine. Roncommock acknowledged him with a hand to his shoulder, but kept walking down the trail. Ascopo fell in beside me and whispered, "It is great to see you again! It's been ages since we talked. I am sure that I can now identify every single tree and bush, whether they have leaves or not. This apprenticeship with Memeo is getting more interesting now that we are carving utensils out of wood."

"Carving!" I said. "That must be fun! What have you made so far?"

Ascopo self-consciously pulled a spoon from his belt. It was gracefully carved, with a long handle and a smooth, shallow bowl.

"Hey, this is nice! You should be proud of it!"

"Takes forever," he said, "to hollow out the bowl with a piece of quartz and then smooth it with shark-skin. Memeo makes everything smooth. Thankfully this is a soft wood and easy, supposedly, to work. He faulted me on the handle because it is curved rather than straight, but I think it is okay for a first attempt."

"What is it made of? It is a pretty, tan color."

"*Rakiock*. It darkens as it ages."

"Hey! That's my favorite tree!" In the spring, the trees bear hundreds of large, colorful, bowl-shaped, open flowers. Each flower is painted with a strip of orange near the base of the yellowish petals. Below the orange strip, next to the cone where the stamens of the flower attach, there lies a sweet band of nectar. Insects often visit the flowers to lap up the nectar, but as children, we lick the sweet bands just as happily. Few of our foods have that sweet taste that we like so much. We even collect the petals and dry them to store for later in the season, but we often consume them as quickly as they dry. My mother puts the crushed, dried leaves into hot water to make a sweet tea that tastes of flowers. The big trees bloom for a short time in the late spring, well after they put on leaves but while everything is still spring fresh. *Rakiock*s, or tulip-tree, are among the biggest trees of all, often growing so wide that it takes six men touching hands to encircle the tree.

While I was remembering all this, we suddenly appeared in the forest glade where the selected cypress tree was standing. *Rakiock* wood is soft and easily worked, but both cypress and pine are harder and longer lasting. Bald cypress, however, is an unusual tree, for although it has tiny needles, it loses those needles in the wintertime the way a balding man loses his hair in old age. All other needle trees are evergreen, like the pines that we also use for canoes. But the most important aspect of cypress wood is that it does not decay. A canoe built of cypress just might last forever.

I turned to Roncommock. "Did you mean that all canoes built of cypress wood might last forever, or were you suggesting that this *particular* canoe would?"

Ascopo looked confused.

Roncommock chuckled. "I see that our sessions together have encouraged you to be thoughtful and to question the meaning of my statements, Skyco. Attending to your own words and ideas as well as those of others is an admirable trait in any person, but a necessity in a leader."

He paused and looked seriously at both of us.

"You were right to ask. While it is true that any canoe built of cypress might last forever, Eracano has foretold that this canoe in particular is destined to travel to a world far beyond our own. This canoe

that you build, boys, will be passed down to many future generations. Build it with pride and care, for it will represent our people to another. The people of the future will come to understand us based on what we pass on to them, their hands will touch what you have touched, and their minds will wonder how you lived. Descendants always learn, or should learn, from the knowledge and wisdom of their ancestors. Just as ancestral wisdom shapes our present lives, careful attention to present actions is the best offering for our future. Remember this when your muscles ache from the work and you are tempted to quit rather than to continue. Pour your heart and your spirit into this canoe, sending it forward as the best representation of yourself and your people. It will test your patience and perseverance, but you must imagine, and be confident of, the long-term importance of quality."

I suppressed a shiver, stunned at the importance of the task ahead of me. Ascopo gaped, his mouth and eyes wide open. Never before had I been told that the job I was about to undertake was certain to matter in the future. On the other hand, any job worth doing is worth doing well. As chief, I will represent my people in many different ways and might never know which particular action is destined to matter more than another, thus, all my actions should be considered potentially important and worthy of my best effort. Ascopo shut his mouth and just nodded.

Roncommock left us near the cypress tree that would soon become a canoe. Memeo, our tribe's master woodworker, started a small fire near the base of the enormous tree as the first step in the long process. Chacháquises, his main assistant, packed handfuls of pine rosin, bound together with a little moss, in a band around the base of the tree. Once he completely encircled the tree trunk with the mixture, he ran a fuse of rosin from the tree to the fire, and soon the fire began to creep around the tree like a flaming necklace. Ascopo and I impatiently hoped to start carving the canoe immediately, but Memeo motioned us to sit down instead.

We had to wait while the fire did its job, providing old Memeo time to describe how he selected the tree we would convert into a canoe. Our inaction, coupled with his rather monotone voice, caused my mind to wander. Suddenly, I saw the flames leaping menacingly around the tree's base and I tried to direct Ascopo's eye, but he was already staring at the flames too. Chacháquises was nowhere to be seen.

"Sir!" I shouted, but Memeo was so intent that he didn't appear to hear me. Just before I leapt up and really got myself into trouble with Memeo, Chacháquises walked into the glade with a *macócqwer* of water and poured some on the highest flames, reducing them instantly. Ascopo and I both relaxed, realizing the fire was not getting out of control as it had first appeared.

After this short period of excitement, my mind focused better as Memeo related that he was named for the biggest woodpecker and Chacháquises for the smallest. Men often, but not always, changed their names from their birth name to a name that better reflected their skills and professions when they became adults. These men carved trees the way woodpeckers did. As might be expected, the men of the bird clan were typically the best wood carvers and the women of the clan were the best weavers. The baskets woven by Poócqueo, Memeo's sister and Chacháquises's mother, held our precious crop seeds from year to year.

Since neither Ascopo nor I knew what was expected of us, we simply sat near the tree and waited. Soon, Ascopo's older brother Kaiauk joined us and surprised me with a question totally unrelated to the canoe.

"Did you really fight off a bear?"

"Uh, it was not like a real fight or anything. Just sort of an improvisation."

"Are you boys paying attention to this canoe or not?" Memeo cried and we all shut our mouths. "Since you seem to know everything already, Kaiauk, please tell Skyco and Ascopo what lies ahead in the making of this canoe." I could sense Ascopo's delight at his brother's discomfort, but he dared not show it to Memeo.

Kaiauk stuttered momentarily, but found his tongue and described our next actions. He said we would eat our food in the glade and sleep there at night, guarding and protecting the tree. Once the fire burned into the wood around the circumference of the tree, girdling its flow of sap, the tree could not survive. Since we caused the death of the tree, we stayed with it until the canoe was complete. It is how we show our respect to the tree.

Memeo seemed satisfied with his answer and turned away to another task. Kaiauk relaxed, for, like Ascopo, he was apprenticed to Memeo and worked to earn his approval. Memeo was treated with the respect of a shaman, since what he did was to contact tree spirits and to carve most anything we needed. Any man knew how to make a bow and arrow, but Memeo's bows were the best, and most of the men waited until they could get a bow from him.

Kaiauk said, "We have a long time to wait. To put this tree on the ground is not a simple task. Memeo will keep the fire small and under control, or at least that is the idea!" He smiled, indicating that he, too, had seen the flare-up from a few moments ago. "Memeo says this is a good time for learning patience, but I think it is a better time to pick up some hunting tips from the older men!"

Kaiauk wanted to impress us with his knowledge and described how Memeo only carved bows of either black locust saplings or a young witch hazel and was incredibly specific about the particular sapling he used, rejecting nine out of ten saplings that he was brought. Memeo only made arrows of reeds and fitted them with the breast feathers of a turkey. He was less picky about the points, using flaked quartz, cracked shell, or even the teeth of a gar, a fish with big, pointed, sharp teeth.

While only partly listening to Kaiauk, I surreptitiously looked around and was delighted to see

Meemz and Tetepano following Chacháquises into the glade. While Kaiauk was just a few years older than Ascopo and I, they were of middle age and were accomplished hunters. Ascopo and I flopped down on the ground on our bellies, heads resting in our hands, and listened with rapt attention. Kaiauk, being older, tried to pretend otherwise, but was also hanging on every word. Tetepano was the best storyteller of the group, but at first I couldn't tell whether or not he was the best hunter.

My favorite hunting story was about how a big buck outwitted Tetepano. The men were out hunting, searching for deer, but the buck was lying in a bed of grass, hunkered down so that he was invisible to the hunters. The buck waited until the men had passed by him, then jumped up and ran back in the direction from which the men had come. The men were startled and missed the chance to shoot at close range, but they saw where the buck had disappeared into a *pocosin*, so they tracked him there. Figuring that he would come out of the opposite side, Tetepano went to the left and his companion, Meemz, to the right, with a plan to meet on the other side of the *pocosin*. Tetepano swore that he could hear the buck moving in the thicket, and pulled his bow, ready to unleash an arrow. Just then, Meemz emerged from the other side and came face-to-face with an arrow strung in a bow. It was a close call, but even small children learn never to release the string until they see the eye of the prey.

The two men decided to plunge into the *pocosin,* and in such close quarters, thought they could probably dispatch the buck with their spears rather than the bow and arrows they normally use, so they unstrung their bows to prevent them getting tangled in the brush. Working together, they moved back through the *pocosin*, which was slow going because there were so many green briers that bound everything together. When they finally reached the other side, they were surprised to see that there was no buck and no evidence that he had come though the *pocosin*.

Just as they were wondering what could have happened, Tetepano noticed the tall grasses were moving out beyond the western edge of the *pocosin*. When he called Meemz's attention to the movement, they were stunned to see that the huge buck was creeping along on his belly and was already well away from the thicket. Only his antler rack gave him away. When the buck realized he was visible, he leapt up and dashed away before the warriors could even think about stringing their bows. The huge old buck had outsmarted them.

By the time this story ended, the fire had burned around the base completely, and we set to work with stone hatchets, chopping out the burned wood. Then Chacháquises set another band of rosin into the groove, which was easier to pack now that a section was hollowed out. It burned a little deeper, and again we chopped with the hatchets. It took most of the day to fell the tree, but the day was full of stories. It was not very hard work, just waiting for the fire to do the work for us, but it took a whole day before the tree was on the ground, and then we had to use the same process on the top to get rid of all the branches. This was a little more exciting since we let the flames get larger. They crackled and popped, but as soon as they really started to get hot, Chacháquises poured water to slow the fire down. We worked until dark, when it was fun to watch the fire sparkle as we listened to good stories.

Tetepano seemed to be the one who most loved to hunt. Many of his stories were funny ones about being outsmarted by the animals he hunted. Meemz whispered to me that the reason Tetepano was a good hunter was because he never made himself out to be too important. He humbly gave the animals their due, making himself look inept while the animals seemed to win, but he always brought home food and was recognized as the best hunter among the other men in our village.

In one story that particularly intrigued me, Tetepano described his prowess with an atlatl, as well as how he learned humility. The atlatl is an old tool, used less frequently than bows and arrows, but Tetepano boasted that he could throw a spear with the atlatl as fast as his companion could shoot an arrow from a bow. It was not an idle boast, but to boast of a kill in the presence of the animal is inviting bad luck.

When his hunting party discovered several deer grazing at the edge of a meadow, Tetepano made his boast. Both Tetepano and his partner disguised themselves with complete deer skins, reducing their human smell and providing camouflage. By pretending to be deer, the hunters could get close enough to kill the deer with a well-thrown spear or accurately aimed arrow after standing up and tossing the hide aside. When Tetepano and his partner leapt up to shoot, a covey of six *chúwquaréo*, or red-winged blackbirds, burst from the ground where just a few moments before, six deer had been grazing. Tetepano understood immediately that his boast had been heard by the deer, causing their transformation and escape, and he knelt right there, broke both of his spear-points, and asked forgiveness for his offense.

I asked many questions of Tetepano, especially about the atlatl. Ascopo asked many questions, too, but his were mostly about the hunt and how the animals reacted. Without a man around the house, I had very little experience with the bow and found it intimidating. The atlatl seemed more intriguing, perhaps because of its rarity. Ascopo was already proficient with bow and arrow, providing his family regularly with small game animals and competing with his brother to bring back the most. Boys were not allowed to kill deer until their preparation for the *husquenaugh,* and Kaiauk loved to remind us that he hunted deer regularly.

As we lay down to sleep that night, Ascopo and I next to each other, I whispered nervously to him, "Do you know if we are the only two undergoing the *husquenaugh*? I haven't heard a thing from Roncommock, but you've been out with these other men."

"Yeah, I have heard," Ascopo replied sleepily. "The twins will be with us. Four of us in total."

"The twins?"

"Yeah. Andacon and Osocan. They are already such good hunters, I bet they get a deer the first day. Haven't missed a rabbit since they could pull a bow, I am sure. I hope you can kill a deer before the *husquenaugh* begins, Skyco."

I slept fitfully that night with stories of deer and atlatls dancing in my dreams. What if I didn't kill a deer? I couldn't even make it into the *husquenaugh* in that case, defeated before I could even try.

Once I awoke to the howl of a red wolf, calling to its hunting partner. I shivered with unease, though I knew the wolf was not really dangerous. Red wolves hunted in pairs and, like us, deer were their favored prey. While red wolves never harmed healthy adult people, there were stories from tribes in the high mountains farther west about larger, rangy grey wolves that hunted in packs and could kill a human. Ascopo made a little snort in his sleep and I nearly jumped out of my skin. I suppose after my encounter with the bear and what with thinking about the upcoming deer hunt and *husquenaugh,* I felt a bit anxious, and it took me some time to fall back asleep after being awakened by the howl.

Morning arrived at last and I was the first one up and moving about, adding wood and stirring the coals of the fire to life so that we could cook food. Ascopo awoke as soon as he heard me stirring. He was probably dreaming about the hunt.

Ascopo and I wondered about the process of hollowing out the tree into a canoe, but our ques-

tions were soon answered. It turned out to be not much different from putting the tree on the ground. In both cases, we smeared a section of the tree trunk with rosin, producing a small, controlled fire that burned the wood and made it easier to chop out. However, when we hollowed out the trunk, we used oyster shells in addition to our stone hatchets. The shells were sharp and cut the wood quickly and cleanly, but they broke frequently and dulled rapidly.

Ascopo said, somewhat wearily, "Look at that huge pile of oyster shells at the edge of the glade. Do you suppose we will go through all of them before we are finished with this canoe?"

I just nodded my head. Since oysters did not occur in the fresh waters of the Chowan or the western sound, they must have been collected during a fishing expedition to the coast. It turned out that Ascopo was correct: we worked through entire the pile of shells over the next few days. When I cut and scraped with a shell, I could usually work the whole area I was assigned before my shell wore out, but the stronger men, by pressing harder and cutting away more wood with each effort, typically used up two shells before we fired the section again. As the shells wore down, we put them into a basket for later disposal.

Roncommock's emphasis on quality and the importance of this canoe to future members of our tribe was well intentioned and helped to ward off our fatigue, because it was easy to tire from the repetitive and slow-going tasks. As soon as we had the initial shallow opening carved, we divided our group into pairs. I worked with Tetepano, Ascopo worked with Chacháquises, and Kaiauk worked with Meemz. Memeo joined one pair or another. With three sets of workers, Tetepano and I worked the middle section while the other two pairs attacked the ends. We burned and scraped, burned and scraped, as the shallow hollow slowly grew deeper. At least it was easy to keep the fire alive because some section of the trunk was burning nearly all the time. But with the fire burning constantly, smoke was often blowing into my face and making me cough. It was hot, too. Even before the sun reached its zenith on the first day, I was already wearying of the work, and we had barely begun to cut into the canoe.

Luckily, it was time to break for food. Chacháquises added a few handfuls of dry corn and beans into a pot along with some water.

"Skyco," he called to me, "please bring me a few bay leaves to give this some flavor. You can find them, can't you?"

"Sure," I replied. Bay trees were common in this glade near the creek, and I found the pungent leaves in a moment.

While we waited for the food to cook, Memeo asked Ascopo to carry the basket filled with worn shells out to the midden. The basket was woven of reeds and reinforced with slender willow branches added to the weave around the mouth of the basket and across its bottom.

"Could I help?" I queried, eager to try something different. Ascopo glanced at Memeo, who nodded his head in agreement. Then, Ascopo helped me put a strap around each shoulder and another—the tumpline—across my forehead, just above the hairline. With the basket loaded, the tumpline bore some of the weight, relieving my shoulders of the full burden. The tumpline also helped steady the load as we hiked over some rough terrain on the path to the midden. Our village midden, where we dumped all our refuse, was at the edge of the village, not particularly close to the glade where we were building the canoe, but we hauled the shells there anyway. Ascopo walked with me.

"Is it heavy?" he asked.

"You bet it is," I grunted.

"I'll carry the next one, then."

We spent many days carving the canoe. Whenever I grew tired and the quality of my effort began to suffer, I took a break. Sometimes I carried away a basket of worn shells and other times I sprinted to the now dwindling pile of unused shells and selected those with the sharpest edges, distributing them among the scrapers. It felt good to exercise my leg muscles instead of just my arms and back. Sometimes, Ascopo and I worked close together and could talk to each other, but often Memeo stationed us at opposite ends of the canoe.

One night, as I lay next to him, I said to Ascopo, "Do you think Tetepano would teach me to throw the atlatl?"

Ascopo laughed out loud and was immediately shushed by one of the men.

"He'd better. You are going to be in trouble when we get to weapons training. You never hunt with me anymore since you missed that rabbit by the length of your whole body!"

My face burned as I remembered the incident. We had gone out to hunt together at his urging and when I missed the rabbit, it started to run away, but Ascopo hit it from behind me with a single arrow. Not only had I missed an easy shot, but Ascopo hit a difficult one perfectly. We hadn't been out together on a hunt since that day. I'm still embarrassed.

At first, our work on the canoe was just rough work, scraping out hunks of blackened wood and leaving long grooves behind. However, as we approached the more delicate phase of the project, the work slowed because Memeo began to oversee every aspect. Now, the fires were smaller and we scraped out less wood. After each round, Memeo inspected our work and determined how large an area to fire next. Through this deliberate process, he slowly sculpted the wood, and the tree trunk began to take on the shape of a canoe. As the pleasing form appeared before our eyes, the once tedious tasks of hollowing and scraping gave way to a sense of accomplishment and feeling of pride.

Ascopo and I had plenty of time to talk with one another because Memeo slowed the work down to a crawl as he carefully considered the final shaping required to complete the canoe. Although Ascopo and his brother Kaiauk were in the same family clan line, the bird clan, as Memeo and Chacháquises, and were expected to be good carvers for that reason, both were more interested in hunting than in carving. Ascopo's name came from a sweet bay tree, important to carvers because they used its white, sweet-smelling wood to create food utensils.

His brother, Kaiauk, was named for a gull. How his mother knew he would turn out to be a noisy busybody was beyond my ken, but his name sure seemed to fit him.

Kaiauk kept asking me to tell the whole story of my encounter with the bear, and with Ascopo's additional urging, I soon acquiesced. Both of them said more than once that they wished they had been there, which struck me as strange, but then Ascopo said that if he had the encounter and been able to draw his bow while looking the bear in the eye, he would feel like a seasoned hunter. The bear was a test to Ascopo, a test of hunting skill, but when I faced the bear, it was just a dangerous animal that I wanted to scare away from my friend. I never even considered killing it, but that was all that Ascopo thought about. I decided to keep the suggestion that the bear was my guardian spirit to myself because that knowledge might make Ascopo jealous. Even Kaiauk seemed more interested than I would have liked.

For five days with nearly perfect weather, we carved and scraped under Memeo's careful eye until the canoe achieved the proper depth and shape. We shaped the outside, too, but only slightly, by removing the bark and tapering each end. Then, old Memeo took the rough skin of a shark and rubbed the inside of the canoe to perfect smoothness. It was his self-appointed responsibility to polish the interior of the canoe, and he did not allow anyone else to assist him. When he finished, the canoe was truly beautiful, smooth as a stone tumbled in a stream.

This canoe was large enough to easily hold twenty men and their gear. Ascopo and I climbed aboard, and the sides rose nearly up to our armpits. Each end tapered to a blunt point on both the inside and outside. The canoe was wide enough that two men could sit side-by-side, but they rarely did so because it cramped their paddling. For Ascopo and me, it was easy to lie down side-by-side, which we quickly did when Memeo unexpectedly walked into the glade. Concealed as we were, he passed by without seeing us, never casting a glance into the interior of the canoe. He was too busy fussing about paddles.

We carved paddles from small *rakiock* trees that the men hacked down with hatchets. The men quickly whittled the paddles into shape, but Memeo was a hard taskmaster. He pointed out to Kaiauk that his paddle was too thick, and to Tetepano that the two sides of his paddle were not the same shape. Both held their tongues, but kept on smoothing the handles and removing any rough spots with shark-skin. After Memeo left the glade, however, Tetepano handed his paddle to me and found another project that needed doing.

I was working on the paddle when Roncommock reappeared in the glade. Although I felt as though I had learned a lot about building a canoe, what I really wanted to do was paddle it, and I asked Roncom-mock if I could help launch the canoe and partici-pate in its maiden voyage down the river and into the sound. He looked at me closely, and when he agreed, I nearly yelped in excitement. Ascopo elbowed me in the ribs and whistled in appreciation. He was already going, of course. But then Roncommock tempered my excitement by saying, "This trip will form the basis of your spirit quest, Skyco."

When Ascopo heard that, his eyes widened in astonishment.

"Skyco will begin a spirit quest *already*? He hasn't even been *husquenaughed!*" Ascopo seemed almost offended.

"It has been decreed," is all that Roncommock would say. Ascopo closed his mouth and his eyes changed back to normal size, though they now watched me warily.

In order to pick up the canoe, we needed twenty strong men from the village including all those who

had been working on it. Neither Ascopo nor I participated in the haul because we were both significantly
shorter than the grown men, but we followed eagerly
along behind the party.

Kaiauk and the other men had to carry the canoe
a long way through the forest to the nearest water
with enough depth, which was a small creek that was
a tributary of the big river. Memeo walked ahead of
them, clicking his tongue whenever a man stumbled,
and constantly pointing out roots and overhanging limbs until one of the men said that the reason
he was stumbling so often was that Memeo's excessive attention to the roots caused them to grow in
self-importance.

As Ascopo and I trotted beside the men, he kept
looking over at me, but he never said anything about
the spirit quest. That could only be a bad sign, for
Ascopo never held back his thoughts.

The men launched the canoe into the water carefully, and only Memeo climbed into it. He walked
up and down, checking for leaks, even though none
of us expected any. Still, it was his right as the canoe
builder to be the first to enter the canoe. Once satisfied, he motioned to the rest of us to get in, and the
six others who had worked on the canoe construction climbed aboard. I took a paddle and went up
to the front of the canoe and Ascopo sat just behind
me, since we were the two lightest of the group. The
heavier, grown men sat in the middle, but Meemz,
who was the best paddler and did most of the steer-
ing, commanded the rear, with Kaiauk just in front of

him. We were staggered, first man paddling on the right, next one on the left, and so on down the line. Ascopo and I were given strict instructions not to wiggle around in the canoe, which would unbalance us and might cause the canoe to roll over. I could feel the canoe rock from side to side as each man stepped in.

We paddled down the creek and out into the river, floating downstream along with the current. I was surprised at how fast we moved. It made me a little nervous. The river was deep and wide downstream of the village, and we paddled long enough that I thought we must be nearly to Ohanoak before Memeo finally gave the word to turn back upstream. As we slowly turned the canoe around and passed close by the riverbank, I noticed how the trees along the bank seemed to reach out toward us, almost straining to reach the water with their branches. I hoped we wouldn't become tangled up in one of them. Small birds darted among the branches and mosses trailed down into the water. Once we were facing into current, it slowed us down a little so that it took longer to paddle back upstream, but I must admit I liked the slower pace because the canoe seemed steadier and less apt to overturn.

The best thing about moving more slowly, however, was the longer time to watch the fish in the deep, clear water. Sturgeon, which our tribe called *coppáuseo*, were easily my favorites. They were the biggest fish in the river, some of them half the length of the big canoe and twice as long as a man. On their

backs were thick, bony scutes. In our village, we used the scutes as decorations or as hide scrapers. They swam slowly along, sweeping their massive bodies back and forth, always facing into the slight current, and sometimes poked the tips of their strange snouts up above the water's dark surface. Their slow, gentle movements gave the impression of a dance as they weaved back and forth, up or down, always to a rhythm that seemed to emerge from within the river itself. The river whispered a gentle song, calling softly to me. I never saw the giants crash into each other, as one might expect from such gargantuan beasts; instead they seemed to flow as the river flowed, elegant in their immensity. The biggest had to be ancient animals, the elders of their tribe.

I swayed sympathetically as I watched them, holding my breath the way they seemed to, and was startled back into awareness when I heard Tetepano, just behind me in the canoe, softly whisper, "Wake up, Skyco."

When we finally reached our village, Ascopo and

Kaiauk chattered about the new canoe, how it handled well, and how many fish they would be able to catch from it. They kept trying to get me to join in, but I was thinking about the *coppáuseo* and the dance of the river.

At the landing place on the riverbank, where the dark river water slowly shoaled onto white sand, many of the other villagers gathered to see the return of the new canoe. Chaham, who loved to fish, was the first to call out with his youthful exuberance, "Where is Roncommock? Can we bless this canoe now and go fishing in it tomorrow?"

"Don't be so impatient, Chaham," Roncommock replied as he appeared from among the throng of villagers on the riverbank. "Why are you in such a hurry to go fishing?"

Manchauemec, another great angler who was never far from Chaham, spoke up before Chaham could reply.

"Roncommock, you know that it is time for us to take a group out to the sandy banks and fish in the saltier waters. Striped bass—*mesickek*—will enter the inlets there and start their runs inshore and we will follow them. It is time."

"Yes, Manchauemec, it is time. Tonight we will celebrate the new canoe and tomorrow you can prepare for a trip to the sandy banks. Come to my wigwam after you have finished here. I need to speak with you about the expedition."

The crowd parted and let Roncommock through, but quickly coalesced again around the paddlers, everyone babbling now about the celebration tonight and the upcoming trip. A trip to the sandy banks! Kaiauk was hopping around with excitement and talking animatedly with Chaham, who was just a little older than he. The men went every spring and occasionally at other seasons. Children and women stayed in the home village, but sometimes they took boys my age, who had begun their training but not yet completed it or been *husquenaughed*. Ascopo would likely be part of the trip since he helped carve the canoe. Would I? I padded quickly along to Roncommock's wigwam and found him sitting by the fire inside.

As I entered the wigwam, Roncommock looked up with a slight smile on his face. "Did you enjoy the paddle on the river in the new canoe, Skyco?"

"It was wonderful, Roncommock," I replied, beaming. "We saw more *coppáuseo* than I have fingers on both hands, and all of them were longer than a man is tall. They are impressive beasts, and they swim as if they were dancing."

"What else did you see?"

"Tiny, pale, green leaves of both the giant *rakiock* trees and cypress were just emerging, barely beginning to cloak the dark limbs in greenery. Long, grey mosses hung down to touch the black water, enhancing the impression that the huge trees were elders with grey hair. The magnificent trees and enormous fish must be ancient, the elders of their tribes. They deserve our respect. A small, energetic, yellow bird with a big voice was calling again and again from a limb that branched and bent slightly toward the water like the fingers on a skeletal hand."

"Is that all you heard, Skyco?" he asked, as if he already knew.

"I heard the song of the river. It called to me. Was it the spirits, Roncommock?"

"Yes, Skyco. Do you think you are ready for them?"

"I think so, but I feel anxious, too. Even while the river sang to me I could imagine the great blue ocean and the tall sandy banks. I have heard the men describe these things, but this felt different. I need to see them myself."

"Then it is time for you to go, Skyco. But first you should learn a little bit about being a fish. Come sit down beside me." With those words, Roncommock opened his medicine pouch and added a pinch of his special mixture of sacred *uppówoc* and other herbs to the fire.

I Am a Fish

Although a moment ago I sat close beside Roncommock, inside the warm wigwam and next to the fire, I suddenly realized that I was no longer warm. Neither did I feel cold. The temperature felt just right. I saw many rounded rocks below me and, as I somehow hovered over them, their patterns grabbed my attention. Some rocks were black with white stripes, some brown with darker swirls in them, many were grey with wavy streaks of white curls. Then I saw a dark grey rock that contained small, red jewels of pebbles, and I tilted over to take a closer look.

How did I do that? I was looking at the rock, but yet was somehow above it. I looked around for Roncommock. Where was he? I saw a shadowy cave over beyond the rocks with something moving in it. What was *that*? Could it be a bear or cougar stalking me?

But then the dark shape moved out from the shadows and into the sunlight where I could clearly see it. It was a largemouth bass. I must be a *fish!*

Now I understood. Up above me glowed the shimmering, silvery surface and the rocks I examined formed the river bottom. I floated in between. I looked back at the big bass as it moved toward me. Suddenly I panicked. How could I breathe underwater? I shot up toward the surface and took a gulp of air, but it hurt. Something was wrong. Then I heard Roncommock in my mind, telling me to relax.

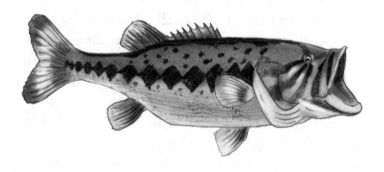

"You are a fish, a bass like me," he said. "Calm down. Feel your gills working for you. There is no need to breathe. Your gills will extract the oxygen from the water for you. Feel it. I am here with you now in the bass beside you. I required a moment for my own mind to locate a fish and join you, but you nearly leaped out of the water before I arrived."

I stopped struggling and drifted down next to

him. I felt the water flow over my gills. I squeezed the muscles in my throat and felt my gill flaps open. Almost immediately, a sense of well-being poured over me.

"The oxygen," Roncommock began, "is flowing through your blood now. Feeling better?"

"Yes," I answered him as our minds touched.

"Now keep calm and connect with your body. Feel how it responds to this new element. It will feel different from the ant, closer to your own form, and that familiarity caused your panic. Like the ant, however, this fish body will perform all the necessary life functions if you allow it to do so."

I noticed a slight pressure along my head as I faced into the current. My tail automatically gave a little push to move me forward. Arms and legs still seemed to be in the right places, but they were fins instead, and I moved them slightly to better orient myself in the water.

"Roncommock," I queried him, "why don't I feel cool in the water? I feel neither warm nor cool, just right. But when I was still me, I mean, still human, sitting beside the fire, I was too warm. Now the temperature feels just right. Why is that?"

"Now that you are a fish, your body temperature is determined by your surroundings. As a human, you made your own heat instead. When the temperature of the air dropped, you felt cold, and then you might shiver or move to generate more heat from within. Or, when you sat by a fire that was warmer than your body, you felt warm, so you sweated to cool yourself or moved away from the fire to a cooler spot. As a fish, your body temperature is always the same as that of the water, so you don't notice any difference. You can't tell whether you are cold or hot."

I thought about that for a minute, and Roncommock entered my mind again.

"Let's swim!" he said. "We are fish, and fish swim!" He darted upstream and I followed. Without thinking too much about it, I just flexed my tail and shot forward. My arms, which were now my forward fins, automatically helped me balance. I came to rest to the right of him in a deep pool of water. Just before he dashed off to another pool, I felt a strange itching sensation along my left side. The whole length of my body, from just behind my gill flap, which used to be my neck, all the way down my body onto my tail, felt like an itchy feather had been drawn along my skin. I swam after him and caught him in the next pool.

"What was that weird itch? When you took off, the side of me that was next to you felt strange. I didn't feel anything like this at all when I was an ant. What was it?"

"It is the lateral line of a fish, a sensory organ unlike anything a human has. Fish use it to detect pressure waves in the water the same way that ears detect pressure waves in air."

"You mean I could *hear* you start to swim?"

"No, I'd say you felt it, wouldn't you?" Roncommock seemed to smile at me even though his fish face was more of a pucker than a smile. "You felt the water pressure wave I generated as I thrust my tail and darted forward. This ability to sense the movement of others helps fish stay together in a school and warns them of a hungry predator's approach."

"Hey, this is interesting. What else can we do?"

"Try this. Swim with me and tell me when you notice a different odor to the water." We took off, swimming faster than before, but still moving upstream. As we passed the roots of a big tree, which created dark overhangs and swirling eddies in the current, I noticed that water was flowing from two directions, one still straight ahead, but another one pushing me from the right side. My lateral line was tingling again.

"I want to go this way. There is less force of water on me from that direction. And my nose tells me that it smells better somehow than the main stream does."

"That's it!" Roncommock said to me. "You feel and smell the water from your home stream. Its headwaters are where these bass hosts hatched and first swam as tiny fry. The waters flowing downstream *should* smell better to you than any other stream. You can smell your home."

Roncommock paused and we both looked toward the smaller stream. I had to turn my body to see the stream, and realized I was looking at it with one eye while my other eye was looking across at the other side of the stream. I moved back and forth a few times, finally understanding that I could never see the same image with both eyes simultaneously, just one or the other.

"Your eyes are on the sides of your head, not in front anymore. You can see both sides of the stream, a large area, but not directly in front of you," Roncommock said, sensing my struggle.

"Then how am I able to see where I am going? That seems like a problem, Roncommock!"

"Just swim, as you were doing before. You'll see."

And I did. As I swam, the slight side-to-side wobble of my undulating body allowed me to see the world in front. I even had a pretty good view behind me. From nearly all directions, I had a great view of the waterscape and other animals, including food and approaching predators, but less acuity directly in front or behind.

"Time for lunch," said Roncommock. "Watch me hunt and then you try it." I did as he told me, watching as he slowly swam upstream, pausing beside a jumble of sticks and tree roots that stuck out from the bank. Suddenly, he shot forward and grabbed a tiny stick, then backed up, pulling out a stone-fly nymph by its long antenna. It wiggled like a tiny wood roach. He flipped it forward, then snapped it up and swallowed it. "Mmmm. Now you try."

I looked, but couldn't see anything hiding amongst the debris. After a few moments, I impatiently asked Roncommock if he could see anything.

"You are moving too fast and not paying attention!" he said. "Slow down. If you create too much water movement, the prey can feel you coming. Move slowly and watch for the tiniest protrusion of an antenna."

Slowing down and moving more gently so that I barely advanced upstream, I began to notice little extensions of legs and antennae sticking out from behind the wooden debris. There was a lot of prey here, which I hadn't seen before. I selected an antenna that looked particularly thick and juicy, grabbed it with my mouth, and backed up. Out came a very angry crawfish, or *anshaham*, waving its big claws around while I hung onto one of its antennae. It kept flipping its abdomen as it tried to escape, but just as I let go so that I could turn it around to eat it, it grabbed my lower lip with a pincer and squeezed hard. My mouth shot open and I yelped, or tried to. No sound came out, but the *anshaham* knew what it was doing, let go with its claw, and dropped back down to the streambed. Before I knew what was happening, it shot backward with a flip of its tail and disappeared from sight into one of the many crevices along the bank.

"You'll be hungry if that is the best you can do!"

I tried glaring at Roncommock, but without eyebrows, it just didn't work, so I decided that the best response to his criticism was to catch prey like a natural-born fish. This time, I chose a smaller antenna and pulled out a mayfly nymph, an insect flattened from top to bottom so that it fits into narrow crevices. I had no problem flipping that flat morsel into my mouth and crunching it up. It was as crispy as grilled fish skin and as sweet as a roasted chestnut. Delicious!

"So, this time, Roncommock, we are both largemouth bass," I stated with certainty.

"Yes, we are freshwater relatives of the big striped bass, or *mesickek*, that you will fish for when you go with the men to the big eastern sound."

"We are here in the Chowan River, then?"

"Yes. I do not have the power to take you far from your human body. There are largemouth bass in the river here by our village, along with many other fish, but the largemouth are most similar to the *mesickek*. Learn from the largemouth bass and you will understand the *mesickek* and the spot-tailed bass that you will catch as a human."

Spot-tailed bass, which our tribe calls *chigwusso*, are as big as *mesickek*, both reaching a size near that of a grown man. *Chigwusso* are reddish in color and have dark spots near their tail fins. *Mesickek* are silvery with dark stripes from their heads to their tails. Both prefer the brackish water of the eastern sound, but the Chowan near our village was freshwater.

We swam out into the river together, down near the bottom where the current was stronger. I felt a big fish approaching us and moved in closer to Roncommock.

"You feel that?" he asked me. "You sense the approach of another?"

"A big one," I said. "Will it try to eat us?"

"You are a predator here, Skyco. The largemouth bass eats smaller fish in addition to other prey such as the mayfly you just consumed, and the small fish are afraid of you. However, you should keep in mind that there is always another fish that is bigger than you and *that* fish might be your nemesis. Be at ease, though, for what approaches is a sturgeon—a *coppáuseo*—and despite its large size, it is not a predator of large fish."

"What do they eat, then?"

"Watch and learn, Skyco."

I held my questions and just watched while an enormous, greyish body emerged from the gloom of the river bottom. It was indeed one of the *coppáuseo* I had seen earlier in the day, when I was canoeing as a human boy. It moved slowly upstream, and it frequently dug down into the bottom sediment with its strange, elongated nose with ropey feelers, sucking up small insects and worms into its mouth from underneath the pebbles it dislodged. Once it moved over a mussel, and I saw its tube-like mouth extend downward in order to engulf the mussel. The big fish cracked the mussel's shell and worked it around in its mouth, spitting out a few large shell fragments but swallowing the rest.

"This huge fish eats the smallest animals?" I asked Roncommock incredulously.

"Yes. That is why we have nothing to fear from this creature. But smaller fish fear us. Now let us see if you can catch one." Roncommock moved off ahead of me and I followed. "Slowly, now, Skyco. Use your new senses to find minnows and other small fish. Remember that they can sense you, too, especially any quick movements you might make."

We cruised slowly along, near the edge of the riverbank now. I could feel the tingling along my side whenever a small fish darted away. I began to understand what they felt like and sensed where they were located when they moved.

As we came around a root ball, I saw a small, pretty sunfish ahead of me. It was greenish with an orange breast. I darted after it, but it easily escaped my charge and swam into a school of other sunfish a safe distance ahead. They seemed to be laughing at my clumsy effort. I was disappointed and felt foolish. A tiny fish had bested me in my hunt.

"Wait a moment, Skyco. Here is another predator like us. Watch him hunt."

Even before Roncommock finished his thought, I saw a big gar—or *kowabetteo*—emerge from the darkness of deeper water. It was at least as long as Roncommock's leg when Roncommock was a man. With large, yellowish scales and a log-like body, it was similar in shape to the *coppáuseo*. Instead of the flattened nose, feelers, and fleshy mouth, however, the *kowabetteo* had a long beak almost like that of a heron or crane, but full of small, sharp teeth. It glided slowly along, barely sculling with its tail fin, giving all appearance of calmness, slowness, non-aggression. But while I was watching it, in a move so fast that I was not even sure I had actually seen it, the big fish darted forward and grabbed a sunfish from the edge of the school.

One moment it was still and quiet, the next it had seized a struggling fish, which it snipped neatly in half, then swallowed each half in two quick motions. Small silver and orange scales drifted down from the mouth of the *kowabetteo*. All the surviving sunfish scattered in a flash.

"Wow! So the trick is to move slowly and quietly, to lull the prey into a false sense of security, and then strike like lightning."

"That's it, Skyco. That is the way to be a hunter. Never be in a hurry, never rush things. Wait until the prey is within your grasp, then strike swiftly and strike hard. Don't miss or it may be a long time before another opportunity appears."

"I understand, master. Thank you for showing me."

"Now it is time for you to try again. Show me what you have learned."

We moved slowly up the river, along the edge of the bank where tree roots hung out into the slight current and grasses grew up along the edges. I could see a school of small minnows ahead and slowed down even more. I balanced my body with my pectoral and pelvic fins, barely pushing forward with my tail fin. Roncommock drifted back behind me, letting me lead as I stalked. When I felt I was as close as I could get, I flexed all my muscles at once and shot forward like an arrow from a bow. My mouth snapped shut on one of the minnows and I swallowed him down in an instant. My host's stomach felt pleasantly full.

I turned back triumphantly to see Roncommock's reaction at my success, but instead of seeing him in the river, we were sitting again by the fire, with the smell of sacred *uppówoc* drifting from it. I cleared my mind and offered thanks, not just to the bass I had inhabited, but to the *kowabetteo* that showed me the hunt and the sunfish and minnow that were eaten.

"This experience was different from that of the ant," I said to Roncommock. "In both animals I felt strange sensations, and scent was again important. Being a fish, however, was more like occupying my own body, but with parts that were somehow both similar to and different from what I expected. I had fins where my arms and legs used to be, an eye on each side of my head rather than two in front, gills instead of lungs to breathe, and lateral lines that provided whole-body hearing instead of just one pair of ears." Here I paused for a moment as I tried to gather my thoughts and explain the experience. "When I was an ant, it was totally unlike anything I had ever experienced, but when I was a fish, it was somehow familiar. It was as if I actually remembered being a fish—as if I had experienced life as a fish sometime in my distant past. As an ancestor, maybe? But how can that be?"

"It is important for you to understand that all life is linked together, Skyco. Those of us who become shamans simply see those linkages better than most other people and we are able to follow the links. We teach the next generation just as we were taught, connecting the past to the future, both stretching into a hazy distance so remote we can only barely comprehend. If we are connected to our ancestors as well as to our descendants, then perhaps we *can* detect them when we enter the great linkage of life and share experiences with other living beings. As you come to understand other forms of life, you will become a better hunter, and you will also become a better chief."

Roncommock stood and moved from the fire to his sleeping bench.

"I must rest awhile until it is time to bless the new canoe. You should get some rest, too. Your journey will be arduous and you will be gone from the village for some time. I imagine the men will want to be out at the weirs by the time of the full moon, when the tides are best. They will return after the good tides are over, but they will come back slowly, lingering at villages of our kin along the way. You will need those skills of diplomacy you have been learning. I expect you to introduce yourself and to negotiate on behalf of our fishing expeditions with the leaders of the villages you visit. You must request accommodation from them. I hope you learned your lessons." So did I. If I failed, we might be attacked as enemies.

We feasted in the village that night. I could smell wood smoke from the central fire and the delicious scent of bubbling succotash, which was a stew composed of squash, corn, and beans. Haunches of venison roasted over the fire, but the smaller or bony pieces of the deer boiled with the succotash and contributed to the fragrance of the stew. Women uncovered baked roots—some called *okeepenauk* and others called *openauk*—that they had buried under the coals at the edge of the fire. Ascopo was standing near his mother, who was scraping away some embers to expose the baked *openauk*, and I walked over beside him.

At the start of the evening, before we ate, Roncommock blessed the fishing venture. Because he was my teacher and I saw him every day in that role, I had almost forgotten that he was also an important man in our village, our shaman. He kept our customs and blessed our ventures. He was my teacher because he was the keeper of our people's history. First, he thanked the cypress tree spirit for providing the canoe and asked the canoe to stay upright and afloat. He asked the waters to be calm and the winds to be mild for our adventure. He asked fish to come to our weirs and the sun to shine while we dried the fish and transported them to our village.

Roncommock then called forth Eracano. He was the medicine man of the village, not just the healer, but the one in closest contact with the spirits. Roncommock, as shaman, asked for blessings from the spirits and orchestrated the ceremonies, but it was Eracano who could tell us whether the venture would succeed. He entered the spirit world, communicated with the spirits, and received their replies. Now that I knew something about contacting the spirits through Roncommock's training, I understood the ritual. I looked at Ascopo and smiled, but did not speak because doing so would interrupt the ceremony.

Eracano came to the central, sacred fire, which we kept burning constantly. Its embers were never allowed to burn out until we held the busk at the beginning of each new year. When it rained or stormed, we covered the fire to protect it and either Roncommock or Eracano tended it to ensure it was not extinguished.

Like Roncommock, Eracano shaved his hair on both sides, leaving a central ridge down the middle, but he lacked the fringe of hair across his forehead that Roncommock wore. The shamans and medicine men were the only ones who shaved their heads on both sides. All the other men wore only one side short and the other long, and the women and children, who did not shoot bows, wore long hair all around.

Eracano's clothing was also different. Roncommock wore a short, rabbit skin cloak the year-round. All the warriors wore a loincloth of deerskin, like me, and we all added cloaks in the winter. Eracano, however, was the only one of us who wore the skin of a river otter tucked into the belt around his waist. Their pelts were brown furred and very thick. They lived near water, ate fish, and dug burrows into the earth. On land, they had a strange, loping run that looked more like swimming than running. Since the animals were comfortable on both land and water, they were powerful connections for the medicine man, helping him to reach the spirits bound to the earth as well as those of the water. Eracano usually wore the skin of a dried bird attached to his hair and dangling down to his ear to help him reach the spirits of the air.

Eracano danced vigorously around the sacred fire while he called to the spirits, stamping his feet and throwing up his arms until the sweat gleamed over his body. Drummers pounded out a fast beat, keeping up with the pounding of Eracano's feet. The rest of us clapped in rhythm and occasionally a man would add a "humpf" at a particularly strong beat. When it seemed that neither drummers nor dancers could possibly continue at such a rate, Eracano abruptly sat down and the drumming ceased. He took out his special pipe from a pouch around his belt. He filled the pipe with a mixture of *uppówoc* and other herbs from the pouch, and smoked it while the drummers started again with a soft, rhythmic beat. Smoke swirled around his face, wreathing his head in a thick cloud of pure white, but the sweat continued to drip off his body, running in rivulets down his chest and back.

As Eracano communicated with the spirits, swaying to the drums' more gentle rhythm, his eyes closed in concentration, and his lips moved without producing sound, the rest of us waited quietly and patiently. Even Ascopo and I found it easy to wait because we could see his intense focus and wondered what the spirits were telling him.

Finally he stilled his swaying, the drums stopped, and then he stood a little shakily and began to tell us what he had learned. We would have a successful trip, and all would return safely. The spirits would test some of us, however, and we should prepare ourselves for their contact. I sucked in my breath at that and Ascopo looked quickly over toward me. Our traps would catch large fish and we would return with much food for the village, but we would return with more than just food. Some significant event was ordained. We should watch for signs from the spirits and heed them. Indicating that his pronouncements were over, Eracano slumped to the ground from exhaustion. Roncommock helped him back to his wigwam as the celebration really got into full swing.

Ascopo turned to me and said, "What did he mean about testing by the spirits? That sounds like an early *husquenaugh* to me and I sure don't want anything to do with that!"

"I agree, Ascopo, but maybe he means something else. I doubt he could be referring to us. Surely someone else will be tested."

"I think we both already know that 'that someone' will be *you*. And what about that big event? What could he mean by that? Is that something scary or something wonderful?"

"I don't know, Ascopo. Listen, I feel rather tired from the day and too excited about tomorrow to be able to really enjoy the celebration. Let's get something to eat and then I will go to talk with Roncommock. Surely he will have some ideas about what Eracano meant."

"Will you come tell me, Skyco?"

"I will try, Ascopo."

I left Ascopo by the fire. When I reached the wigwam, Roncommock was already there.

"Ah, Skyco," he said. "Tomorrow is a big day. Are you ready?"

"I think so, master."

"You will learn to set the weirs and repair them, no doubt. You will also learn how to spear fish from a canoe and to attract fish at night. You will have many opportunities to catch fish."

"It will be a pleasure to learn these things. And I look forward to seeing the big blue ocean and the sandy banks. These places are new to me and I have never traveled before to see them."

"Skyco, it will be good for you to see these things, but you should also take the time to study the other villages. No doubt, your party will pick up more men from Ohanoak just downstream, but you will also travel through Weapemeoc territory. Have you learned the names of the leaders of each village?

"Yes, master."

"You will certainly stop at Ricahokene,"

"Ribuckon," I interrupted.

"Good, but who is chief of the Weapemeocs?" Roncommock challenged me to see if I had learned.

"He is chief Okisco, and he is in my family clan."

"Tell me your relationship. It is important for you to keep kinship in mind. Our kinships determine who will help you and who you will fight when you become chief. When you succeed to the chief's position, you will make a tour to cement these kinship obligations, and it will be easier if you have been to the villages beforehand. This trip is a good opportunity for you to reconnoiter with the Weapemeoc villages, to see them unofficially. They will be your closest allies."

I recited my family history, at least as far as the tie between Okisco and myself.

"My mother and chief Menatonon were born of Sacquenummener, who is my grandmother. Sacquenummener and her two younger sisters were born of Mamankanois and my sister carries the name of our great-grandmother, as is her right. My sister will be head woman of our tribe. The first Mamankanois, in addition to being the head woman of the Chowanoacs, married a man from the Weapemeoc tribe. His mother was the head woman of that tribe, and the first daughter of her first daughter is the mother of

Okisco, making him chief of the Weapemeocs. Thus the Chowanoacs and Weapemeocs have family ties."

"Remember that, Skyco. Your uncle Menatonon is the most powerful chief in the area, for eighteen villages fall under his eye. Even though his body is now crippled, his wisdom is unparalleled. You must learn as quickly as you can, and as much as you can, for we do not know how long his body will last. Take this chance to study the Weapemeocs when you are in their villages and keep in mind that you will need Okisco and his sister's son as allies." Roncommock paused and I realized that he was studying my reactions.

"Skyco, I have reason to believe that you are the one who will be contacted by the spirits. Both Eracano and I have had visions and communications from the spirits that suggest as much. It is likely that the spirits will lead you on your spirit quest. You will fish, but you must follow your instincts and see where they lead you. Remain alert for their contact. And be careful," he added almost as an afterthought.

Suddenly the thought of my upcoming fishing trip lost some of its luster; it was not going to be as much simple fun as I had hoped. What was I going to tell Ascopo?

My Fishing Trip

Ascopo and I were disgusted. We were stuck at Metackwem while waiting on the weather to improve before we could cross the big sound and make our passage to the east. The Chowan was a wide river and we made good time heading downstream, but as we approached the sound, the wind came up strong enough to throw up some choppy waves. We put in to Metackwem, another village of our tribe, to await better conditions. The men resigned themselves to the delay. They even suggested it was good to have strong wind, because when it calmed down and changed direction, the sound would be smooth for a few days and make our crossing easier. But I was not even out of Chowanoac territory yet!

At least the food was good. On the evening we arrived, the villagers of Metackwem were enjoying the catch from a particularly successful fishing expedition. On a grill over the central fire lay a huge flounder—which we called a *pashockshin*—as large as a warrior's broad back. I had never eaten such fresh *pashockshin* before, for I had never been on a fishing expedition to the eastern sound, where the brackish water attracted fish such as the *pashockshin, mesickek*, and *chigwusso.*

At home, the Chowan River was chock-full of fish that preferred freshwater, such as largemouth bass, sunfish, chubs, *kowabetteo,* and *coppáuseo.* We caught huge catfish—which we called *keetrauk* and were bottom feeders—by impaling a piece of meat on a hook carved from bone, and sometimes hooked big *coppáuseo* that way, too. The big fish swallowed this bait and we pulled them up on a rope made of nettle fibers that was tied to the hook. If a *kowabetteo* bit the bait, his sharp teeth cut the line.

To catch other fish in shallow creeks, we built a stone weir by piling up the stones to create a sort of fence across the width of the creek. The women and children entered the water upstream, splashing and scaring the fish downstream, where they encountered the stone fence.

The fish swam along its sides, becoming ever more panicked as the women came closer to them, until the fish found a single break in the fence, where the women had already placed a large woven basket. The fish darted through the opening into the basket-trap, and the women simply lifted the basket and took home a mess of fish. Clearly, the technique worked well in a shallow creek to catch small fish, but

I was curious about how the men could build a weir in deeper water to trap larger fish.

Since the weather was comfortably cool and breezy at Metackwem, we ate outside the wigwams on a reed table mat. Each of us had his own wooden plate, and we served ourselves from the big fish, already cooked over the fire. The *pashockshin* was so big that its tail actually draped over the edge of the wooden grill. It was the only fish cooked over the big central fire. I wish I had seen how they turned the huge thing over to cook both sides. At least it was flat so that the whole body cooked evenly.

Not so for a huge *chigwusso*. The meat was filleted from the backbone before being cooked because it was so thick behind the head while thin along the tail that it would never cook evenly if left whole. It was so big that four large families of warriors fed from that single fish. The bulk of the catch was smaller *chigwusso, pashockshin,* or croaker—also called *man-chauemec.* Everyone sat outdoors as we did, enjoying the late afternoon warmth from the returning sun of early spring.

The whole village smelled of wood-smoke and the pleasant tang of fresh fish. With all these fragrant aromas in the air, raccoons, skunks, and opossums would visit the midden tonight. I was sure that some of the older boys would lie in wait for these animals, proudly bringing home food for tomorrow, just as they did in my village when we had a great meal like this one.

With my stomach full and my obligation to the

head table completed, I was free to join Ascopo and wander around the village. We found Keetrauk contentedly resting on the ground, leaning back against the wall of the wigwam along with his brother Tetszo. Both were from the fish clan and had fish names; not surprisingly, they were good fishermen and leaders of this expedition. Keetrauk was named for the catfish, Tetszo for mullet. With everyone relaxed and full of food, now was the time for a suggestion.

"How are those great big *pashockshin* caught?" I asked the two men, winking at Ascopo.

"Oh, now *that* is fun," Keetrauk said. "We spear them from the canoe."

Tetszo added, "But a fish as big as the one eaten tonight can't be hoisted up on a spear as we do with the small ones. With one of those monsters, you have to jump out of the canoe and lift the big fish in with your arms. It takes a lot of shoving and grunting to get the beast into the canoe. Got to watch those teeth, too. They are sharp!"

"Do you remember the first time we took Chaham night fishing for *pashockshin?*" Keetrauk asked.

"I will never forget it. That is when we knew he was going to be a great fisherman like us. He is still young, but he is already accomplished, and since he is named for the shad fish, his prowess will only grow," Tetszo added proudly. "It was his first trip as one of the spearmen in the canoe. As we glided over a shoal, he said that he saw a giant *pashockshin* buried in the sand. I asked why he didn't strike it, and didn't believe him when he said it was too big to lift into the canoe. I even laughed when he said that our canoe had passed near its tail, but its head was too far away to strike. 'Chaham,' I said to him, 'it can't be that big!' But he said, 'Yes, sir, it is. Please back the canoe so that I can hit its head.' I chuckled, but maneuvered as he indicated, and when he struck with the spear, there was never so much thrashing and splashing and water flipping up everywhere! Chaham and the other spearman jumped overboard into the water and together they lifted and shoved the biggest *pashock-shin* I have ever seen into that canoe. I don't mind admitting that I was astounded."

"Yeah, and next time Chaham said he saw a big fish, you believed him," Keetrauk added.

"You bet I did," Tetszo agreed.

"But the *chigwusso* are usually caught in the weirs with the *mesickek*, aren't they?" Ascopo asked the two men.

"Yes, Ascopo," Tetszo answered. "To learn how to build and set a weir is an art. To build one correctly and fish it successfully requires knowledge and skill that you can only gain by practice. Because it has been so long since we visited our weirs at the coast, it is likely they have degraded, so we will no doubt start your training with repair work."

"But I thought *women* fished the weirs in the streams that empty onto the Chowan," I said.

"Everyone needs to know the fishing weir, Skyco. You are correct that women often set the weirs in the small, freshwater creeks, but we men set a different version of the weirs in the sound where the bigger fish run. There, we build our fence of strong stakes and weave a larger and stronger basket, or pen, out of rope and saplings. Our weir must be strong enough to hold a fish as large as a man, and we must be strong enough to manage them! It is nearly time for the striped bass, the *mesickek*, to start their yearly movements, coming in the inlets and making their way up to the rivers where they spawn. Those are the fish we are going after this time. They are as big as men, silver with dark stripes. Their meat dries well and we will take it back to the village to eat until our crops are ripe. The spring is the season of *mesickek*."

Tetszo paused and glanced up at the trees, then looked around at Ascopo and me, careful to get our attention.

"Notice, boys, that the wind has dropped. In the absence of wind and choppy waves, we will cross the sound rapidly and without the danger of overturning the canoes. We have two days of heavy paddling ahead of us. Tomorrow night we will stop at the halfway point, the village of Ricahokene, and the next night we will be at our fishing camp. Once there, you will night fish for *pashockshin*, and the next day you will be setting the weir to fish for *mesickek*."

Ascopo nearly leapt up in delight.

"Night fishing!" he cried excitedly. "I can hardly wait!"

Manchauemec said, "You boys had better find something to occupy your time. You'll drive yourselves insane with waiting unless you focus on some other project."

"Let's go check Metackwem's palisade, then. If we built one of them around our village, I could get interested in carving!" Ascopo said.

"I know what you mean. The palisade is impressive, but you know that we will never build it because when we host the other villages of the tribe, the huge increase of visitors swells the size of our village," I replied. "We couldn't build a palisade large enough to hold them all."

"We could still have a palisade and just have the temporary wigwams set up outside it," he argued.

"Well, let's see how it is built. Maybe you can make the suggestion to Menatonon when we get back," I suggested.

"Or maybe I will just wait until there is a new chief," he smirked.

Because Metackwem was located close to enemy Mangoak territory, the villagers built a palisade, or wall of posts, around their village to protect it. To build the wall, they had cut down trees and removed all their branches, which was a major undertaking. They set these posts side-by-side, with the base of each post buried in the ground and the top sharpened to a point. Each post was about three times as tall as a man. There were two openings into the palisade, one to the east and one to the west, and to enter the village, a single person could just fit through the narrow chute. At night, all the villagers retreated inside the ring of trees that they had essentially planted around their village. The palisade made a sturdy wall of defense should the tribe be attacked by enemy warriors. Only the wigwams and central fire were inside the wall, which kept the size of the palisade manageable. The crop fields and the dancing circle were outside it.

Ascopo pointed out that we could build a palisade around our own village and still accommodate additional people during celebrations because the temporary wigwams were set up near the crop fields, which would be outside the palisade, rather than inside the protected center of the village. One aspect of the palisade bothered me.

"Ascopo, don't you find it surprising that Metackwem's palisade has gaps between the posts that are large enough for an enemy's arrow to penetrate? Seems like the village is unnecessarily vulnerable."

Ascopo looked doubtful and replied, "Perhaps, but the enemy warrior would need to be close to the palisade in order to shoot through it and would have to cross the open fields. There are guards stationed at each opening, and they would certainly see enemies coming before they were close enough to shoot."

"What if, instead of a palisade, we envisioned it as a weir? Did you hear Tetszo describe how they wove rope and saplings between the sticks of the weir and made the whole fish trap strong enough to hold a big fish the size of a man? What if we did that here and made the palisade impenetrable?"

Ascopo thought for a moment and smiled at me. "That is a good idea, Skyco, something that a chief might think of as a way to protect his tribe. I like

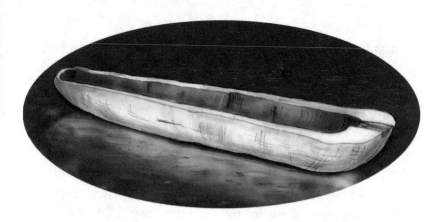

how you put together a village palisade and a fish weir, because they don't seem alike at all, yet what you propose might just work! It is a good improvement to the basic structure they have here."

As I fell asleep that night, I felt rather proud of myself. The extra time in Metackwem was not wasted after all; it had given me some ideas.

The next morning, we departed early and almost immediately gained the sound. It looked immense, with the water stretching away from us in all directions. I could still see land on each side of us, but straight ahead was only an endless expanse of water. We encountered a few small waves in the sound that splashed against the sides of the canoe, but the water's surface was mostly flat, unlike the previous day when the choppy waves were large enough to endanger the canoes.

In addition to two canoes from Chowanook, two more canoes from Metackwem joined us to reduce the immediate demand on their village's spring food supply. In the spring, food supplies are always lowest, for the winter uses up much of the preserved crop food and the new crops have yet to produce. The villagers had meat and fish available, but without the added pressure from two canoes of hungry men, the food would last longer. Each canoe held about fifteen men plus fishing gear, which was much of the adult male population from the village. The elders and boys, as well as any man whose wife was pregnant or had recently given birth, stayed behind with the women to continue to provide game animals to eat. In each canoe, ten men usually paddled while five rested and they changed places as the paddlers tired. In this fashion, we kept moving the entire day.

I paddled for a while, learning to coordinate my stroke with the others so that our paddles dipped in the water at the same time. Since I was shorter, my strokes were also shorter, and I had to pay attention to keep in time. To help us keep rhythm, we often chanted a song that had an accented beat, "Hey-um-HUH!, Hey-um-HUH!" We dipped in our paddles and pulled with each forceful "HUH!" We kept along the northern edge of the sound, traveling in Weapemeoc territory, but where a river opened up or a bay formed along the shore, we cut across the mouth to shorten our trip.

We carried water, dried berries, and dried strips of smoked deer meat in the canoe, eating and drinking as we needed, but that created a problem. We were paddling all day with no stops, and I had to pee. Putting it off as long as possible in the hopes that someone else would have to go first, I waited until I could no longer stand it. I leaned over to Ascopo, seated next to me and whispered, "Ascopo, do you know how we are supposed to pee?" His face turned bright red and he just shook his head, not looking me in the eye, so I leaned back toward Chaham, who was seated close by, and whispered, "Chaham, I have to pee. How do I do it?"

Chaham laughed aloud and Manchauemec yelled from behind me, "Hey Skyco, notice all this water rushing by? Hear that sound of the water flowing? Drips of water everywhere?"

The other men started to snigger.

"Water sure is clear. Not a yellow streak any-where!"

Chaham said, "Just ignore them. They made bets on how long you could last. You have to stand up and pee over the side. But don't fall out, don't let the pee get in the canoe, and whatever you do, pee downwind so that you don't hit someone else with it."

It was a lot to remember, especially when I felt like I was about to burst. I moved back so that I would be downwind of the paddlers. Balancing was tricky in a round-bottomed canoe, but I managed to wedge one foot under a basket loaded with gear so that I felt a little more secure. Lifting up my loin-cloth, I relaxed and the pee shot out into the water, foaming up because it hit with such force.

"This canoe is floating higher now!" Tetszo shouted.

"Oh, I think the water in the sound has risen, brother. That is what is happening back here." The other men chuckled and I felt my face redden, but I could do nothing else until I was finished, and that seemed to take a long time. As soon as I sat down, however, each of the other men also had to take breaks to empty their bladders, and I felt somewhat vindicated while also embarrassed. They had been waiting on me to do it first. Even Ascopo seemed to know the joke.

Before dusk, we could see the smoke from the village fire of Ricahokene, near the midway point along the sound. When I dipped my hand in the water and scooped up a handful to drink, it was too bitter and salty for me to swallow, and I spat it out. Ascopo saw me and tried it too, with the same result.

Along the shoreline near the village grew a huge bank of oysters. We pulled our canoes to shore, and Chaham took both Ascopo and me with him to explore the bank. He carried a big basket and gave us each a stone tomahawk that had been flaked to make a sharp edge. There were narrow paths or channels that had been cut through the bank by prior parties of fishermen from the village, and we walked carefully along the sandy paths and knocked loose clumps of the oysters. Despite the well-worn paths, there were sharp shells scattered about and we all donned moccasins to protect our feet. We quickly filled the basket and carried it with us to the village.

Diplomacy was a little tricky because the villagers of Ricahokene didn't expect us. It would be easy to mistake four canoes loaded with men for a war party, and the last thing we wanted was such a misunderstanding. Now we'd see if Roncommock's training was effective and if I really knew what I was doing. I was nervous.

My canoe coasted slowly forward to the landing place while the other three floated back beyond the range of arrows. Men of the village had gathered on shore and they held strung bows, although they had not yet nocked in arrows. I stood up and moved slowly forward to the front of the canoe, so that the onlookers could see that I was just a boy not painted in war paint. No one in our canoe held bows, but I could see Tetszo's hand tighten nervously on the paddle as I made myself an easy target should something get out of hand.

I called out, "Village of Ricahokene, ruled by Ribuckon, son of Marangahockes, I come to you in peace from the Village of Chowanook. Menatonon, son of Sacquenummener, sends his regards through his heir Skyco and asks that you house us tonight. We bring oysters to the evening meal."

On hearing my address, the men along the bank visibly relaxed and lowered their bows. A youthful man, wearing a copper gorget that marked him as the chief, replied, "I am Ribuckon and we welcome you, Skyco. You speak well."

Our canoes pulled ashore and we climbed out, glad to stretch our legs after a long day of sitting in the canoe. While I went ashore a little anxiously to meet Ribuckon, the other men unloaded the oysters and other gear. Ascopo stayed with them and helped to refill the *macócqwer* that held our drinking water.

I turned my attention to Ribuckon. His tattoos

were extensive. Many of the men in my village were tattooed around their arms and legs, and all men are marked with the symbol of their home village on the left, back shoulder, at the conclusion of their *husquenaugh*. Ribuckon, however, sported extensive tattooing on his chest and stomach in addition to the tattoos that encircled his calves and upper arms. A complex coil descended from his shoulders down his chest, mimicking a necklace of wampum, and dark outlines encircled both nipples and belly button. He also wore a V-shaped mark on his forehead between his eyebrows. In total, he looked intimidating, which was the point.

I took a deep breath, and he began to talk. He was very curious about the Mangoaks and was glad to hear that we had made a successful raid on one of their villages to avenge an attack sustained by one of the Chowanoac villages. It was important to keep a balance among the raids. We killed only the number that they had killed. While I was listening to Ribuckon, answering additional questions that did not require much thought, I suddenly wondered how war could have ever started, or how it would ever end, if we killed just the number they had killed of us, but presumably they were killing just the number that we had killed of them earlier. It was confusing, and something I would have to ask Roncommock when we returned.

By then Ribuckon had asked all his questions and it was my turn to question him. Menatonon had specifically instructed me to ask about the Roanoacs, a tribe to the south of the sound. They were Algonquin, but both the Chowanoacs and the Weapemeocs had allied themselves together to fight the Roanoacs in the past. Ribuckon had no further news about them. They had not ventured to the north side of the sound into Weapemeoc territory, and the few contacts with them on the sandy banks did not result in bloodshed. We still held an uneasy truce.

I liked Ribuckon and felt that our alliance would remain strong. We would support each other when I became chief. After our conversation, we walked over to the central fire, where the women of the village were already preparing the evening meal.

Ironically, the villagers had also collected oysters for the evening meal, undoubtedly because they were so abundant and so near the village. They were also delicious, especially after roasting over the fire. In Chowanook, we held an oyster roast once or twice a year when the fishermen returned from the fishing expeditions, but there were always other items to eat in addition. Tonight we only ate oysters, and it took piles of them to feed us all. Ascopo and I really out-did ourselves, eating as many as the grown men. We left a huge stack of discarded oyster shells at the village's midden and I slept like a contented bear that night.

After another full day of paddling, we reached our fishing camp, which was located on a point of land at the eastern edge of Weapemeoc territory. Near the end of our journey, we seemed to be farthest out in the sound, more distant from the northern shore than ever before, and I grew a little anxious. I glanced over at Ascopo and thought his face revealed his discomfort too, but neither of us spoke. Soon, however, we sighted the point of land that was our destination and began to approach it. I grew more confident that we would actually reach it before the winds piped up, and when I looked over again at Ascopo, he smiled reassuringly at me.

While Ascopo helped the other men pull up the canoes and unload gear, Tetszo took me aside.

"One of the other important tasks for any fishing expedition is to bring back the spring leaves of the yaupon holly, with which the shamans make the black drink. The trees surround this fishing camp and we harvest their branches every year on a spring fishing expedition. Go get Ascopo and I will show you the trees while the others build up the fire."

I ran back to where Ascopo was unloading. "Come on! Tetszo has something to show us!" Indeed, just a few steps from where he waited, he pointed to a shrubby tree with pale bark. The trees weren't much taller than a man and their trunks were slender and contorted. Their small leaves, borne on short, twisted branches, were about the size and shape of the last joint of my index finger. Some of the trees had bright red berries.

Ascopo and I whispered thanks to the tree spirits, and then broke off twigs until our arms were full. We carried the small branches back to camp, where we piled them up carefully to one side of the fire. "Tomorrow one of the men will set these up to dry while the rest of us are fishing, and in a few days, whenever the leaves are fully dry, we will pick them off and place them in a basket to take back with us. When we return to the village, Roncommock will prepare the leaves to make the black drink," Tetszo told us. We felt honored to be involved in the important task.

It was interesting to learn about the black drink, but I really wanted to fish. The gear was unloaded, the fire was burning inside a rock ring, and some of the men were off collecting fresh water. As Ascopo and I finished our task, Keetrauk called out impatiently, "What's keeping you? Chaham and I have the boat ready to fish!" We needed no additional encouragement, but ran immediately to the boat.

Ascopo asked, "What about my brother?" Chaham replied, "He works with the other boat. He has a lot to learn, just like you, and we can't have all the untested fishermen in a single boat." Ascopo seemed relieved and pointed to the funny-looking spears that we carried with us.

"Do we use these to fish?" he asked. Instead of the normal stone spear point joined to the wooden shaft, these two spears bore a trident of sharpened, fire-hardened wooden points that formed dangerous-looking spikes.

"Yep. These are the fishing tridents," Chaham said.

We also carried a fire in the canoe with us. Now that surprised me. How could we carry fire in a wooden canoe? It was an ingenious method. After starting the fire on shore, the men transferred coals to a shallow clay pot. They wedged the pot in the canoe with rocks around and underneath it, and we carried reeds and small sticks to keep the fire burning. That became the task to which Ascopo and I were assigned, to tend the fire in the canoe while one man steered and two men speared fish.

"When will we get to fish?" Ascopo asked, somewhat impatiently.

"Soon enough, Ascopo. Be patient. Someone must attend the fire just as someone else must steer the canoe and yet another spears the fish. You will perform all three tasks as you become an experienced fisherman," Tetszo said.

We glided swiftly out into the sound and as soon as we were a few canoe-lengths from shore, we turned and began to move parallel to the shore. Chaham and Keetrauk, bearing tridents, stood up in the front of the canoe, one facing to each side. Tetszo, the paddler, moved to the very back of the canoe. Ascopo and I sat in the center, one on each side of the fire. It was still daylight, but the sun was getting low in the sky. We fished so that it shone from behind us; we faced away from its glare.

Before the canoe had even balanced from all the shifting of positions of the men, Keetrauk lifted his spear high and, with a shout, plunged it forcefully into the water. Tetszo, who was paddling, backed the canoe slightly as Keetrauk, in a single, swift, arching movement, lifted the spear with its impaled struggling fish from the water, and in the same continuous motion, swung the spear inboard to slip the struggling fish into the basket near my feet.

I looked down into the basket and saw a *pashock-shin*, a flounder, flattened from side to side, its two eyes on the same side of its head looking up angrily at me. Ascopo stood up and leaned way over so that he could see too, tilting the canoe, and Keetrauk snapped at him, "Hey, watch it back there. I am trying to fish here!"

Ascopo sat back down, but not before jabbing his finger into the fish's body. It snapped its small, toothy jaws and flopped around in the basket, trying to jump free, and Ascopo jerked his finger back out of the basket. "A *pashockshin*," he said proudly, as if he'd caught the fish himself.

Chaham, the other fisherman, gave a grunt as he too thrust a spear into the water. He landed a huge crab, a *seékanauk*. The enormous round crab had a long spiky tail, which it kept trying to use to turn itself back over. Ascopo was laughing at its antics as it frantically tried to gain purchase to right itself, but just continued sliding around in the smooth canoe. When it was upside down, its ten long legs, each with small pincers on the end, grasped helplessly at the air. Its mouth set forward of the first pair of legs and was mostly just a grinding plate. After the legs ended, a short section of abdomen supported flapping gills, which looked like thick leaves stacked up in a row, and then the heavy, spiky tail protruded from the back end of the animal.

"Is there any meat on this animal to eat?" Ascopo asked.

Chaham replied, "Not enough to bother with, but this one has such a long tail that it will make a good spear point."

"Then maybe we can use its tail to spear more *seékanauk!*" Ascopo suggested.

I peered over the side and realized we were in very clear and shallow water, which is how the men were able to see and spear the fish. I thought the men used the light from the fire in order to see, but realized that the low sun, soon to be followed by a nearly full moon, cast enough light to see by.

"What is this fire for?" I asked of anyone in general. "Do you need it to see?"

"It lures in the bait fish, which attract the big *pashockshin.* Sometimes we get *chigwusso,* too." Chaham paused, and with a satisfied grunt, said, "Like that!" as he dropped a big, reddish fish into the basket. It was an attractive, coppery-red color, with two large black spots near its tail.

Gingerly, I leaned over so that I could see over the side of the canoe. The water was clear, and I could see all the way to the bottom. A few small fish darted away as the canoe passed them. A jelly with long streamers drifted past, then another just like it, except it was the color of freshly crushed grape juice instead of plain white.

"What are those jellies? Do they sting?"

"You have many questions, Skyco!" Tetszo said. "But that is, after all, why you are here. The jellies are called sea nettles because they sting like the nettle plants on land do."

He paused, then added, "Watch also for sea plums, or comb jellies. They too are jellies, but lack long tentacles and do not sting. The sea plums are worth a close look in strong daylight. As they swim and turn, they glint with the colors of the rainbow in stripes along their oval bodies." Now Ascopo was leaning over, too, trying to see the jellies.

"Why are some of the sea nettles red and some white?"

"Now you have asked a question that I cannot answer," Tetszo said.

"I think the red ones have eaten something that makes them red," Chaham said from up front.

"You mean you think they are animals instead of flowers or fruits of the sea?" Tetszo said with surprise.

"That blob right there is an *animal*?" Ascopo said as he pointed to one of the jellies in the water.

"That is what I think," Chaham said firmly.

"Hmmph," was all Tetszo replied, making me believe that he disagreed, but did not want to argue further with Chaham. Were these creatures animals or plants? I thought more and more about that question while we continued to fish. I definitely saw one move, contracting slowly like a disembodied heart, but it had no eye, no mouth, nothing that seemed to make it an animal. Yet plants did not move, did not contract. The problem intrigued me.

Soon we were back at the landing place, guided by the light from the moon and the fire on shore. The men who'd stayed at the fishing camp had already constructed a high grill over the fire. They filleted the big fish and laid them up on the high grill to smoke and dry slowly. We also had a normal-height grill ready for the smaller fish, and we ate those hungrily. Ascopo grabbed a small croaker off the grill while it was still smoking and switched the hot fish rapidly from hand-to-hand as he pulled out the fins. Not one to fall behind, his brother Kaiauk grabbed one too, and though I was sure it burned his fingers, he never let on that it did.

"This new canoe is a good one," Tetszo said. "Old Memeo selected the right tree. You know, boys," he continued, "even when a tree agrees to become a canoe, sometimes it changes its mind in the water and dumps out the paddler and the fishermen when they try to spear fish. It is a good sign that this canoe barely budged as we speared fish and shifted our positions. It is definitely happy to be a fishing canoe."

I felt good about how I'd helped to build the canoe, and glad that the fishermen agreed that it was a good one.

"We should get some sleep. Tomorrow we will set the weirs near the inlet, where the waters of the land meet the endless water of the sea. It will be hard work."

Ascopo, Kaiauk, and I walked up the short path to the camp's sleeping quarters under the spreading boughs of a huge, live oak tree. It was no protection from rain, but its leaves would keep the morning dew from forming on our bodies. We lay down in sandy depressions that other fisherman must have used. Ascopo and I lay close together and relived the day of fishing, but Kaiauk moved further away, closer to where the older men settled down.

"We caught lots of *pashockshin* and *chigwusso,* Skyco. Do you suppose they will let us try our hand at spearing the fish tomorrow?" Ascopo whispered to me.

"I sure hope so. Tetszo said something about fixing the weir, too. I want to see how that works," I replied. "But don't forget that we speared *seékanauk,* too. We don't want to offend them."

"You are so careful about offending the spirits, always thinking about them. That was the first thing you asked me when we were building the canoe. Why do you think about spirits all the time?" Ascopo paused, but when I didn't answer, he went on, "I wonder what those *pashockshin* look like when they are buried in the sand. Did you hear Chaham say how they could be hard to see when they buried in like that? I hope we get a really big one."

I started to feel sleepy. As I looked up from my warm, sandy nest, the stars shone through the branches of the oak tree. "What did you think about those jellies? Do you think they are plants or animals?" I asked him.

"Oh, they just float in the water like plants. Must be plants since they don't have mouths."

"I am not so sure of that, Ascopo. I think Chaham might be right. I think they are eating something that makes them red. Otherwise why are some red and some white?"

"Well, aren't flowers different colors, too? Some

flowers even start out pink and then fade to white. Now I am sure they must be flowers of the sea. The white ones are just fading in color."

"If so, then where are the plants they come from?" I asked him. "You never see flowers that are not connected to a plant. Besides, they contract and move, unlike any plant I know of." That shut him up.

"You boys quit talking and get to sleep," one of the men called out.

"I sure hope we get one of those big *pashockshin*. Don't you think they'll let us fish? Surely we will be allowed to fish when we are on a fishing expedition." Ascopo couldn't be quiet for long.

"You know, Tetszo, if you'd just tell them what they are doing tomorrow, I bet they would be quiet and let us get some sleep!" Keetrauk called out.

"Right," I heard Tetszo grunt. "Tomorrow the boys go with us first thing in the morning to fix the weir out near the ocean's inlet. In the afternoon, they can try their hands at spearing fish."

"Now hush, Ascopo," Keetrauk said.

"Yeah, Ascopo. Do what you are told," Kaiauk added, just to let Ascopo know he was still his older brother even if out here they were on equal footing.

I fell asleep to the sound of katydids and grasshoppers, but just as I fell asleep, I remembered flytraps. They were green plants, but they moved.

I Am Almost Eaten

NEXT TO THE day when I was almost shot by that arrow, the worst day of my life was when I was almost eaten. The sky was dark when I awoke, but I felt refreshed and no longer sleepy. *Dawn must be close*, I thought. I punched Ascopo on the shoulder to awaken him, and he was alert almost instantly.

"Why did you let me sleep so long?" he asked peevishly.

My feet knew the path to the riverbank where we launched and stored the canoes the evening before. We sat down on an overturned canoe and waited. Soon, I heard the soft footfalls of others traveling the path. Both Tetszo and Keetrauk appeared, emerging into the faint light of the riverbank from the dark forest.

I was surprised to see that when we rolled one of the canoes upright, the head and attached backbone of a big *chigwusso* from last night's feast had been stored beneath it. Only now did I realize that yesterday another canoe, not ours, had brought in such an enormous fish.

"Why is that carcass *here?*" I exclaimed with some astonishment.

"We keep the big ones to trap blue crabs. Look at all the flesh left on the head of this *chigwusso!* It should attract enough blue crabs to fill a basket with them. Really, we should have cooked the head in a stew pot over the fire, but instead of eating the meat ourselves, we'll use it to catch crabs and eat those instead. Did you remember to bring the rope, Keetrauk?"

"Yes, sure I did. You don't think I would forget basic fishing equipment, do you, brother?"

The men dragged down a smaller canoe from high up in the marsh, placing the fish carcass, some thin rope, and some thicker rope into the midsection.

"We are taking this smaller, faster canoe today, boys. You'll be back in the big one a little later." Keetrauk voiced what was on my mind before I got to it. "Don't worry, Ascopo and Skyco, you'll get to fish from the big canoe later, but first we want to repair the weir and this small canoe will get us there much faster."

"We'll need some strong reeds and stakes to repair the weir, too, brother," Keetrauk said as he rummaged around in the canoe.

"I left them over at the edge of the woods yesterday. Go look for the bundle, Skyco, while I load the canoe with the rest of the gear." Tetszo pointed toward the woods in a rather general manner and I wondered if I would be able to find the parcel. "Run along. Look for a pile of sticks all bundled together and tied with a rope. You should stumble across it."

Stumble I did, ramming my foot right into the bunch, and skinning up the top of my big toe. I couldn't see the dark mass of sticks against the slightly darker trees when there was still barely any light in the sky. I hobbled back with the bundle, afraid to complain about my sore toe. When we had more light, I would check for a splinter. It hurt enough that I thought there might be a splinter of wood under the skin.

Tetszo and Keetrauk pushed the canoe to the water's edge. "Hop in, boys. Today we visit the sandy banks."

"Will we come back here or stay there?" I asked.

"Depends on the weather. We'll see," Keetrauk replied.

Ascopo and I climbed into the middle of the canoe. It was smaller and shallower than the big one we had helped to build. It held the gear and all four of us comfortably, but any more would make it crowded.

"Where did this small canoe come from? We had only big canoes with us." I couldn't help but ask because I knew this small canoe wasn't with us on the journey. Did I miss something?

"We leave this canoe here, high up on the shore where the water can't reach it. Out here we often want speed, not a lot of room for fish. The big canoes are necessary for carrying men and fish back to the village, but this little girl here is for getting somewhere quickly. The weir will certainly need repair and we don't expect to catch any fish today." Keetrauk spoke from the front of the canoe where he sat already positioned with his paddle.

"Unless there is something so big it can't escape," Tetszo rejoined from behind as he pushed us out into deeper water.

"Sure, sure. Giant fish. Ha-ha," his brother said as Tetszo jumped carefully aboard without spilling us. I hadn't seen him add the basket for crabs until now, when he abruptly pushed it toward me, explaining, "Need a little more room for my feet back here."

"Those big feet get in the way of everything. Maybe you could wiggle your toes to attract the crabs and get those feet nipped back down to size, Tetszo!"

Soon they pulled with strong strokes, leaving no more breath for jokes. We skimmed across the surface, almost flying. The water was flat and clear. The horizon was pink and orange, but the sun was not yet visible. It was beautiful out on the vast but calm water, and we moved so quickly that the wind was blowing Keetrauk's hair on the longer, left side.

We rounded a point and Keetrauk cried, "Across the last river to the sandy banks! They are dead ahead of us now, boys. Let's get across this expanse before it gets rough!" And the two men pulled even harder than before, which I could hardly believe.

All too soon, we approached a sandy beach that

provided a little protection and made for an easy landing, and the brothers beached the canoe. They took out the fish carcass and the thin rope, tying it in two places: around the backbone just behind the head, and through the mouth and around the lower jaw. Ascopo got out of the canoe and helped them. They put the carcass in the shade of a bush and tied the other end of the rope to its branches.

While they were busy with the crabbing preparation, I took the time to examine my toe. Indeed, a splinter stuck out of the top of it, with just enough protruding that I could get my fingernails on it. I pulled and nearly fainted from the pain, but the splinter did not budge. Taking a deep breath, I tried again, and this time the splinter came free with a spurt of blood.

My toe looked nasty. It was purple near the nail, where I had probably jammed and bruised it, there was a gash right at the joint where the splinter had split the skin, and now there was a pool of blood drying around it. I was about to get out and wash it off, but the three were already turning the canoe around in preparation for heading out again. I put my other foot over the worst of the bloodstain to hide it.

"We'll come back here to catch crabs as soon as we get the weir repaired," Keetrauk said as he leaped into the bow, his brother pushed us off from the stern, and we headed out again into open water. The first run that morning was just plain fun, skimming the surface as the sun came up. But now we were heading toward the inlet, which joins the sound to the open sea. There was a little wind and small waves, and I could see the current roiling along. The shore seemed a far distance away, certainly farther than I could swim. I was apprehensive.

"Don't worry, little ones. We have made this run many times. Just don't fall out. The current is swift."

"Are we going out the inlet to that great blue sea?" I had never seen such an expanse of water, endless to the horizon.

"No, we set the weirs in the sound, but close to the inlet. At this season, countless fish enter the sound through the inlet and run up to the rivers to lay their eggs. We catch a few of those with our weirs after they swim in through the inlet."

As Tetszo was telling us this, I turned to look at him in the stern and was astonished to see a big canoe, with twenty men in it, rounding the point we had left behind. A quick surge of fear coursed through me. Who were they? I pointed and Ascopo looked back too.

"A canoe, behind us, with twenty men!" he exclaimed breathlessly. Both brothers paused in their paddling and looked around briefly. "I thought you said we were the only ones coming out this morning."

"It is okay, boys. It is the rest of our fishing group, come out to tend the weirs. They are bringing along the two big canoes and all the fishing gear. I knew they would come right behind us when we said we were taking you boys to teach you weir repair. Now they can rest while you are working. In fact, another canoe should be right along behind the first."

"I thought maybe it was the Roanoacs instead of our group," I tried to explain, and Ascopo nodded vigorously.

"You are right to be concerned. Sometimes we do encounter other tribes out here, but generally, these banks are uncontested land. The Roanoacs claim the central island because their village Dasemunkepeuc is right across from it. At low tide, you can walk across from the village to the island. As you get farther south, the Croatoans occupy the wider islands permanently. But up here, north of the Roanoac's island, we stay out of conflict." Tetszo paused and Keetrauk added, "Just don't go south by yourself. A boy is too tempting a target. They'll make a slave of you."

"Or worse," Tetszo filled in. "Get back to paddling, brother! Let's show them how we can move."

Even with twenty men paddling, the big canoe was slower than we were. A second canoe finally did appear, but it fell even farther behind. We landed before it rounded the point. I leapt out as we beached the canoe on shore, and my toe throbbed from the impact. The blood that had congealed across the wound began to ooze again.

My sore toe only briefly distracted me from looking around, for the banks were different in appearance from the mainland. There was none of the sticky black mud so common everywhere else in the sound. Along the Chowan, we had a sandy beach where we walked down to the river to bathe, but here most of the marsh shoreline was sandy even though we were still on the protected sound side of the banks. I couldn't even imagine what the sea side of the island looked like, but I wanted to see it.

Most astonishing, however, were the great dunes of sand that pushed up above the trees. Men talked about the sandy banks, but not about great dunes of sand like these. They were immense! I was curious about them.

We got out of the canoe and pulled it well above the water onto the dry marsh sand. Tetszo said, "We are close enough to the inlet that we get tides here, boys. The water rises and falls regularly, powered by an internal drive instead of by the wind as it is on the mainland. See that line of flotsam on the upper part of the beach? It is the high-tide line and the canoe should rest above that line to prevent the water from washing it away when the tide rises. Here, near the sea, you must pay attention to the tides. A low tide can leave you stranded on a mudflat if you are not careful. But it is not a big problem, because the water will come back a little while after it leaves you, as long as you are considerate and do not curse at its going."

"You are silly, brother. The tides do not move the water very much. Only a careless man would mindlessly beach his canoe. And only one in a hurry to return to his pretty woman would even consider cursing the water, causing it to hold him even longer!" Keetrauk teased Tetszo.

"You hush, now! I am trying to teach the boys something of the water here."

Keetrauk snorted and said, "Pull, brother, pull!"

With a final great heave, the brothers beached the canoe well above the high tide line.

I glanced up toward the sand dunes, shielding my eyes from the glare. "What are those mountains of sand?" I asked, nodding toward them with my head. I was accustomed to the landscape around Chowanook, which was flat and level. Men talked of the mountains to the west, where the Cherokee tribe, relatives of the Mangoaks, lived, but never had they spoken of sand mountains, only dunes, to the east. When I imagined those sandy dunes, I thought of small hummocks of sand blown by the wind, perhaps as tall as a man, but these were mountains, taller than the trees.

Tetszo looked up briefly and said, "They are big hills of sand. No animals there, no water, and you have to go over them or around them to find a shallow pond on the other side." Ascopo, the hunter-boy, glanced at the dramatic sand mountains disinterestedly and abruptly redirected his fish-seeking gaze to the water.

To me, the sand mountains were awe-inspiring, but they held no intrigue for the others. They thought only of fishing. In fact, Tetszo was already explaining the weir. *I had better listen.*

"The weir is located down along the shore of the marsh. See the line of stakes protruding from the water?" I followed his raised arm and did indeed see dozens of stakes in the water. But how they would function to catch fish was hard for me to determine.

We walked toward the contraption while Tetszo explained it. "You see this row of stakes in front of us? This is the fence, which extends from the beach out into the water as far as we can wade and still push the stakes into the bottom. The stakes are far enough apart to allow water to flow through easily, but close enough together to prevent any good-sized fish from pushing through it. Instead, the fish move along the fence, searching for a way through. Over there, near the middle section of the fence, is an opening, but rather than leading to freedom, the gap opens into an enclosure that traps and concentrates the fish. Once they are in this pen, we either spear the big fish or dip out the smaller ones with nets, so we must locate the pen where it is deep enough for the fish to survive but shallow enough for us to spear and net the fish."

As Tetszo described how the weir worked, I could imagine how it looked under the water by following the line of emergent tops of the stakes. What had initially appeared to be a forest of random stakes now had a visible pattern.

"The pen's construction is paramount because that is where the fish are trapped and concentrated, and they mill around in there, bumping against the sides. The fence is just a series of stakes, but the pen must have strong walls. To strengthen the pen, we weave willow branches through the upright stakes to make a strong wall from which no fish can escape. When the fish are really running and quickly fill the pen, we must keep pace with their increasing numbers by spearing and removing them. Even as strong as we build the walls of the pen, they cannot withstand the combined force of too many fish."

"What keeps the fish from just turning around and swimming back out of the opening they entered?" Ascopo asked.

"Nothing!" Tetszo replied, grinning. "The weir concentrates the fish into the pen and holds them temporarily while we catch them. They are coming in the inlet with the rising tide and they want to swim upriver to their spawning ground. Any fish can turn around and swim out, but because the opening is relatively small, only one fish can enter or leave at a time."

"There aren't any fish in the pen today because there is a hole in the pen opposite the entrance, so when fish enter, they can just swim straight out the other side. Last time we were here, a big, angry *chig-wusso* thrashed around so vigorously that it created a hole in the pen's wall before we could spear him and get him out of the pen. We left the hole unrepaired because it was the end of the season and we did not want to trap fish in the pen when we were not available to harvest them. Our normal practice is to open the pens when we leave." Tetszo looked over at me with a critical eye and said, "You know, Skyco, that *chigwusso* was about as long as you are tall. Probably weighed nearly as much as you do too. It was a big one."

"Was it coppery red with black spots on its tail like the one we caught? I mean, the one *you* speared yesterday?" I asked a little sheepishly since all I did was ride in the canoe while the brothers fished.

"Yes, but the spots differ among individual fish. Some have one, two, or more spots, the spots have different shapes, or they are in different places. Every spot-tailed bass looks a little different from every other one and I find that interesting because among most types of fish, the individuals all look the same."

Tetszo paused, then added, "Boys, we all worked together to catch the fish. You were right to include yourself as a fisherman, Skyco. Someone must paddle and someone else must tend the fire while the spearman fishes. A single spearman wouldn't get many fish by himself."

Ascopo broke up the serious discussion by saying, "Is it true that some of those striped bass, the *mesickek*, get as big as a man?

"Oh, yes, Ascopo, and when they are running, we catch dozens. We must keep watch and get those big ones out of the pen so there is enough room for the rest to come in! You are going to love it!" Keetrauk said.

"Enough about what might happen, Keetrauk. Let's get this pen fixed and see what *does* happen!" Tetszo slapped his brother on his back and they pulled out the bundle of sticks from the canoe.

"Why did we bother to bring that bundle in the canoe?" I asked the men. "Looks like plenty of sticks are right here."

"I know it seems strange to bring materials with us when the low woods here have unlimited numbers of shrubs, but these essential materials are not available here in the salt marsh. We need both long, stout reeds and flexible but tough willow branches, and they grow only in freshwater marshes. We harvested them a couple of days ago, before we left the big freshwater marshes. We will weave the reeds and branches between the stakes already in place. The stakes that form the fence go down into the bottom and protrude up above the water, but the willow branches and thick reeds are woven from side to side between the stakes. You need to practice on land first, before we put you in the water to make the repair. See how this works, boys? Once you get the hang of it, the task will be easier."

Ascopo and I set to work practicing with the stakes, reeds, and branches on the dry beach. First, we pushed a line of stakes vertically into the sand, and then, with Ascopo on one side and me on the other, we began to weave in the reeds and willow branches. Beginning at the top of the line of stakes, we wove in one reed, bending it repeatedly behind one stake and in front of the next until we completed the row, then we pushed the reed-row down to the base of the stakes. We continued this process, alternating between a row of reeds and a row of branches, until the stack of woven material reached the tops of the stakes. Then we stopped to admire our work, hoping for approval from the men.

"Hey Ascopo!" I said, stepping back to appreciate the short wall we'd set up on the shore, the woven branches supporting it. "Isn't this exactly what we were talking about for the palisade? The vertical stakes are just like the palisade logs. By weaving the branches in between, we strengthen the whole pen. It would work on the palisade, too." As I considered our project, I was also reminded of Roncommock's teachings. Like the strong wall of stakes and woven branches before me, interlacing everyday actions with guiding principles of the spirit world built a strong tribe.

The two brothers and Ascopo looked at each other and back at me. "You are thinking like a chief, Skyco," Keetrauk said as they all grinned. "You have some good ideas, but now let's get to work."

Ascopo, Keetrauk, and Tetszo waded into the water along one side of the fence while I entered along the other. We walked along the fence until we came to the pen, and Keetrauk said, "We three will stay on this side of the pen. You come into the pen through its entrance, Skyco, as a fish would. We need you on the inside to help work the weave with Ascopo on the outside, just as you did on land. Feel each stake with your hands and make sure it is still in place. If the stake feels loose, push it down deeper into the bottom. While you and Ascopo work on the pen, Tetszo and I will check all the stakes in the fence that go out into deeper water."

I did as he instructed, finding several stakes that were lopsided or loose in the fence near the opening to the pen. By the time I made it to the opening, I was already chest deep and wading deeper. "This is too deep for me to walk easily. Let's hurry up and get done with this repair before the tide makes it any deeper," I said anxiously as I stood in the water already up to my armpits.

"Sure. We've already started back here. Come on, we need your help along this wall of the pen. We can do the rest of it without you. But before you leave the opening, double check those stakes on either side. They get pushed by the fish most frequently and probably need to be reset."

Indeed, as I shuffled along, I bumped into one of the stakes that was bent over so that its top was not even above the water. I tugged at it to right it, but without my feet firmly planted, couldn't move it in the bottom. Instead, I managed to bump my injured toe again. Suddenly I felt a strange sensation: the water, which had been at the level of my armpits, suddenly rose up to my chin! Puzzled, I immediately looked toward Keetrauk, Tetszo, and Ascopo on the outside of the pen. Was the tide rising? From outside the pen, they were looking back in at me, but their eyes were wide, and suddenly I saw why. A dorsal fin was between us, heading my way.

"Skyco, quick, get out of there!" the brothers yelled simultaneously. I tried to back up quickly, but it was difficult to move fast enough in the water. I realized in panic that I stood helplessly right in the opening, between a big shark and its freedom. I had no chance. The fish was upon me, but instead of biting, it thrust past me as it swept out through the entrance of the pen. The impact of its body and the turbulence of the water tumbled me off my feet and my head went under water. After an eternity, I finally surfaced outside the pen, sputtering and hurting, my arms and legs paddling frantically against the water.

"Hurry, hurry!" I heard Ascopo shouting, but I was disoriented from the dunking. At last I got my feet under me and turned toward the shore, but then I felt another wave rising up my back and realized

that once the shark was free of the trap, it had turned around and was charging toward me again as I rushed along the fence trying to make it back to shore. It was my bloody foot that it was after! Why hadn't I thought about that?

I pushed my feet against the bottom with all my might, flailed my hands like paddles in the water, and rushed headlong toward the beach. I heard the brothers give an alarm yell just as a wave broke and helped push me onto dry ground as I flew up the beach. I looked over my shoulder to see the shark whipping its massive muscular body from side to side as it struggled against the sand to swim back into deeper water. It had come right into the shallows after me. It was a menacing creature, dark, brownish gray with a broad, flat, depressed snout and tiny, dull eyes. It snapped its mouth and I saw pink gums and rows of gleaming, white, triangular teeth.

I collapsed down onto the beach as the others rushed up. My hip and side where the shark had brushed past me were raw and bleeding, the skin scraped away so deeply that the exposed surface was stark white, with red streaks from which blood was welling up. My toe was bleeding too. I thought of that flat head and tiny eyes and white teeth, imagining that the teeth must have scraped without actually biting me in half. All of a sudden, the memory overwhelmed me, and I leaned over and vomited.

"Okay, okay," the brothers said. "You are going to be okay, Skyco. Sharkskin is as rough as teeth if it rubs you the wrong way. Don't worry, the shark didn't bite you."

"Skyco! Are you dying?" Ascopo's face looked terrified.

"He'll be fine. Go get him some water, Ascopo," Tetszo said as he supported my shoulders. "There should be a *macócqwer* full of water in the basket in the canoe." He turned to Keetrauk and said, "We'll need to get this wound patched, too. Can't have him bleeding in the water. It will attract more sharks."

"Here, Skyco, drink this water," Keetrauk said, handing me the big round gourd with a long thin neck while crouching down to look at my injured hip and side. "This is going to ooze blood for a long time because it is scraped down to white and pink skin over the whole area."

Ascopo said, "You've been sanded like a canoe!"

"Shut up, Ascopo," Tetszo said. "There is no need to describe what he can plainly see."

Keetrauk said, "And what in the world happened to your toe? That is something different. No shark did that. It is black and blue as if you hurt it earlier, but it is bleeding. Tell me you didn't go in the water with a bloody toe, Skyco!"

I hung my head, admitting that I had.

"No wonder that shark turned back on you! He was just trying to get out of the trap at first, but then he smelled your bloody toe. You got lucky there. Remember that guy from Ohanoak who had his hand taken off, Tetszo? Now he is crippled. Can't shoot a bow anymore. A warrior who can't shoot. He is useless," Keetrauk commented with scorn in his voice.

The thought of that lost hand turned me as white as the bark of a sycamore tree, I am sure, and Ascopo looked as if he might vomit, too.

Tetszo glared at his brother, then said to me, "Tell us what plants to gather to treat your wound and stop it from bleeding, Skyco. I heard you did a great job with Roncommock when he was hurt. Come on, little medicine man. You've got to help yourself now."

I could see that he was trying to help me and distract me from focusing on the scare and the injury. "Okay, then," I struggled out, but my breathing was shallow because it hurt to flex my rib cage.

"Let's get him up to the campsite where we stayed last time we fished. He will feel better if he can lie down flat."

"Wait," Tetszo interrupted. "Rinse off that wound with some of this fresh water. The salt must be stinging like a whole nest of hornets." He poured most of the remaining water from the *macócqwer* over the wound and I winced in pain. The two men carefully supported me as we made our way up the beach. Ascopo danced around, trying to be useful. A short way into the forest lay an opening with a ring of stones for a fire.

"Ouch!" I gasped as they helped me to lie down. "Okay. Herbs." I made myself focus on the problem of which herbs would be best for this type of injury, imagining I was someone other than myself, someone who was nearly eaten by a shark. "See if you can find some willow bark for me to chew on. It will dull the pain. If you find willow, there should be some elderberry nearby since both like fresh water. Gather enough leaves to cover the wound."

The brothers looked at each other. Keetrauk volunteered, "The only fresh water is over the big sand dunes. I will go with the *macócqwer* and get more water for us to drink and look for the willow bark and elderberry leaves. Ascopo, you come with me."

"Agreed," Tetszo said. "I will stay here with Skyco. Where are those other men? I thought they were right behind us!"

Keetrauk replied with some irritation, "I noticed they went north, closer to the inlet. They are probably spearing fish there. If they don't paddle down here soon, I'll go up and get them, but first, water, willow, and elderberry."

Once I lay down in the shade, I began to feel a little better. By the time Keetrauk and Ascopo returned, I was even feeling drowsy as the effects of the scare wore off. I sat up, drank more water, and chewed the willow bark while Keetrauk pounded the elderberry leaves as I told him. The wound was barely bleeding now, but we covered it with the leaves and wrapped it with my loincloth.

"I think if I rest here for a while, I will feel better," I said to Keetrauk. "I am so tired now; my energy has been sapped."

"Yes, rest. We'll go find the other men and will be back shortly. Ascopo, you stay here and guard him. Get him whatever he needs."

"Yes, sir," Ascopo said. I thought he was glad to

have something to do, but then he continued as soon as the men were out of earshot, "First a bear and now a shark! You've even been on a war raid! How come you get all the great adventures? Roncommock said you will go on a spirit quest before you have even finished the *husquenaugh*. It's not fair!" Ascopo stomped his foot and plopped down on the sand beside me.

I looked over at him in astonishment. "You have *got* to be kidding! You can have *all* my great adventures, Ascopo! That thing nearly ate me! Go away and leave me alone."

I turned away, rolling over on my uninjured side, and must have fallen asleep because I awoke suddenly to the smoke from a fire and the delicious smell of cooking fish. I was very hungry. Several men were around the fire and two were farther up the beach testing a repaired net.

"Hey! Welcome back, Skyco. How are you feeling now?" Keetrauk asked me as I started to sit up and move around.

"Much better, thanks. It only hurts when I move or breathe," I chuckled out and immediately regretted sitting up and talking at the same time. I found out quickly that if I kept my torso rigid, barely turning my shoulders or hips, I could move without a lot of pain. It ached, but the sharp burning was gone. Walking, I discovered, was not much of a problem, but I took small steps.

"Skyco, Tetszo and I think we should stay here on the banks themselves, give you a little time to scab over, before we head back to the main camp. Are you okay with that plan?"

"Sure," I said. "I think I will be alright. But I also think I will stay out of the water."

"Good idea!" Tetszo agreed with a smile. "This is not normally what fishing is like. Usually we catch the fish instead of the fish going after us!"

"Yeah, Skyco. I have never before seen such a big shark in one of our traps. I guess the hole made by the *chigwusso* was too small for him to swim through, but when we started to repair that wall of the pen, he decided to turn tail and head out of the entrance. Thought he might pick up a nice morsel when he smelled that blood on you, too. He was a grown one, alright. Did you see how big? And the size of the teeth on that thing!"

I started feeling a little sick again as I remembered the scenario and Keetrauk poked his brother in the ribs.

"Really, though. We've had some tiny sharks in there, and we've had big fish, but that is weird how a big shark was in there and we didn't even know it."

"Some fishermen you are!" I joked back, but then worried they would take it the wrong way. I hadn't meant to insult them. The statement came out of my mouth before I thought about it.

Luckily Keetrauk just laughed and Tetszo joined in too. "You got us there, Skyco. A fish bigger than any of us and we didn't even know it was in the pen. Bad form!"

"Where is Ascopo, anyway?" I asked. I felt a little bad about ignoring him. It was just that his timing was poor.

"He has been out fishing this afternoon. Speared his first *pashockshin* with his brother and Chaham, I heard. You should congratulate him, Skyco."

The men kept the fire burning long into the night, and I rested beside the fire after wolfing down several of the cooked fish I smelled when I awoke. Warm and full of fish, tired from the enervating events of the day, I drifted off to sleep again listening to their fishing tales.

When I awoke the next morning, I felt much better. The wound had formed a brown scab and, though ugly, at least it wasn't raw and bleeding. I still felt sore, but could move more-or-less normally. I asked Tetszo if I could walk over the big sand dunes and see the ocean and he agreed, but only if both brothers attended me, so the three of us set off immediately.

"Hey, Ascopo, would you like to come along?" I asked, but he replied, "No, Skyco. I am going fishing again with Chaham. We expect to have some fish in the weir before long, and you aren't allowed in the water. I'll have to do it."

I could sense that he was proud to be doing something that I was not, so I let him go without any further comment.

The great dunes were even more spectacular than I had expected. The sand rolled from one dune into another, swallowing up a forest at some distance on each side. The vast expanse of sand was so impressive that it was hard to comprehend the width and height of the whole area until I looked down from the top of one dune to Keetrauk standing at its bottom and finally realized the immensity of scale. There were no plants, just sand, until the dunes sloped down to the forest, the sound, or the sea.

From the top of the highest dune, I could see back across the sound to the mainland in one direction, and out to the horizon in the other. The water in the sound was brownish and calm. The inlet north of us was clearly visible, and I could even follow the channel and the sandy shoals that swept in the inlet's mouth. The slipway where the other men had pulled up their canoes close to the inlet was a flat, white path. Where the sea met the land on the beachfront, wave after wave crashed, casting a line of white foam onto the beach that curved around and into the inlet. Past the beach and the breakers, the blue of the ocean water met the blue of the sky along the thin horizon and seemed to stretch away into infinity.

This is a place to contact the spirits, I thought, and wondered whether Eracano or Roncommock ever came here. *I am higher than a hawk! And I feel just as majestic, perhaps even more so. I have a white loincloth instead of a white tail like an eagle—the* nahyápuw— *but close enough.*

I hated to leave the dune-top, but Tetszo was motioning me to join him down at the bottom. As I walked down, my feet sank into the sand, and although I felt like I might topple over, I never did. Tetszo and Keetrauk awaited me at a muddy pool, where a few stunted trees and shrubs grew. As I walked up to its edge, the ground started hopping, and unbelievable numbers of tiny frogs erupted from the damp ground. The pool itself was thick with tiny, black tadpoles. What an amazing place!

"This is where you must come to get fresh water, Skyco. It pools up here in this depression between the big dunes and the forest. You may have to dig down to it, but it is always here."

We climbed back up a shorter, but still impressive, dune and worked our way through a stunted forest before we finally emerged on the open beach. More wonders awaited me there. As far as I could see in each direction, up and down the beach stretched a ribbon of white sand. It actually burned my eyes to look in the direction of the sun because so much light was reflected off the sand and from the waves. And waves! I had seen plenty of choppy white-capped waves during windy periods on the sound, but nothing like the magnificent rollers spilling onto the beach. And their sound! The surf was rumbling like a great beast's stomach during a hungry time. It spoke clearly to me of the spirit world. The white foam flew up as each wave crashed onto the beachhead and hissed like a great snake as it retreated. I walked down to the edge and gasped as the spray from a wave struck me. What a place!

I knew then that I had found the sacred place, the location of my quest to enter the spirit world. The spirits were nearby. Is this what Roncommock meant when he said that I should follow my instincts? I knew this place was important. The sea, the dunes, even the inlet, held significances greater than I could imagine.

party ate most of the smaller fish, but we smoked and dried the larger ones to take back to the village.

One afternoon, Ascopo and I finally fished for blue crabs—the training we were to have received before my fishing accident postponed the crabbing adventure. It was fun because the bait carcasses attracted more than just blue crabs. We did indeed catch blue crabs, but we also caught hermit crabs that lived inside whelk shells or other shells that they carried on their backs and retreated into when they were disturbed. Some of these crabs had brown, striped legs and were big. Others had white legs and were smaller. After a while, we attracted a few of the big, round crabs—the *seékanauk*—and hauled them up on shore. When we turned them upside down in the sand, they struggled to right themselves by folding their tail-spike forward, thrusting it into the sand and then using the anchored spike to pole themselves upright. When a small shark with a rounded head came to the carcass, I quit fishing. The little shark was not so scary with its gently rounded head, and I couldn't even see its eyes and mouth, but the rest of it looked too much like the monster that attacked me.

Ascopo already knew how to prepare a fish carcass for use as crab bait. He tied a rope through the gills and around the head, tossed it out into the water, and then tied the free end to a stout branch that he'd broken from a tree. He said we should be patient, but it was hard to wait and wonder what was happening to that carcass in the deep water. Before long, Ascopo pulled in the line very slowly, hand over hand, with

the carcass still attached. As it gradually appeared out of the depths, we saw that two large blue crabs were clinging to the head while tearing away bits of fish-flesh with their pincers and passing them to their busy mouths. The sight of the two big crabs so excited Ascopo that he gave the rope a jerk, pulled too hard, and the wary crabs dropped off and scuttled back into deep water. Disappointed, he turned over the line to me, and I tossed the carcass back out into the water. After a short time, I slowly and steadily pulled it back in. The crabs were again feeding on the carcass, so I continued my slow and smooth retrieval until the carcass, with the crabs still attached and feeding, began to clear the water as I pulled them up onto the beach.

Once the bait was clear of the water, Ascopo used a forked tree branch that he had already stripped of its leaves to rake the crabs off the carcass and cast them high on the beach. The beached crabs scuttled around angrily, snapped their upraised claws, and frothed madly at their mouths, thoroughly intimidating both of us.

"Okay, Ascopo. *Get them*!" I yelled.

"No *way*! Do you see those claws? If they pinch my finger and make it bleed, I won't be allowed in the water to work the weir. Those crabs are *fast*."

"Well, how are we supposed to pick them up? Aren't you the one who has been fishing? What have you been learning from those fishermen?"

"How to catch *fish*, not crabs! I'll get Keetrauk. You keep the crabs up here on the beach." Ascopo ran down the beach to the camp. I left the branch on top of the crabs to slow their scuttles and to provide a target for their aggression.

Keetrauk sent back Kaiauk instead, who was happy to show off what he knew, and then we learned that the hardest part of crabbing was handling and cleaning the catch. Their claws were sharp and the crabs were fast. Kaiauk showed us how to pin the fearless crabs down to the ground with the branch, which they aggressively attacked with their jagged claws, firmly grab each menacing claw from behind so that the crabs couldn't pinch our fingers, then to snap the claws free of the body. Pulling off the other legs was easy, but wedging the carapace loose from the body was a bit of a trick. Kaiauk jabbed his thumb below the edge of the shell between the crab's eyestalks and pulled up until the shell tore free of the body, but I thought that was a little gruesome. The crabs were looking at you when you ripped off their backs. He also showed us that you could peel up the belly flap and wedge your thumb there to pop off the shell. I preferred that technique.

Some of the females, with rounded belly flaps instead of the triangular ones of the males, held reddish eggs, which we scooped out and ate without bothering to cook. We boiled the rest of the body over the fire in a clay pot with seawater. Picking the cooked crab meat from the body took some time to learn, but it was so sweet and delicious that it was worth the effort.

I noticed that the other men brought back whole live crabs in a basket, dropped them into the boiling seawater, and *then* cleaned them. Kaiauk was just showing off by cleaning them alive, challenging us to handle them without getting pinched.

By our third day on the banks, my wounds were healing and I felt much better. I wanted to return to the dunes, but needed to convince Ascopo to join me. While we picked flower buds from the prickly pear cacti, I began my effort to get Ascopo to go to the dunes with me. Kaiauk showed us a sandy spot that was loaded with the prickly cacti and left us with a basket to fill. As we picked the flower buds, I said to Ascopo, "These buds are rather small. The fruits, the *metaquesúnnauk*, must not yet be ripe, because I know they are larger than these buds. I hope these taste good when we roast them tonight."

"I agree," Ascopo grumbled. "I've never eaten buds before and I don't really like the fruits either. It is more fun to dye sticks red with the juice than to eat the fruits full of those little black seeds that you must constantly spit out, even if the juice is sweet. Those men, especially my brother, are always finding something for us to do so that they don't have to."

"Aren't you getting tired of them?" I asked, setting the trap.

"Sure am. I've had enough of working like a slave for them!"

"Well, then, Ascopo, let's get away for a bit. We can spend the night up on the dunes and not have to clean up after the evening meal. The men can do it themselves."

Ascopo realized he was caught. "But we are here to fish, Skyco, even if it means that we have extra work because we are the youngest. If we leave tonight, the men might go without us tomorrow and I wouldn't get to fish."

I'd thought he would bring up fishing, and I was ready to parry. "Since we will be up high on the dune, the sun will wake us early, and we can run back to camp before the men set out. You know they like to get up slowly. The last two mornings we had to wait on them for a long time before the fishing started."

I stumped Ascopo with this. I could see he was thinking.

"Oh, come on, Ascopo. You won't miss a thing, plus you will get to see the sun rise out of the sea, something I know you have never seen before. What could be better than that?"

"Oh, all right, Skyco. If you promise we can come straight back, first thing, in the morning."

After our evening meal, we climbed to the top of the highest dune and pushed our bodies down to form a slight depression in the sand, which held a little warmth. The sun had already set and drained the sky of color. Because it was past the full moon, the sky grew completely dark before the moon rose and during those first few hours of complete darkness, the stars were incredibly brilliant.

Ascopo asked, "Do you think the *husquenaugh* is as difficult as Kaiauk suggests?"

I answered, "I don't think it will be easy! It is a training time for our minds and our bodies. It's supposed to make us tough enough to withstand war raids and hunting trips."

"And fishing expeditions," Ascopo volunteered.

"Yes, you can think about it this way: we have already been preparing for the *husquenaugh*. The *husquenaugh* itself is just the final test. Maybe it won't be so overwhelming."

Ascopo snorted and said sarcastically, "Yeah, *right*."

From our lofty position high on the dune, I could see the campfire at our nearby fishing outpost on the banks, but I could also see across the sound to the distant fire of the mainland camp, where the majority of our party was at work drying the big fish.

"Kaiauk doesn't say much, but all of it is scary. He says I need to toughen up," Ascopo recalled.

"You know he is not supposed to describe the experience in any way."

"I know, but I thought a brother might tell me more. Give me some warning, or something."

"Sounds like he did give you a warning, Ascopo."

"I guess you are right."

Ascopo and I sat quietly for a few minutes. I turned my back on the sound and looked out to the sea. After a while, it became so dark that I could just barely see the white line where the waves crashed, rumbled, and hissed on the beach. They glowed and sparkled with greenish phosphorescence as they broke. At last, the moon rose and cast a silver glow over the landscape even as the brilliance of the stars and the phosphorescent waves dimmed.

"It is beautiful here, Skyco. Thanks for encouraging me to come up here with you."

"Yeah. I am glad you came along, Ascopo. Look, I am sorry about telling you to go away when you were helping me after the shark attack. It was just that I hurt and was still in shock, and couldn't believe you really wanted to be in my place."

"It was silly of me to say so. I shouldn't have."

"Right. Let's get some sleep so that we wake early enough to return in time for fishing." I fell off to sleep and dreamed.

I was a bear. It was the same sensation as when Roncommock helped me into the other animals, but this time the bear itself seemed to be a spirit bear. I felt few sensations, but I saw through the eyes of the bear. We were back at my home village, but I hardly recognized it. In fact, the village was not there at all, just the crop field, grown immense and stretching away into the distance. Instead of growing interplanted with beans and squash, the corn grew all by itself in long, straight rows. I stood at the edge of this great field and saw in the distance, at the other end of the rows, a strange, gigantic beast rumbling toward me with an evil-sounding growl, and I turned and fled back into the forest. I awoke in a sweat. Ascopo was snoring.

The strangeness of the dream kept me awake as the moon moved across the sky. Finally, I jostled Ascopo and he turned over and stopped snoring. Eventually I fell asleep again and once again dreamed that I was the bear. This time, I felt a little more securely lodged in the bear and noticed odors as well as sights and sounds. What I smelled was a man, but not like any man I had smelled before. Then the strange man walked into view. He was completely clothed from head to foot and these clothes were what gave him the strange odor of a wet animal, but no animal that I knew. He wore a long knife at his waist, a shiny plate across his chest, and a gleaming cap on his head. Black, curly hair covered his face everywhere except a small area around his eyes and nose. Perhaps his whole body was hairy like that of a bear, and that was why he wore the clothing, in order to cover it up. Even his hands and his feet were clothed. He strutted around in his fancy clothing and yelled at some other men in a tongue that I could not understand. It was very different, even from that of the Mangoaks, who spoke Iroquois instead of Algonquian. It was confusing, but not frightening, and I awoke slowly from the dream.

I thought about my dream until the sky attracted all of my attention, and I punched Ascopo awake. The sky was a glorious sight. The whole sky turned pink and then a deeper shade of orange and red. A few clouds hung low on the horizon where the water met the sky, and they picked up the colors of pink, purple, orange, and red. I could tell where the sun would appear because one area held the brightest, most intense color. It was so strong that I could barely look at it, but then Ascopo said, "Here it comes!"

I kept peering and then looking away until I saw a small, intensely orange band appear. Quickly, the huge disk of the sun sprang up out of the sea, becoming perfectly circular as it leapt free from the water. What a sight! Within a short time of its appearance, the sky became uniformly light blue, the color show ended. We had witnessed the birth of the sun from the sea.

"Time to go," Ascopo said. "Fish are waiting."

"Let's fill our gourds with water before we leave. The water here tastes better than the water back at camp," I suggested. I was surprised at how easily he agreed. He must not like the taste of the camp water either.

Down at the foot of the dune, the tiny frogs in the muddy pool began hopping frantically as we disturbed them, but we needed to enlarge and deepen the fresh water hole so that we could fill our containers. The digging was easy. When we sat back to rest from our work, I saw my face reflected in the pool of water. A little frog hopped back in the pool, and as the ripples reached my face, I thought I saw a bear face reflected there instead. I jerked back, about to

ask Ascopo if he saw it too, but he was already calling me to come see a fox track he'd found.

The tracks went from the pool to a copse of shrubby trees. I recognized them immediately as wax myrtle shrubs and knew that my mother would welcome some dried leaves for her medicine bundle, so I broke off several branches and laid them on the sand not too far from the water hole where they would receive unobstructed sun. I would return for them later, perhaps tomorrow. Their heady fragrance swirled up in the air as I breathed it in.

Ascopo continued tracking, but said that the fox tracks were harder to follow in the sand under the trees than in the muddy area near the water hole. I came over to help and the two of us were barely able to discern them. Soon, however, Ascopo had located the foxhole at the roots of one of the wax myrtle trees.

"Now what?" Ascopo said as he turned toward me, indicating the fox's lair. "Should we dig him out?"

"For what reason? We have plenty of fish to eat and there is nothing we need that the fox could provide. Let's leave him. It was fun just to be able to track the animal to its den."

"I agree," Ascopo said. "We need to be heading back anyway."

Back at the water hole, the sediment stirred up by our digging activities had settled back out, leaving the water clear. While not as clean and nice as the water from the Chowan, it was fresh, unlike the brackish water of the sound, and better tasting than the water near the camp. We each filled a *macócqwer* with water and stoppered it with a wooden plug carved from a tree branch. Again I thought I saw a bear face reflected in the surface instead of my own.

"You go ahead on back to camp, Ascopo. Tell Tetszo that I am staying over here today."

"What, and miss the fishing?" Ascopo couldn't believe what he was hearing.

"Yeah. I had some really weird dreams. Roncommock told me that I should follow my instincts when I was here, and I think maybe I should stay here a while longer. I know you want to fish, so go ahead without me."

"Are you sure you will be safe here by yourself?"

"Sure. Go ahead. I'll be fine." I could see that Ascopo was reluctant to leave me, but fishing easily won out after his brief, internal struggle. He headed back toward camp, and I headed toward the sea. I could smell the myrtle here, too, its essence reminding me of the *winauk* that Roncommock often used when summoning the spirits. My mother used it for calming coughs or breathing problems, but maybe it was a spirit herb, too.

Over on the beachfront, it was clearly low tide. The wrack line of flotsam was high above the waterline on the upper part of the beach. There was an immense curve of white sand in each direction, but I turned toward the north. I knew this was the right way to go. I felt a little dizzy from the bright sunlight on the sand and felt disoriented from the constant wind and sound of the waves, so I looked down at my feet and began to walk in the direction that they pointed. Eventually I would come to the inlet.

As I walked the beach, my senses sharpened and time slowed down. I was not sure whether I was in the real world, or the spirit world, or both at the same time. My vision was sharper, sounds were louder, scents more intense. The wind was strong enough to move the hairs on my arms and legs and set them tingling. Even my lips tasted of salt and the briny sea. Were the spirits insisting that I pay attention?

I could hardly believe the incredible numbers of interesting shells that seemed to be everywhere. I looked at all the different shapes and colors, and found a whelk shell that was so big I just had to pick it up and carry it in my hand. It would make a great head of a hoe or maybe even a war club if someone could carve the handle so it would fit tightly enough into the shell's opening. Perhaps Ascopo's carving training would come in handy; if not, I bet Cossine would know how to affix it. Next, I came across a cockleshell so large that each half would hold a mouthful of water. I picked it up too. I could use it as a bowl or ladle. In one place where the waves had left a slight depression, the shells piled in a heap. I found a bunch of shark's teeth and picked up every one. Since I escaped the teeth of a shark, it felt only right that I should claim them. When a beautiful, tiny, white, intricately coiled wentletrap revealed itself, I wanted to keep it, but I already had too much to hold in my hands and needed to adjust.

I looped the string from my water container around the whelk so that I could carry it over my shoulder, and packed the small shells and teeth into the bowl-like half of the cockle, leaving my other hand free. Some broken shells of the wampum clam were already partly rounded and polished, so I picked them up, thinking that they would be easy to finish into purple wampum disks for Menatonon to add to a wampum necklace. Next, I found a translucent shallow shell that resembled a glossy toenail. It was even marked in the center with what looked like a miniature footprint. I kept an eye out for those and collected many more, which my mother and sister

would appreciate as decorations for their skirts.

Soon, the cockleshell was full and I was in a quandary over how to carry my growing shell collection. I drank as much water as I could hold, brushed the sand off the shells, and dropped them down inside the water gourd. I strung a few more of the larger shells on the string over my shoulder, but I still had to carry some of the bigger shells in one hand. It would do for the time being. I kept walking and picking up more interesting shells. Was this what I was supposed to be doing? It was strange to feel such a compulsion to pick up shells and to think about their uses for myself and others of my tribe.

A flock of terns stood on the beach ahead of me, facing into the wind, and I studied them as I approached. There were big ones and small ones, but all were white and light grey with black feathers on their heads. They made their loud "kak-kak-kak" and lifted up from the beach without apparent effort. One wheeled out over the swash of waves and immediately dove straight in, like an arrow shot from a bow. It came back up, flapping vigorously and shaking water off its back with a silvery minnow in its mouth. Another tern made a half-hearted lunge at it, but the one with the fish flew on safely ahead. Another bird caught my attention as it began to flutter like a hummingbird high up over the water, peering down at the water. All of a sudden, it dove straight toward the surface, just like the other bird, but this one pulled out of the dive before it hit and I rocked back on my heels and gasped at the speed of it all. They were consummate hunters, surprising their prey of tiny fish by swooping down from above.

I walked on farther down the beach, enjoying the warmth of the sun and the feel of the sea air blowing across my face. It was moister, with a more noticeable tang, than the air of my home village on the river. The loose sand crunched under my feet, grinding away at my toes unlike the mud or soils I was more accustomed to feeling. Little bits of sand blew against my face and lips, some even entering my mouth. It was a strange sensation to feel them grind against my teeth, as if I'd broken a part of a tooth. As I felt all these sensations from my body, the sounds, scents, feelings, and even tastes of the great beach, I simultaneously saw myself outside my body, observing it.

A giant cloud obscured the sun, then moved in from offshore, sweeping through the inlet ahead, dark, menacing, and fast. Wind whistled around my ears. I was cold—shivering—and sand pelted my legs. The shiver seemed to shake me back into myself and I saw there was no cloud after all. Even the wind and blowing sand ceased. What had I seen? Was it real or imagined? I sat down abruptly, light-headed and confused.

Up ahead I saw more birds flying toward me, and I focused on them as a way of clearing my mind from the image of the cloud. They differed from any I had ever seen. Three of them traveled together and they glided right along the edge between the water and the sand, where the big waves washed up and left a shimmering sheet of water before disappearing down into the beach itself. These birds glided barely above the shining pools, and their lower bills left a line behind them where they cleaved the film of water in two.

As I stood awe-struck, watching the birds fly while skimming the surface, one hit a fish with its lower mandible, flipped the fish up into the air, and caught it on the wing. He flew up and gave a little shake, then glided back down and starting fishing again just behind the other two. It flew as if it were a sunbeam, animated light and shadow rather than a living animal. It wheeled and turned back to make a loop, starting another fishing run well up the beach ahead of me. It drew a line with its beak that perfectly outlined the swash of each wave on the beach. The birds flew on past, still skimming down the beach until they disappeared into the hazy white distance. I shook my head in wonder, stood up, and walked on.

Behind me I heard a ruckus and turned around just in time to see a bald eagle, enormous in comparison to the delicate skimmers, as it struck the forward bird and drove it down to the water. Black and white feathers flew into the air. My chest hurt as if I'd been struck instead of the bird. The skimmer flopped feebly once or twice in the shallow water and then the eagle swooped in and scooped it out of the water, clutching it tightly with deadly talons. Its beautiful white breast turned ochre from the blood seeping from the wounds made by the eagle's talons as droplets fell from the red bill. The other two skimmers skittered away, calling angrily to each other. The roar of the waves crashing on the beach intensified and confused me. Just a moment ago, the skimmers had flown away ahead of me, disappearing into the distance. How had they suddenly appeared behind me?

The slope of the beach to the water became steeper, and I struggled along as walking became more difficult. A few white mounds of sand pushed up above the surface of the water, forming tiny islands surrounded by deeper water. The islands of white sand appeared bright and attractive, but the dark swirling water surrounding them suggested otherwise. I considered wading out to one of the islands, but the dark water discouraged me. The breakers were striking farther off the beach, making the water muddy instead of clear pale blue. I was nearing the inlet, with currents and waves much more pronounced. Here at the inlet, dark and light swirled together.

Now I could see across the inlet to the land on the other side. The current was rushing out, sweeping along bits of seagrass and brownish twigs so quickly that I became dizzy watching it. Some tiny fish swam by, little minnows that would swim in toward the beach, hunker down in a depression behind a pile of sand pushed up by the current, then dart out after food and be swept a little farther out the inlet.

Suddenly, a skimmer sailed in the inlet, leading the flock of terns. Their white underwings flashed so brightly in the light that I felt blinded in looking at the flock. The whole sky filled with white billowing feathers. Again I felt the cold, strange, shadow sensation of the dark cloud, and I shivered.

A bigger wave suddenly swept up the strand, splashing against my shins and startling me, forcing me back to reality. "Look at what is actually here! See this place as it really is!" the water gurgled and murmured around my feet. As the water retreated, scouring away the sand under my feet and making me sway, tiny coquina clams colored in rainbow hues spewed out of the sand and washed down toward the ocean, where they rapidly reburied themselves. They were incredibly numerous and I considered collecting them for a clam stew, but, instead, I picked up empty coquina shells that were piled in windrows higher up the beach.

Many of the shells already had holes drilled into them at the apex of the shell, exactly where you'd want a hole in order to string them onto a necklace or sew them to a garment. My mother could cover a deerskin with these colorful shells and make a magnificent cloak, fit for a powerful chief. If she were to give me such a wonderful gift, I would hold an enormous celebration and shower her with presents in thanks.

In addition to the coquina clams, funny, little, rounded crabs dug like moles down into the beach sand when a wave washed them out. I dug in after one and caught it just under the sand's surface. Its back was smooth and curved, hard and slippery, and its small feet dug constantly into my hands. When it found a little purchase in between my fingers, it nearly pushed its way out and escaped, but I caught it in time. I held it in my fingertips and turned it over, its feet still moving. It was hard to see a mouth anywhere, unlike the big round crabs whose mouths opened at the base of the feet, or the blue crabs who bubbled up froth around their mouths. This little one just kept digging frantically, and when I set it back down on the wet sand, it disappeared in an instant.

While watching the mole crab dig back in, I crouched down close to the sand where I saw dozens of tiny forked lines on the surface of the sand. I scooped up a handful of sand around one of the strange forks and found another mole crab. I tried again; another mole crab. These crabs tried so carefully to hide, but now I could identify them while they were buried under the sand, and as I looked down the beach, I could see hundreds of them, hidden in plain sight. I laughed aloud at the thought that they left some part sticking up above the sand, like a person hiding under a basket with his feet sticking out. I also saw structures that were tufts of some rooted material instead of the perfect V-shapes.

Scooping up one of these, I discovered a big coquina with a nearly transparent, branched, plantlike growth on its shell. It looked like a plant, but was not green, so I wondered whether or not it was a plant. Perhaps it was like the ghost plant that grew in the forest, poking up from the leaves of the forest floor, white or pinkish colored instead of green, but still with a flower atop a strange short stem. Or maybe this had something to do with the sea plum question: were they animals or plants? I would have to ask Roncommock.

As I completed my turn around the headland, I could now see back in the direction I had come, toward the big sand dunes and the fishing weirs. The weirs were not far off, and our men were working the weirs, spearing the big fish in the pen and tossing them up onto dry sand. A few *mesickek* flopped on the beach where they'd been tossed until men dispatched them with wooden clubs. Other men cleaned the fish and carried them up to the fires to dry and smoke. I looked for Ascopo, and finally saw his smaller form helping with the *mesickek* as they came out of the weirs. He was right in the thick of the action, of course.

As I watched them, they seemed to shimmer from the heat rising from the beach, and suddenly none of them were there. The weirs still stood, the canoes were still there if strangely altered by the mirage, but not a single person was visible. I nearly started forward in terror when the heat mirage ceased and I could see them all once again. This spirit quest was confusing. One moment I was totally absorbed in reality, the next I was sure I was walking with the spirits. What was happening to me?

The dark cloud-shadow descended on me, thick, black, and menacing, and knocked me flat on my back. I lay in the darkness, hearing no sounds, seeing no images, sensing nothing. It was flat black emptiness. Then, slowly, I began to see a white, blinding light growing closer and closer. I felt warmth on my skin again. I felt my chest rise in a breath. I was lying on the beach again, totally alone, the waves gently murmuring, the sun warming me, bringing back life.

During the remaining couple of days that we spent on the banks, I tried to make sense of all I had seen and felt. I spent another night by myself up on the dunes, but no other dreams came to me, nothing to clarify the images. I collected the leaves and berries of the wax myrtle for my mother and stored them in a basket separate from the yaupon leaves we collected previously, but their heady scent did not transport me anywhere. Ascopo and I became quite good at spearing fish from the boats or in shallow water, and we caught and ate baskets of crabs, but I was never again able to enter the weir. Every time I waded in along the fence, the water seemed to rise, and I expected to see a great, grey back and snapping white teeth.

When we had piles of dried *mesickek*, Tetszo began to mutter about heading back to our home village. The winds came around again to the southeast, and clouds built up in the afternoons. A period of rainy weather seemed to be approaching.

He spoke that night around the campfire. "We have had good fishing here and our canoes will be loaded with the harvest we have made. Our bellies are full and yet our women await us, hungry for meat. We should begin our voyage of return before these dried fish that we have prepared with so much effort are ruined from rain or from water slopping into our canoes. Is it agreed?"

Chaham, too young to have a wife and children relying on him, spoke up and said, "I doubt the canoes would be completely filled with fish. I bet if we stayed a while longer, we could fill them up. The *mesickek* are still running, if a little slower than when the moon was full."

Ascopo looked hopeful for a minute, but then Manchauemec said, "We need some space for oysters that we'll collect on the way back home. Memeo told us that he needed more shells because he used so many to scrape and form the new canoe. And you know those we left in the village would love to eat these sweet oysters."

Chaham said, still hopefully, but with a bit of resignation in his voice. "Won't we eat some of that dried fish on our journey and make more room?"

Tetszo said, "No, Chaham, we will catch fresh fish on the return voyage. We will need some good spearmen to spear enough fish to feed the whole crew. You won't mind having to catch more fish, now, will you?"

"No, Tetszo, I think I am ready to leave now!" Chaham said, and Ascopo joined in with, "Me, too! Chaham can't catch all the fish we need." Kaiauk spoke up quickly too, afraid to let Ascopo get ahead of him.

"Okay then. Are we all agreed?" Tetszo asked.

Chaham looked up and murmured, "Yes." Kaiauk was a bit more spirited with his affirmative reply, and the other men followed suit in agreeing to prepare for an early dawn departure on the morrow. As in all important matters, consensus is reached before action is taken.

We made a stop at Chepanoc on the return. Well before arriving, we paused at a point where the oyster beds were enormous. These banks were farther out into the sound and the oysters were larger than those near Ricahokene where we stopped on the way out.

First, we put on moccasins, then wrapped our feet in another layer of hides. I was surprised, but then I remembered that we used oyster shells as scrapers and that these upright oyster shells were incredibly sharp. So sharp, in fact, that they would easily slice into our feet if we walked on them without protection. Ascopo and I, as the lightest of the group, were the first to step out and were given baskets and thin stone axes, which we used to knock loose the oysters. Chaham helped, but most of the other heavier men stayed in the canoes. Once we had a basket full, it took two of us to walk it back to the boats. We filled a canoe in no time at all, and not one of us slipped and cut his feet. The speed of our oyster harvest left us with enough time to catch fish for our supper before we arrived at Chepanoc.

Later that day, as we arrived at the town, the villagers welcomed us warmly. Like the village of Ricahokene we had visited on the way out to the banks, these people were Weapemeocs. Okisco was the chief of both villages.

Again, I announced our intentions, and it seemed easier the second time. I was less nervous, but they also knew we were visiting, having heard from Ricahokene. I felt at home in the village that night and enjoyed the celebrations. Still, I felt apart from the other men. I was sure that the spirits had orchestrated my experience of walking the beach. They were telling me something. But what? I was ready to get home to Roncommock so that he could help me understand.

Since the head woman knew that I was Menatonon's heir, she invited me to sit with her family nearest the central fire. I could see this privilege rankled some of the other men from my village, for they all sat together at the mat that was spread for guests. Soon, however, they set aside their annoyance, for the head woman asked to hear their stories and they loved being the center of attention. I just hoped that Ascopo and the others would not hold a grudge against me. While our men were recounting their tales, I tried to talk to their shaman about my vision experiences, but as soon as I sat down next to him, he touched me gently on the forearm, shook his head, and withdrew. He knew something, but left it unspoken.

When Tetszo began the story of the shark that nearly ate me, some of the women began to wail, and he immediately slowed the tenor of his voice from that of an excited, proud warrior reciting a battle engagement to more of a concerned and caring friend or father. He told the remainder of the story less dramatically, while keeping it equally engaging.

As it turned out, a large shark had attacked and killed a boy my age from this village as he too, was tending a weir. No one knows for sure, but it seems likely the boy injured his hand and the blood attracted the beast. It rammed the boy against the outside of the fence and bit him in the stomach. Other fishermen tried to drag him to safety, but the boy was already dead before they pulled him out of the water, with most of his belly gone and one leg sheared off. They abandoned that weir, though they kept fishing elsewhere.

We stayed one night and left early the next morning. While en route, we landed at Mascomenge, but only long enough to pay our respects. We caught fresh fish before entering the village and presented it to the headman. He, in turn, provided us with something of equal value. The villagers of Mascomenge had killed a big sturgeon, and they gave us some of its bony scutes. They were useful items for decoration and for hide scrapers.

Late in the day, we entered Warowtami, the Weapemeoc village closest to our territory, in a pretty bay located on the eastern side of the Chowan River. Again, we fished and quickly filled up several baskets with fresh fish before we entered the village, and again we were rewarded with an enjoyable celebration of dancing and stories and mutual sharing of food. Anxious to get home, we departed at first light.

We had slower going as we paddled upstream, against the flow of the Chowan, but we made it to Chowanook by nightfall and unloaded our harvest into the chief's wigwam for distribution on the next morning. Before returning to Roncommock, I stopped at my mother's wigwam. She had already heard the hubbub and knew our group had returned.

Seeing her felt soothing after my adventures.

"Tell me what you have done, my son," she said after releasing me from a comforting embrace.

I sat down and began my stories, telling my mother first about the sandy banks. Even my sister Mamankanois was listening, though she was pretending otherwise. Trying to explain their magnificence and the significance I felt from them was nearly impossible, so I told of walking the beach instead, leaving out any reference to the spirits, though I was confident that the spirits were telling me something important. I brought out the shells I had gathered for mother and gave them to her. I also gave my sister the wentletrap since it was so pretty. I knew she would like it, and she did. They both thanked me, but then my mother said, "What is this I hear about a shark nearly eating you? Those men were supposed to take good care of you and protect you from harm. I hear they had you repairing the weir, walking into the trap yourself!" Somewhat indignantly, she crossed her arms and bored her eyes into me.

"Well, mother, it was really pretty scary and a close escape." She took a deep breath, but I plunged on. "However, it was no one's fault. All of us thought the pen was clear. I checked it too, and never saw the shark until too late. In any case, the men helped me treat my wound."

"You were injured," she interrupted. "And you recovered from the bite of a shark?"

"Not a bite, mother, just a scrape when the shark

pushed by me. Their skin is very rough, you know. We use it sometimes for making wampum smooth."

"Yes, yes. I know all that," she muttered impatiently. "Now tell me what happened."

I related the story and could see that even my sister's eyes got big and round when I described how the shark came up after me, thrashing around in the shallows. Perhaps I embellished it a little for the benefit of my sister, but when I finished the story and poured out the teeth from my *macócqwer*, she jerked back from them, touching them only hesitantly. As I stood up to leave my mother's wigwam for Roncommock's, she hugged me and told me she was glad I was home. So did my mother, but I expected it from her.

I stumbled along the path to Roncommock's wigwam and lay down on my sleeping bench, happy to be back. Roncommock didn't even turn over when I entered the wigwam, but Jackáwanjes got up from her sleeping bench to see that I was comfortable.

"Do you need anything, Skyco? Something to eat or drink? Another warm skin?"

"He is fine," Roncommock said irritably as he rolled over, but then he sat up and opened up his arms to me. "Welcome back, Skyco. I am proud you have learned from the fishermen and pleased you have returned. Tomorrow you will describe your journey to me. I know that you achieved significance." He patted my shoulders and looked at his wife. "Now if you don't mind, I am going back to sleep. Skyco needs some rest, I feel sure."

I did. I didn't even get completely underneath the skins. My sleeping bench was so comfortable after sleeping on the ground for days that I felt as if I were lying on a cloud, covered with soft animal skins. I slept deeply, my body so physically tired that I didn't dream at all.

I awoke the next morning to find Roncommock sitting up, looking at me. Jackáwanjes was already gone, attending to another duty. Immediately I started to explain, "Roncommock, my teacher, I have so much to ask of you. I need your guidance and explanation of my experiences."

"It is not yet time for that, Skyco. You have another duty that comes first."

"What can possibly be more important than interpreting the will of the spirits?" I asked incredulously. "Haven't you been training me for this? I think they contacted me several times and showed me what lies ahead, but I am not sure. Once I even fell into a black stupor, where nothing existed at all. I need your advice."

"Before I can take you further down the pathway of the spirits, Skyco, you must complete the hunt."

"Oh, no!" I nearly wailed at him. "What if I fail?"

"Well, that is simple, Skyco. If you fail, you are finished."

"Finished?" I echoed as I looked at him in disbelief.

"It is time for your weapons training," he continued, "time for you to begin. You must take this seriously, Skyco. It is another test of the spirits' favors, one you must successfully pass in order to be accepted by them." He paused, and I felt barely comforted when he continued, "But I can relieve your mind by talking with you and hearing what you have to say. We will talk tomorrow, once Cossine releases you from your first day's training. Not until the hunt is complete, however, can I interpret for you. I can only listen until then."

I stumbled out of his wigwam in despair.

The Hunt

I MANAGED TO put it off long enough. What with fishing, building a canoe, and Roncommock's teaching, I avoided the master of the bow, but it couldn't last forever, and today was the day I dreaded. Every other boy my age was already skilled with a bow and arrows, but I was barely competent. Today everyone will find out. Ascopo already knows.

In my village, boys are given small spears when they're young—five or so winters old. We learn to aim and to throw, but we have little strength to strike anything other than frogs and the occasional snake. Those who show promise, or who just worry their fathers to distraction, often receive small bows with reed arrows so that they can learn the mechanics of drawing the bowstring and aiming the arrow well before their tenth year. I had received such a bow from Menatonon after I survived my seventh winter, but without anyone to practice with and little inclination, I rarely used it after the initial excitement had passed.

I wish I had been more interested or learned sooner, but I didn't, and now I must face the consequences. I held a full-sized bow of witch hazel, strung with a dried sinew. Clumsily, I nocked an arrow—a lightweight reed with turkey feathers on one end and a small triangular piece of flaked quartz on the other—onto the sinew. I took a deep breath, held it, and then drew back the string while holding the nock of the arrow in the fingers of my right hand, my left arm stiff and straight while holding the bow. I let loose the arrow, and the string snapped forward, hitting the wrist of my bow hand, while the arrow flopped to the ground about one arm's distance away. *Ouch!*

Sighing heavily, I relaxed my bow arm and rubbed my sore wrist.

"Come now, Skyco. You can do better than that." My teacher that day was Cossine. We have many good hunters in the village, but Roncommock had selected Cossine as the master of bow. Later I would learn atlatl from Tetepano, who is the acknowledged master of that weapon.

"Open your stance. Where the bow leads, the arrow will follow."

"I know, master. This new bow is hard to draw." It was true. The new, large bow of witch hazel was much stiffer than the childhood bow I had received from Menatonon. It required all my strength to pull the string back to my cheek while keeping my bow arm stiff. When I pulled, my arm started to shake.

"Hold still, Skyco. You can't shoot while your arm is shaking. Take a break."

I relaxed my pull, gently releasing the force on the string, and brought down my bow.

"Now watch me," Cossine said, and he brought up his bow, drew the string back to his cheek, and released the arrow in one smooth fluid motion. "Don't waste time holding back the arrow. Draw the string, then let fly. Your eye should already be on the target. Hasn't anyone taught you this before now?"

"No, sir. My father died before he could teach me and my mother has never remarried. Menatonon is unable to teach me because he can no longer draw the bow."

Cossine hung his head and sighed, "Yes, I know. Forgive me, Skyco. That is why I am here. It is just that you are old to be learning the fundamentals."

"Your turn, Ascopo," he said, and turned to Ascopo, who was standing next to me. He hit the target with all five arrows. Three were inside the inner circle and two were on the line.

"Now you, Andacon, and then you, Osocan," he said to the other two boys in line. Andacon and Osocan were twins. While Ascopo and I were slight of build, these two were sturdier. They already looked the part of warriors. Because they were so skilled with deer decoy skins, they had already participated in hunts even though they could not shoot the deer. That was part of the preparation for the *husquenaugh*.

Not only must we show competence in weapons, but we must demonstrate our skill by killing a deer. Our instructors will take us on a hunt, and we must each come away with a kill. Only after we succeed at the *husquenaugh* can we take part in the men's hunt, and we must make our first deer kill before we can be *husquenaughed*. It seemed insurmountable to me. *How will I ever kill a deer, never mind survive the husquenaugh?*

Andacon, who always led his twin, stepped up and delivered five shots, all of which hit the mark straight on. His brother, in what I suspected was a nod to the other's skill, hit the first four, but pulled the last one just barely outside the marked ring. Elders often said that the younger twin of a pair carried the wisdom of the shaman while the older was destined to be a strong warrior, and these two fit the description exactly.

Embarrassed now, I determined to do a better job. I picked out the target first, nocked the arrow in the correct position on the bowstring, then brought up the bow and arrow together, pulled the string to my cheek, and let fly. While I didn't hit the mark dead on, at least it was a good shot, within a finger's breadth of the mark.

"Nice one!" Cossine said. "Now the others just like that." My next three shots were also acceptable, hitting the target, but not the central circle.

"Retrieve your arrows, boys. Another round, please."

During the next round, some of my arrows hit the

central mark, but all the arrows of the other boys did. If I thought Cossine would praise me for getting the hang of it, I was wrong. He kept exacting accuracy, urging each of us to hit the center target every time, dissatisfied with anything less than a direct hit. We kept going, shooting arrow after arrow. My shoulders started shaking from the effort of drawing the bow, and my accuracy declined. When the arrows of the other boys also began to hit wide of the mark, Cossine called an end to practice.

"You will gain in strength and in accuracy. Tomorrow we meet here again. We will not hunt until I am satisfied that all of you can hit the center of the target every single time. It requires strength and accuracy to bring down a deer." He looked at me and my face flushed. I heard the two brothers snicker, and Ascopo glared at them.

"This afternoon Tetepano will teach you the atlatl. Maybe you will find that more to your liking, Skyco." I felt humiliated.

Glad to be finished with Cossine, we left the practice field, and Ascopo walked out with me.

"I can't believe he called me out like that," I complained to Ascopo.

"Well, Skyco, it is true that you need some more practice. Just keep at it. You'll improve."

Since I didn't feel much like continuing the conversation with Ascopo, I thought that perhaps I would visit my sister to see how she was doing with her training. Mamankanois sat on a reed mat just outside our mother's wigwam, sewing some of the pretty coquina shells onto a white deerskin cloak. As I approached, she set aside her work to greet me.

"Skyco!" she called out. "How glad I am to see you! These shells you brought mother are beautiful even if sewing them onto the skin is a bit of a challenge."

She was using a fish bone with a slight curve to it to pierce the skin and pull through a short length of dried deer sinew, nearly identical to the method that Eracano used to sew up Roncommock's wound. She tied down the coquina through a hole at its apex so that the shell lay flat against the skin, but not so tightly as to prevent the shell from swinging slightly when the wearer moved.

"See how these shells will dance as the wearer dances, making a nice sound as they clap together. We will add the other shells you brought us, too, and they will jingle together to make music." She shook the cloak, and the shells created a pleasing tinkle. "I can look forward to the next dance now."

"This is a beautiful cloak you are making, Mamankanois. You will look good in it."

"Oh, I am slow compared to the older women. They can sew much faster than I can, but I am learning. And I hope that I do look good in it." She paused momentarily, looking off into the distance with a slight smile on her face, but then returned to her practical self. "How was your bow training this morning?"

"I am not as good as Cossine thinks that I should be. The bow is hard to draw. But later today I work with Tetepano to learn the atlatl, and I think I may be better with it."

"Well you had better get good with one of them, because you must kill a deer before the *husquenaugh*. You don't want to embarrass our family by not being able to even participate in the *husquenaugh* this year. Menatonon would disown you."

My face reddened when I realized that she was right. Not only must I kill a deer for the spirit quest to be interpreted for me, the kill was the first step in the *husquenaugh* ritual, too. I must work harder tomorrow with Cossine. "I am off now to talk with Roncommock. Is there a cornmeal cake left from this morning's breakfast? I am hungry."

"Yes, there on a stone by the fire. Still warm, I imagine."

I took a swig of water from the water gourd, the *macócqwer* that my mother always keeps just inside the door, and found the cake of cornmeal on the stone by the fire as my sister had said. Although I now lived in Roncommock's family wigwam, it was nice to visit home and find it as I expected.

"I will stop again this time tomorrow to see how you are progressing with the cloak. Tell mother I will be here then. I missed seeing her today. Where is she anyway?"

"She is attending the birth of a new clan member. Cháppacor felt the labor pains early this morning and we expect the baby to come later today. All the women of the clan are there to welcome the new member of our clan and of our village."

"Why aren't you there, then, Mamankanois?" I chewed my cornmeal cake thoughtfully.

"Only those who have already given birth assist in the delivery. I haven't started my courses yet, haven't entered the woman's wigwam even once."

It was time to get out of here. "See you tomorrow, sister."

Roncommock was waiting for me when I arrived at his wigwam for our session together. "How was your bow training? Both the spirit quest and the *husquenaugh* require that you kill a deer."

Him, too? Was everyone going to remind me of this? But Roncommock's unwelcome comment focused me back on the problem of the *husquenaugh* itself. Although Ascopo and I talked about it, and even asked Chaham, no one really knew what the *husquenaugh* was like until he experienced it. It was a ritual that must be completed in order to become a full member of the tribe. Some boys never returned from the *husquenaugh* wigwam. We heard that they were dead, and I have seen their mothers wail just as they do when one of the tribe dies. However, last year one of these "dead" boys came to the busk at Chowanook, traveling with his kin from another village. He was clearly not dead in reality, even if he was dead to the kin in Chowanook. I wondered what had happened.

"There is plenty of time yet," I said with some irritation as my nervousness showed itself.

Roncommock sighed and said, "You will be prepared, Skyco. You will be successful at the hunt. You must." He looked at me and I understood the importance of what he was telling me. He will prepare me, but I must be successful. There was no margin for error.

"Tell me what you have learned now that you have experienced the mind and body of an ant and a fish," he said without further elaboration.

The dry cake seemed to stick in my throat. "First, I learned how differently they sense the world around them. The ant smells everything using its antennae. The fish feels the pressure changes in the water but does not feel the temperature of the water."

"Good. But what else?"

"I learned hunting technique from the fish: to wait patiently, to stalk quietly, to strike quickly and with all effort." I paused and considered for a moment. "When it is time for me to hunt, that is what I must do. You showed me, didn't you?"

"Yes, Skyco. I told you that you would be prepared. Everything you are learning is important and may affect you in ways you do not anticipate. Learning occurs not only when you are memorizing family clans, but every time you have a new experience. If you pay attention, take the time to consider the experience and understand its significance, you will grow in knowledge throughout your whole life. Part of Menatonon's wisdom comes from his age, for he has seen and experienced much, but part also comes from his thoughtfulness and consideration. He has never quit learning, even now in his old age and crippled body." He paused, then asked, "What else can you tell me of the fish and the ant?"

"The largemouth bass was a loner, a solitary predator. The small fish schooled together for protection, but both the largemouth bass and the gar were predators on their own. The ants, on the other hand, were always part of a large village. They did everything for the village so that the individual hardly mattered. They fought and gathered food, not chiefly for themselves, but instead for all members of their village."

"And what does this mean for you, Skyco? What can you learn from these different ways of life among the other inhabitants of our land?"

"We are in between these extremes, I think. Our village, like that of the ant, is how we organize our lives; our village deserves our support and protection. We work together to bring in food. We hold a great celebration with the whole tribe when we harvest our crops. We function best as a community. But we also hunt as individuals and bring down our prey like the bass or the wolf or the cougar does. And even if we are young or old or wounded, we can still participate in the village life, the way we send children and elders to guard the cornfield. The ants care too little for the individual, the bass too much. I am glad to be a human in between, part of a village with my family near me, but also able to be myself."

"Well done, Skyco. You have learned your lessons from these animals. Our initial training together has been successful and prepared you for the hunt."

I nearly interrupted him, "But can I at least tell you what happened to me on the banks even if you can't interpret it until I finish the hunt?"

"Certainly you can tell me what you saw and what you think you learned."

"Well, point number one is definitely never to enter a fish weir with a bloody toe!"

Roncommock had to chuckle at that. "Interesting that you bring that up. When your mother passed by here this morning, she left this for you." He held up a necklace of shark teeth, the very ones I had picked up and given to Mother along with the shells. I put on the necklace and felt the sharp teeth against my collarbone. I was glad the teeth were not in the mouth of the shark. "Few people wear shark teeth as a talisman, Skyco. Truly you have the favor of the spirits."

"I am not boasting or offending the spirits, am I, Roncommock?"

"Not when you earn the right to wear those by feeling the teeth of the shark."

It was true. Roncommock now wore a bear's tooth dangling from his left ear after surviving the fight with the bear in the early spring.

"But back to work. Tell me, Skyco. What did you see while you were on the sandy banks and what did you learn?"

For a few moments, I just thought about it, and what came to my mind was the image of standing on top of the giant sand dune and seeing the ocean stretch out into the distance—the blue of the sky meeting the blue of the sea in an uninterrupted line as far as I could see, and closer, the break in the white line of sea meeting land, where the inlet with its sandy shoals provided a passageway between the sea and the sound. I remembered the sunrise, and the stars at night, and the walk on the beach when my senses were altered; all these impressions passed through my mind's eye, but the images that returned most strongly were the endless onrushing of the sea and the turbulent currents of the inlet. Then I remembered the menacing, dark cloud over the ocean as it rushed ominously onshore and suddenly disappeared. Clearly, *that* was an image sent by the spirits.

"It is a place to seek the spirits. I feel a strong connection to the sea. The view from the top of that highest sand dune is spectacular, with the sea stretching out to infinity and the path of the inlet from the sea into the sound so clearly outlined. The water connects it all: from the river to the sound to the sea, fish, or men in canoes, can pass from one to the next. The water breaks the land into islands or into the banks and the mainland. As animals of the land, we often think of the land as providing the connection, but it is really the water that connects. Being the fish taught me that. This place of unification is an important place, a place where distinctions dissolve as the water and land—even the sun, moon, and wind— unite in harmony. I saw the sun itself rise up out of the sea, and I felt the wind as it blew in from the sea to the land. The water connects them, too." I paused and looked at Roncommock, who was watching me intently, and then I continued, "I think that the spirits walked with me, for I saw details so clearly and time seemed to slow down. A cold cloud was there at first and then not there in another heartbeat. A bird was struck down by an eagle and then another came skimming in the inlet, leading a whole flock, stark white and bigger than life. As I watched the men work the weirs, they disappeared and reappeared. I was not sure if what I saw was real or not real."

Then Roncommock stood up and began to walk around the wigwam. "Could he be the one? It is still too soon," he muttered to himself. Then he stopped pacing and looked at me again with that intensity of concentration that he showed before. "Is there more?"

"A dream," I replied.

"Tell me of this dream," Roncommock said as he sat down curtly.

I replied, "It was actually two dreams, but related to each other. I was in the body of a bear," I could see Roncommock draw a sharp breath at that, but I continued, "in a manner similar to how you placed me in the ant and in the fish, but less firmly lodged there somehow. I could see and sense through the bear. First, I saw the village disappear, replaced by vast, straight rows of corn—of *pagatowr*. It was not just our crop fields grown large, because the planting was completely different. It seemed so unnatural to have *pagatowr* planted without its companions and in such long lines without regard to the shape of the land, the forces of nature, or the people who planted it. This dream frightened me and I awoke when a great beast roared at me." I paused, remembering the sensation of awakening in a sweat, still hearing roaring in my ears and slowly recognizing it as surf and Ascopo's snoring.

"After I fell asleep again, still as the bear, I saw very strange men. These men wore unusual clothing that covered all parts of the bodies except their faces, but their faces grew hair like a bear. They even smelled of a wet animal; I remember thinking that I had never smelled such an animal before. This dream was not as frightening, but just as confusing.

"Then, the next day, I saw my own face replaced with that of a bear as I looked at my image in a pool. After that was when I walked the beach and saw all I have told you. I cannot understand these strange things, but they trouble me."

Roncommock looked at me a long time without speaking, and I could see his mind turning.

"Skyco, I am not permitted to interpret your dream before you complete the *husquenaugh*, but I can reveal another's. Eracano made an important prediction for Menatonon. Men will come from the ocean to the east, through the inlet, and here to our village. They will bring with them great opportunity and grave threat. Eracano is not able to clarify what the benefits will be or what the threat actually entails and he cannot predict when the strangers will arrive."

I sensed that Roncommock was holding something back from me, but he had already revealed so much that perhaps I was just imagining it. A prophecy from Eracano about our village and white men! Of course! It had not occurred to me, but the bear-man in my dream must be a white man. The fancy clothes and hairy face were the clues, even if I did not see his skin.

We had heard the stories of men with white skin, hairy faces, and fancy clothing that visited other tribes. The strange looking men have long sharp knives that never dull and extremely long pipes whose poisonous smoke kills us but spares them. Sometimes, they steal away the people and take them to the spirit world, never to return. At other times, they leave behind an invisible fire that kills the people in the village and against which the medicine men are impotent. These strange men come from the south, marching over land, but I had never heard of them coming from the sea.

"From the sea?" I couldn't help but utter. "How can they come from the sea?"

"Eracano didn't say. I suppose they have canoes as we do."

"But we never go to sea in them. Our biggest canoes traverse the sound, but not the sea. There is not a tree big enough from which to make bigger canoes," I said, brimming with confidence after my training period with Memeo the canoe builder.

Roncommock sighed. "I don't know, Skyco. That is what he said and that is all I can tell you." Addressing me less directly, Roncommock continued, "I wish we had started your bow training earlier. You may need the skills sooner than I thought." About to add more, he caught himself in time. "Never mind. Your training is progressing at its appropriate pace. We will know when the time comes."

I was getting a little worried with all this discussion of my future while I was standing right in front of him. He seemed hardly to see me. "Tetepano meets with me later today for atlatl training, master. I am busy learning bow technique from Cossine. I will apply myself."

"Do so, Skyco. And reveal nothing you have learned about the prophecy given to your kin. Eracano made his prophecy to Menatonon. The spirits do not look kindly on their sacred words passing from man to man, or boy to boy, without their consent. It seems the spirits are calling to you as well, revealing themselves in the form of the bear and giving you advice on the future. I thought you would receive such a guide, but for the spirits to make contact before the *husquenaugh* is complete—even before the sacred hunt has begun—has never occurred before, and I am keeper of our tribe's knowledge. This must be the reason the spirits sent you on the quest; they could contact you because you were on the sacred dune. There is no doubt you will play a central role in what is coming. Perhaps that is what Eracano foresaw on the night before you departed. I must consider what you have told me and consult with Eracano." Roncommock bustled out of his wigwam in an atypical rush. So did I.

When Tetepano arrived at the practice field, I already awaited him, well ahead of the other boys.

"I like to see an eager student," he said as he pulled out the equipment from a large basket slung over his back.

"I wish to learn, master."

"Okay, then, tell me what you know of these," and he indicated a jumble of items as the other boys walked up.

I picked up the three spears first. Each was as long as I am tall. "These are the spears, with shafts that appear to be made from black locust saplings and flaked quartz heads tied on with a strip of leather made from deer hide." I turned them upside down, pointing at the end opposite the head, and said, "These are the feathers that help the spear fly true, and behind them the spear ends in a notch into which the atlatl is set." I set the spears aside and picked up a shorter stick, about the length of my forearm, with a handgrip carved at one end and a peg carved in the other. "This is the atlatl." I picked up one of the spears and fitted its notched end onto the peg while holding the handgrip of the atlatl firmly.

"Excellent, Skyco. Now let's see you throw it."

That turned out to be the hard part. I couldn't get the spear to remain positioned on the atlatl and its peg. Holding both the handgrip of the atlatl and the spear itself was more than my fingers could keep organized. The spear kept falling off the atlatl peg before I could throw it.

"Let me show you a trick to help you learn the technique," Tetepano said. "All of you gather round me here and observe." He quickly set the atlatl and spear in his hand. "Hold the spear gently between your index finger and thumb, but bend your wrist back so that the atlatl rests on your palm and is firmly gripped by your remaining fingers. Your thumb and index finger should hold the spear in the correct position. The force of the throw will come from the forward motion of your arm, but the atlatl will amplify it. Using the atlatl lengthens your throwing arm and causes the spear to fly faster and with more force than you can generate from throwing the spear with your arm alone. Make your throw smooth and end it sharply with a slight flick of your wrist as the spear releases. Like this," he said and threw a spear perfectly so that it sailed through the air like a giant arrow, embedding itself deeply in the ground where it hit.

"Okay, all of you pick up an atlatl and a spear. Let's see what you can do."

At first, all of us made throws that were awkward. The others were not ahead of me on this weapon! In my first few attempts, the spear mostly just fell out onto the ground in front of me, but I kept trying until I finally threw one as it was meant to be.

"That's it!" Tetepano proclaimed triumphantly. "Not too forcefully yet; keep practicing the technique. Once you can feel the right position, you can add the power. The motion is much like that of throwing a stone or spear without the atlatl. You need to open up your stance so that your left foot and leg are in the direction of your target," he said as he kicked his foot between mine, gently moving them until the left was a little forward of the right. "Now, when you throw, stride toward the target with your left leg and swing the right leg forward as you thrust ahead with your right arm and body." Here he paused and directed his attention away from me. "You, Osocan, who throws with his left hand, you must lead with your right leg instead." Tetepano turned back toward me, again addressing me primarily, rather than the other boys. "You will gain power if your step and throw are smoothly coordinated. Push off on the ball of your foot. Put your whole body into the throw. Again!"

We kept throwing, each with his own atlatl, and Tetepano wandered up and down between the four of us, providing suggestions and making adjustments. I began to feel comfortable with the throwing motion.

Tetepano paused beside me again and seemed pleased with my progress. Deciding that I could add some power without losing the right motion, I really put my shoulder and bicep muscle into one throw while stepping forward with purpose, and was astounded to see the spear point embed itself deep into the tree that was our target. The shaft of the spear quivered from the impact. The other boys stopped their throws and looked at me, Ascopo and Osocan in admiration, but Andacon glaring.

"Skyco! That was great! It is only your first day and you have control and power, too. Perhaps this is your weapon," Tetepano said to me as Andacon sulked.

"I sure like it better than the bow. Drawing the bow hurts my shoulder and the string stings my wrist, which it hits much too frequently."

Andacon laughed at that, but Tetepano continued, "Then you must practice with the bow. A great chief demonstrates mastery of all the weapons, although I hear your natural bent inclines more toward the healing arts. Perhaps you will be a priestly chief instead of a warrior chief."

"How do you know this? What have you heard about me?" I asked with some apprehension.

"Oh, everyone has heard how you treated Roncommock when he was mauled by the bear. Now the fishermen say that you healed yourself after being bitten by a great shark. They ran off and gathered the herbs you instructed them to find, and prepared them as you described, and you were up and walking around the next day. I am sorry I did not see that myself, but I was here in the village with my wife and new baby daughter while you were fishing."

The steam was nearly boiling off Andacon. Because we had worked on the canoe, Ascopo and I were allowed on the fishing expedition, but Andacon and Osocan stayed in the village with the other children, the women, the elders, and a few men such as Tetepano whose wives were pregnant or had just given birth. Instead of traveling away from the village on hunting, fishing, or war raids, they provided game animals as food for the villagers while the rest of the men were away.

"Now, Tetepano, those stories have been embellished a little bit." The last thing I wanted was to have all the other boys angry and jealous. I remembered how Ascopo reacted to my adventures, and he was on my side. Andacon and Osocan were not.

"Any story worth telling has been embellished a little bit, Skyco, but the best stories are born from an honest seed that simply grows a little in the retelling of it. See, you wear the teeth of a shark, so it must be true," Tetepano said with a wry smile. "And believe me, I know a good story!"

Thankfully, Ascopo jumped into the conversation. Laughing aloud, he said, "Yes, Tetepano, you can certainly spin a highly entertaining tale. We heard many good ones while we worked on that canoe together. Tell us again of the time the buck outsmarted you. That one is my favorite."

Tetepano launched into the hunting tale, and Andacon and Osocan were hanging on every word, just as Ascopo and I did the first time we heard it. Finishing the story, he cried, "Ah, but you have distracted me. Back to work, all of you." By the end of the practice period, I felt comfortable with the weapon. Every one of us could hit the mark, but I was the only one who managed to combine force with accuracy.

"We will continue with atlatl training tomorrow. See you all then." Tetepano dismissed us. I was the last to return my weapon to his basket, and as I did, I said to him, "Your stories are so entertaining that I think you should become my master of storytelling in addition to my master of atlatl!"

"I find that both are useful arts. A chief needs many skills."

Over the next few days, I practiced hard at the bow and arrow. Ascopo was even willing to spend what little free time we had in more target practice with me. The other boys were quickly bored with Cossine's bow lessons, but I continued to improve as I listened to his instructions. Soon we were standing at some distance from the target, and we graduated from shooting at a ring drawn on a pile of dirt to shooting at a deerskin stuffed with pine needles and grasses. When all of us could regularly hit the deerskin on the mark at twenty paces, Cossine declared that it was time for a hunt. Truthfully, I think he was ready for his obligation of training to be complete.

Perhaps because the other boys already handled the bow so well, they never really took to the atlatl. I was better than any of them with it. Tetepano did not seem surprised when I asked if I could use the atlatl rather than the bow to make my first kill. He conferred with Cossine, who agreed, if reluctantly.

"You know you need to be skilled with the bow as well, Skyco," Cossine said.

"Yes, master," I replied. "But does it matter whether I use a spear or an arrow to kill my first deer?"

"No, it does not. And your skill with the bow is sufficient. You are as accurate now as the other boys are. You should, perhaps, be required to shoot with the bow so that you will gain confidence, but," he paused and I held my breath, "you may choose your weapon."

I released a sigh. If I could kill a deer, I would be

one step closer to being a man.

Cossine, Tetepano, and we four boys set out early the next morning to test our skills. Ascopo, Andacon, and Osocan each carried a bow and five arrows, but I took an atlatl and three spears. Cossine had his bow, and Tetepano carried his atlatl. Each of us also had a deer hide, which we wore to stalk the deer. We traveled to one of the best hunting locations, a wet, grassy meadow along a small stream that fed the Chowan.

Tetepano showed us the tracks from a buck deer that was traveling with a herd of does and he asked Andacon to identify them. He was proud to show off. The male's toes were spaced wider apart and the prints were deeper, indicating a heavier animal. In addition, the buck's greater size appeared in the longer stride length between the front and rear prints and the wider width between the paired front prints, but it was tricky to keep up with each individual's line of prints. The prints were extremely fresh, little crisp pieces of soil clung to their outline, and indicated that the buck was traveling with a herd of four females.

Tetepano whispered to us that we four boys must work together to take the buck as our first kill, for his strength and power would transfer to us. We were fortunate to find such a large animal as part of our sacred hunt. Apparently, the spirits were watching. All of us needed to stalk slowly toward the herd, getting well within range. Andacon and Osocan, the two accomplished deer mimics, would lead us, but I would give the signal to attack. Tetepano stressed again that all four of us must shoot. It might take more than one arrow to bring down the big buck. We could each identify our arrows, based on the tail feathers and the point, and my spear was obviously different from the arrows, so we would know who hit the deer and who missed.

There was no wind, but we donned our skins to mask our human scent. Walking slowly, with the skins around our shoulders, we paused at Andacon's signal that he'd sighted the deer. The rest of us leaned down and pulled up the heads of the skins, putting one hand up into the skull to move it around. We looked like real deer, moving the deer heads as if they were sniffing the air or leaning down to eat a mouthful of grass. Hunched over so that our size and shape were about right, we approached the deer, looking out carefully between the front legs of the skin. I saw the big buck, which seemed twice as large as the females. In this early season, his antlers were still covered in soft, brown skin.

The deer looked up at us, and we stopped moving forward. I held my breath and looked at how Andacon and Osocan were nodding the heads and stretching the noses up as if our group was scenting the other deer. I copied their movements, as did Ascopo. I lost track of Tetepano and Cossine, who were probably behind us. Andacon and Osocan were a up ahead, and Ascopo was directly beside me. The herd returned to feeding, flicking their tails a little nervously, but apparently deciding that we were acceptable deer.

Andacon motioned me forward. He was agitated, clearly ready to strike, but I knew it was too soon to shoot. I remembered how the *kowabetteo* hunted as we approached the deer slowly and carefully, taking our time to get as close as possible before striking. I stayed calm and hunted like the fish. Once I felt that we were close enough, my heart beat faster. I lowered my deer-skin head toward the ground, as if feeding, then pulled my hand out of the skull, signaled the boys behind me, and readied my weapon. I paused briefly to allow time for the other boys to nock arrows in their bows.

It was hard to hold my weapons while hiding under the deerskin, but I made sure I had the proper placement of the spear on the atlatl, and I remembered to position my feet correctly. I took a deep breath and made a single throaty grunt. Shrugging off the skin, I stood and threw the spear in one motion, and I saw three arrows fly at once. Behind us, Cossine and Tetepano each stood up, but neither released an arrow or spear. The great buck took one gigantic leap and crashed to the ground.

All of us whooped with joy. We jumped up, holding our weapons high. We did it! We ran up to the deer and saw four arrows clustered together in a perfect position, just behind the front leg. My heart skipped a beat because I did not initially see my spear, but then I realized it was because it had gone directly through the ribcage, into the heart, and out the other side. Only a short length, its feather fletching mixed up with that of the arrows, stuck out of the body on the side facing us. The fourth arrow was actually my spear. I made the fatal throw, which stopped the buck cold.

Andacon clapped me on the shoulder, and addressed me for the first time ever in our training. "I thought the atlatl was a primitive weapon, but it was your spear that killed the buck so quickly." He nearly smiled at me, but caught himself in time. "Well, we all hit it; it would have died in any case," he quickly added.

"That's what I've been trying to tell you," Tetepano said. "The spear is larger and can be thrown with more force. I prefer it for large animals like this great buck."

"This is truly cause for celebration," Cossine added. "This buck was pierced by three arrows and a spear. You can all claim the kill. You are all accepted by the spirits to enter the *husquenaugh*. Well done!"

The buck was still moving his head weakly when

we approached him, his lifeblood draining out of the wounds. I saw the light fading from his eyes and my joy at making the kill was tempered by sadness at the great buck's passing. When he finally stilled, Cossine wiped his thumb through the buck's blood and drew a line across the forehead of each of us. We paused to pray to the buck's spirit, thanking him for his death and the food he would provide our village. Cossine and Tetepano stood back at a little distance until our prayers were finished. I looked up and saw that I was the last one to stand.

Getting the deer out of the forest and back to the village took a bit of effort. The buck was too big to carry over any one's shoulders, so we tied it to the middle of a stout pole, allowing us to carry it on the shoulders of two of us positioned at either end of the pole. I was reminded somewhat of the sling we made to carry Roncommock after the bear wounded him, though this one was much simpler—however, the deer was at least as heavy as Roncommock. We took turns carrying it, Andacon and Osocan working together, and Ascopo and me teaming up. We finally approached the village, and all four of us proudly shouldered the deer together.

With the deer on our shoulders and the red smear of blood on our foreheads, everyone knew that we made a successful kill. The news raced ahead, and my mother, my sister, Roncommock, and chief Menatonon stood by the central fire to congratulate us. The chief clasped each of us on our shoulders and nodded to us as a gesture of respect. I had never felt so proud.

After the greetings and congratulations ended, the four of us worked together to skin and gut the deer. We left the steaming intestines on the far side of the midden for the other animals to eat. My mother took the liver and heart and boiled them in a special pot. We four boys would share the organ meat in the evening, again taking on the power of the buck as we consumed his vital organs. We cut up the meat from the deer and set it to roast on the central fire, where all members of the village will share it.

After the meat was cut up and given to our mothers to cook, we four began the process of tanning the hide, carefully cleaning it of any fat or flesh by scraping it with sturgeon scutes. It took all four of us to stretch it out onto a wooden frame, and we propped it up next to the fire to dry all night. The next morning we moved it out into the sun and let it dry there all day. Meanwhile, I boiled the brains in a little water until they were very soft and mushy, then late in the day, a full day after skinning the animal, we met again to rub the brains of the deer into the flesh side of the skin to make it soft and pliable. We took the treated skin off the frame, balled it up carefully so that the brains did not get on the fur side, and let it rest another full day and an extra night.

The last part—making the skin soft—took the longest. We met by the fire on the third morning and stretched the hide back on the frame, where we scraped off the goopy brain mush with dulled shells. We scraped and scraped, then took it off the frame and stretched and pulled the skin in every direction.

It was helpful to have four of us participating. After several rounds of scraping and stretching, which took most of the day, we had a soft, tanned hide.

Since my mother was head woman, we presented the hide to her, and from it she cut four new loincloths. It was a good thing that the deer was so large and we were relatively small, for getting four cloths out of one hide must have been a challenge. My mother managed to make them so that most of the cloth that hung in front of the belt was white from the belly fur, and the portion that was tucked in under the belt was brown, from the back of the animal. My loincloth was the most attractive of the four. It had red dyed fringe at both the top and bottom to indicate my status as heir, and it also had two bands of red, one for Roncommock and one for me, both indicating a dangerous encounter that drew blood but was successfully treated. My sister added a few of the jingle shells to the fringe, which made a nice decoration and reminded me constantly of my trip to the sea.

With our hunt completed, we continued regular, but much less frequent, weapons practice with Cossine and Tetepano. The practice rounds ensured that we did not lose the skills we gained, but they lacked the urgency of previous days. We had more time to talk to each other and our teachers were much less strict. Now that the four of us had shared in a kill, I found that Andacon and Osocan were friendlier to me, and we concluded the end of most practice sessions in a discussion of the *husquenaugh,* all of us wondering what we would face. Not knowing could be even worse than knowing, because we can imagine most anything.

The other boys' training for the *husquenaugh* was minimal. They focused chiefly on weaponry and hunting skills. At least Ascopo also learned the skills of canoe making and fishing. None mentioned the spirit-world training that I received from Roncommock, and I didn't bring it up. I was happy enough just to seem like a regular boy, reliving our hunting success and wondering about the *husquenaugh*. *When would it begin?*

Roncommock soon suggested to me that it was time for another of his lessons and we walked out to the edge of the field where it looked out over the river. He built a small fire and fed it with sacred powder from his medicine pouch. What would I become next?

I am a Falcon

This time, I became a falcon, and not just any falcon, but a duck hawk, the swiftest of all birds. The duck hawk was sitting in a tree overlooking the river when I entered her mind. I sensed at once that she was female and hungry, ready to begin the hunt.

I was hungry, but I couldn't see anything moving yet. Then, across the river, I saw prey. A bufflehead duck— a *weewraamánqueo*—floated on the water, its large white patch on his black head making a tempting target. As soon as he took to wing, as long as I was above him, he was doomed.

I jumped from my perch on a tree limb high above the ground and really just sort of fell. I opened up my wings and the air underneath them pushed me up into the sky. I beat my wings and felt incredible lift and power. Within moments, I was sky-high above the river. I could see so clearly and so far!

Below me, the wide river stretched away to the horizon. The land was incredibly green, with the fresh leaves of trees. The leaves were still so new that each tree had its own distinct color, some pale green, some darker. The patchwork reminded me of autumn leaves, when different trees were red or orange or yellow, but now, in the spring, the leaves were all different shades of green.

Narrow creeks emptied into the river, and I followed their courses as winding, darker patterns on the landscape, like giant snakes crawling through underbrush. At the head of a creek, a dark swamp full of water-loving trees sponged up the water and soaked up the sunlight. Huge *coppáuseo* swam slowly through the creeks like mobile logs. My human mind recognized the clarity of my eyesight at such distance and was astounded by it.

The village was a small clearing in the landscape, wigwams clearly visible arranged around the central fire, from which a thin column of smoke lazily rose. The dancing circle, with its soil pounded down in a perfect circle, revolved around the seven posts, empty now of dancers. The crop fields were pale, rounded areas with irregular edges, and the platform where a child usually sat to scare away birds was empty. The canoes looked like short, thick sticks pulled up on the riverbank.

The land stretched away into the distance in every direction. Only the river and its adjoining creeks provided a direction or a boundary. Our village was a tiny place, though it supported the lives of hundreds. The landscape was immense.

But the hunt! I'd become distracted by the magnificent panoramic view.

The duck had just taken flight and was gaining height. I spiraled up higher, knowing that it couldn't see me directly above. Two others joined it, both female and not as gaudily marked, but the male had already gained the most altitude. He was my target. His bold, black and white coloring made him stand out against the dark water below. As soon as he was high enough above the water so that I could grab him without hitting the water itself, I folded my wings against my body and began to plummet. I was faster than any arrow—faster than a spear thrown with an atlatl. I was faster than anything on Earth. I was moving so fast that I felt special structures holding open my nostrils and channeling the air so that I could still breathe at such speeds.

Within a moment I was nearly on the prey. Just before hitting it, I pulled up by extending my wings, which turned me out of the dive and up into striking position. I extended my feet and hit the back of the duck right between its wings with my open talons. It began to fall from the sky, already dead from the terrific impact of being hit at a speed it could never even imagine, let alone achieve.

Now, in a more leisurely descent of just half my former speed, I dove after the prey and snagged it with my talons before it hit the water. It was heavy and I labored with it, pumping my wings to haul it back toward a limb on my hunting tree, where I could rest as I consumed it.

Before I arrived at my tree, however, another bird was suddenly ripping past me, splitting the sky overhead. I turned and veered instinctively, but too slowly with the heavy load of duck, and the bald eagle—*nahyápuw*—was upon me. He flipped upside down as he passed me and snagged the duck with his feet. I gave a couple of jerks, but his talons were embedded too deeply in the prey. We started to plummet toward the water, the eagle twice as heavy as I, the duck interlocking us. I looked at his fierce eyes, huge beak, and thick, yellow talons. His black feathered body and white head were enormous. He opened his mouth in a feint toward my head. It was over. I could not win. I let go and screamed in frustration. *Nahyápuw* righted himself just above the water's surface and with his big wings flapping strongly, pulled away with my catch.

I spiraled upward again, angry, annoyed, and still hungry. All the ducks had scattered, alerted by both my hunt and the eagle's dramatic theft. *I must travel to find more prey.* I turned toward one of the big lakes, where I knew there would be more ducks. Swans and geese were there too, but since they were too big for me to fly with, I avoided them. As I approached the lake, I searched the skies carefully for the presence of other raptors, and, gladly, saw none. If I could make a kill, I should be able to keep it this time.

I saw a coot out on the edge of the lake, separated from the rest of the flock. It was a small, black bird with a white bill. I spiraled higher and higher, waiting for it to take off from the water so that I could catch it on the wing, but it stuck firmly to the water's surface, swimming away into the reeds along the edge where I could no longer see it. All my waiting was in vain. I screamed in frustration again, a high "Cree, Cree!"

Suddenly, from behind me, I heard an interesting "kek-kek, kek-kek." I looked around, and saw a small male falcon following. I kept flying, but slowed down when I heard the call again, softer this time, more friendly. The male had come closer. I flew up higher and he followed, then he turned and flew upside down underneath me, showing off his best acrobatic flight maneuvers. He was a good flyer and he had a nice voice.

He flew out ahead of me, made a loop in the sky, and came back underneath me again, this time holding out his feet. I liked him, so I responded by grabbing his feet with my own, and we began to fall. Our wings were outspread, our talons clasped together, and we spiraled down together, tumbling as we fell. Before we hit the water, we released our grip on each other and flew back up into the sky. I felt elated, invigorated by the fall and delighted with how the male executed the trick. When he flew back toward a tall tree that reminded me of my hunting tree, I followed him, and we landed in the highest branches. He had cached a kill in the tree and offered me a morsel of it, which I consumed hungrily. I stepped toward the food and he backed away from it, allowing me, the larger bird, to have as much as I wanted. He was a suitable provider too. When the time comes to raise young, which I sensed was not far distant, he would be my mate.

Flying felt so good—so easy—that I took the opportunity to enjoy it now that I was no longer hungry, and took off from the tree limb. It was no more effort than running when I was human. Contracting my chest muscles caused my wings to beat down and pushed me up into the sky. While soaring, I adjusted my wingtip feathers slightly to provide either lift, by opening them up, or speed, by sliding them back into a smooth foil. Moving my wings back toward my body began an angled dive, and the steepness of the dive was determined by how closely I tucked my wings against my body. My covering of feathers provided constant feedback about my speed and the angle of flight because my skin detected the position of each feather against it. My whole body responded to the feel of the air against my feathered skin.

From up so high in the sky, the peoples' lands merged together. It was hard to tell when I left my tribe's territory and crossed into another. I started out over my home village, but in only a few wingbeats, it seemed, I passed Ohanoak farther down the river. I swung out in a wide loop, passing far beyond where I had ever been on foot and well into the dangerous territory of the Mangoaks before I turned back. The freedom of flight was exhilarating.

The world was vast, and I was a tiny part of it. The boundaries we people set were arbitrary and barely even recognizable from a distance. If I hadn't known that the longleaf savannah with the *pocosin* was a boundary of no-man's land between tribes, I would have never known that I was in Mangoak territory. It was just land passing into more land, not a single boundary line in sight. Animals, plants, air, and water all passed through these human boundaries. Everything but men. Their presence and boundaries seemed eerily temporary.

I was beginning to tire from the long flight, and I sensed that my host falcon was ready for me to go. She landed on a lower tree branch, near Roncommock, and looked at him. When I returned to myself, I was looking back at her. She was a beautiful bird, her back the color of slate-gray rock, her creamy chest covered with rusty bars. Her sleek head was black, with a wide V down each cheek like a tattoo completely filled with dark dye. Her intelligent eyes sported a yellow rim, making them appear even larger. I saw her mate soaring high in the sky, waiting for her to return.

I was seated in the respectful position, legs

crossed, hands on knees, back straight, and I bent forward at the waist until my forehead touched the ground. "Thank you," I murmured and felt the softest whisper of air as she flew back over me to return to her mate. As I sat bent with my head upon the ground, a flight feather from her left wing drifted down to the ground beside me and I picked it up. My heart swelled with thanks and the knowledge that she accepted me to fly with her on a hunt and beyond.

"What a regal animal," I breathed softly to Roncommock. "The whole time I was part of her, she was always right there too, unlike the ant or even the fish. I used the ant's body, sensed what she sensed, but this was different. The falcon decided what we were doing and just showed me, allowed me to watch, while she performed."

Taking the feather she offered, I tucked it into my hair on the left side, which had grown out a little longer since Roncommock cut it. I wrapped a strand of my hair around the feather's base to hold it. It rode gently in my hair, brushing my shoulder when I moved my head.

"What did you learn from her, Skyco?"

"It was dramatic to kill *weewraamánqueo*, but then have it stolen by *nahyápuw*—the eagle. I thought she would fight back, but she did not. When she realized that *nahyápuw* was bigger than she was, and that it had a firm grip on *weewraamánqueo*, she let the duck go. She was frustrated, but she knew that she was no match for the bigger bird. Rather than chase after him fruitlessly, she just went out to hunt again."

"Yes, Skyco, that is the nature of the bird. Duck hawks are hunters. Eagles are hunters, too, but because they are so much larger than the other raptors, they are also piratical, stealing away the food of others. The duck hawk knew that to hold onto the prey would result in personal injury. By letting go, she protected herself from harm. After all, there are many more ducks for her to catch."

"Still, it doesn't seem fair that she caught the duck and the eagle only had to steal it from her."

"What do you think the other ducks would say to that? Didn't the duck hawk steal from them as well? The male was part of their flock, the mate of another duck. His life was stolen from them, was it not? You could say that we steal from the deer tribe when we kill a deer or from the hickory tree when we take its nuts for food. We offer our thanks and prayers because we recognize that we depend upon those animals and plants to nourish us. We cannot live without taking their lives, but we try to avoid an overharvest, taking only what we need and never hoarding excess."

"Isn't that what we do with fighting, too? We kill the same number of the enemy as they killed of us so that we keep a balance. We satisfy our sense of justice and avoid escalating the violence. But how did we ever start the killing in the first place?"

"Like the birds, Skyco, the first people took from each other just as they took from the deer and the hickory tree, and we have been seeking reciprocity ever since. It is a natural process, occurring constantly, just as a predator takes its prey. The duck eats the weeds from the pond, the hawk eats the duck, and the hawk drops the carcass back in the pond where it grows more weeds for other ducks to eat. When the eagle takes from the hawk but does not kill it, it does not fundamentally alter this circle, it just adds itself to it."

Roncommock paused briefly and then continued, "What else did you learn from the hawk when you saw with her eyes?"

"I also learned that the world is vast and without borders. When I was just human, the whole time we traveled out to the banks and back, I was always conscious of whose territory we were in. It took us days to pass through the territory of the Weapemeocs because they live along the north side of the sound. Our territory extends down the Chowan to the sound and all the way behind us to the heads of many creeks that join it. You have been teaching me to learn the boundary with the Mangoaks because they are our enemies and to enter their territory is foolish, but from up above, the territories are practically indistinguishable except where they coincide with water. As I learned before, water connects land, but now I see that water also provides the edges in nature."

"So you understand then that where we place our boundaries is really rather arbitrary. We skirmish and move them slightly when we win or lose, but in reality, the only boundaries of land are of water, as you saw. This is one of the things that troubles me about the idea of strange men coming from the sea. What are their boundaries? Do they recognize any limits?"

I was beginning to comprehend Roncommock's concerns, and I wondered how I was wrapped up in them. How could there be men in the sea?

"Before you worry yourself with the implications of this news, for there are important consequences as I see you realize," Roncommock said, "I want you to reflect back on the three animals that you have become: the ant, the fish, and the falcon. Each animal's spirit has received you and you have parted with their blessings. You can call on these spirits whenever you need their connection to earth, water, or air. They will help you to make wise decisions of benefit to you, your family, and your tribe."

"This is why Eracano wears the pelt of an otter and the skin of a bird; they are talismans that remind him of his animal-spirit connections!" I cried in wonder as I realized what he meant. Pausing to reflect, I added, "Now I have the feather from the falcon and the teeth of a shark, but what is my talisman from the ants, teacher?"

"When you complete the *husquenaugh*," Roncommock said, and I squirmed because he was assuming that I would successfully pass this greatest of trials, which came next. "When you complete the *husquenaugh*, you will earn the right to wear a medicine pouch. Into this pouch you must add some sand from an ant mound so that you carry it with you at all times. While not a visible talisman, the spirits will recognize the ant sand."

"I understand," I replied.

"Skyco, I feel certain that the spirits have something important in store for you. You have slipped easily into their world on three occasions now, and you recognized the sacredness of the sand dune. The spirits visited you there, too. They were warning you of the arrival of white men, coming in that inlet and bringing change with them. Recall that the bear spirit fought on your behalf before," he said as he stroked the bear tooth hanging from his earlobe. "After the busk you will meet him in the *husquenaugh*."

Time for Feasting

The warm season had finally arrived. It was time to plant corn, which we call *pagatowr*. That season, Ascopo, Andacon, Osocan and I were allowed to perform the duties of the men in planting because we had killed a deer. Every prior planting season, we'd worked with our mothers on the women's tasks. This time felt different, more important. Best of all, the husquenaugh was still several moons away and I had some time to relax without worries of an upcoming black drink ritual, a spirit quest, or a deer hunt. I could almost put the husquenaugh out of my mind. Almost.

"Hey, Skyco! Not long until the season of the *husquenaugh*, and this is your year. Ready for it?" Kaiauk came walking up with Ascopo.

"Oh, be quiet!" Ascopo said, clearly annoyed. "Older brothers think they know everything!"

I shrugged my shoulders and quietly replied, "So do older sisters!"

Pagatowr was our most important crop. We stored it for winter and it kept for the whole year. It was best in the summertime, when it was still green instead of dry, and we roasted it over the fire after soaking the whole cob, still in its husk, in water. In the wintertime, women made succotash, with corn, beans, squash, and deer meat stewed together in a pot, and they made cakes of cornmeal, wrapped in the husks, which they baked on flat stones around the fire. Every stew that the women cooked had a handful of ground *pagatowr* in it, I think.

"Today we began the planting, but tonight we get to celebrate! I can hardly wait for all that food!" Kaiauk continued.

"I am looking forward to the dancing and drumming," Ascopo said. "It makes the hard work easier to bear when I think about how much fun we have during the celebration." He paused and smirked at Kaiauk, "And I know who *you* are looking forward to seeing, Kaiauk. Does Skyco know?"

I looked questioningly at Ascopo, but he just laughed as Kaiauk's face turned bright red.

"Well, then, uh, let's go get started!" he stuttered.

The sun was high in the sky as all the people of the village gathered together at the edge of the field. Ascopo, Kaiauk, and I joined Andacon and Osocan, who were standing together, as always. We each picked up one of the men's tools, the shoulder blade of a deer attached to a long stick. Because the men hunted deer, only the men used the sticks with the deer bones, and this year that included us. We all felt rather proud of ourselves and shared conspiratorial smiles as we selected our special tools for the first time. We were nearly men!

I scraped out a clump of green grass by its roots and left it on the surface to dry out. My sister, with one of the pointed sticks that women use, was concentrating on the old stalks from last year, prying them up out of the ground. Since the ground was dry and the sun was hot, the weeds died quickly once we jerked them out by the roots. My back was already warm in the sun and a few droplets of sweat accumulated on my upper lip, where they tickled. After we worked through the whole field, we turned back and raked the dead plants into small piles.

After we finished the first field, all the villagers took a break together under the shade of trees to drink cool water that some of the women had

thoughtfully hauled up from the river in a large *macócqwer*. Andacon complained about the heat, and my sister made a little snort of disbelief. We were all hot and thirsty. My stomach growled, making Cossine look curiously at me, but we did not eat anything, fasting instead until the evening's celebration. I drank some more water to quiet my stomach. We would sow this first field with the initial planting of *pagatowr*, but two more fields for the later plantings and one field for the sunflowers remained. We had much yet to finish, and soon Tetepano led us back into the field.

While we worked steadily along in the second crop field, I heard the piercing whistle of a red-shouldered hawk, and Pooneno, who was close to Ascopo, stopped what he was doing to look around. The hawk was his spirit animal. I paused, too, and followed his gaze to the line of trees that bordered the river, but I could not see anything there. I kept looking, scanning from tree to tree, and then I saw the big bird move.

She perched high in a big oak tree, on a limb that gave her a good view across the whole field. Her chest and shoulders were reddish; her tail had alternating bands of white and black. She was bigger than the duck hawk, and broader of wing and tail. The duck hawk was slender and elegant, relying on her incredible speed to catch prey, but the red-shoulder exuded strength and raw power.

We were about halfway across the field, working toward her perch, with a cleared field behind us and a grassy, weedy strip still between the trees and us. I was surprised when she leaped off the limb, opened her wings, and glided across the field toward us. By now, most of the other men who were working the field had seen her too, and they all paused to watch as she swooped to the ground in the weedy section and came out with a mouse gripped in her claws. She screamed again in triumph, her whistle longer and more penetrating than before, and flew off out of sight to eat her catch.

When we finished the field, we gathered again for water under the shady trees. All the talk was about the hawk and her catch.

"Did you see how close she came to us?" Andacon asked the group in general. "I was on the edge nearest her, and I bet I could have touched her when she hit the ground to grab that mouse." Andacon was so interested in hunting that he even evaluated the bird's prowess.

"Yes, it was a close pass. I've never seen a hawk that was willing to come so close to us," Ascopo volunteered. He was hoping to sound knowledgeable, I could tell, but Pooneno stepped in.

"She was hunting the edge of that field from which we flushed the mouse with our scraping and digging. I think that she knew to wait there while we flushed out animals for her. I could sense her watching and waiting; she was hunting."

"You should know, Pooneno, since the red-shoulder is your spirit guide," Kaiauk replied to him.

"She is a smart hawk, then. What is the chance she will come to the next field?" I asked aloud to no one in particular.

The hawk did not return to the third field, or at least I didn't see her. I strained my eyes as I searched the trees, but she did not reappear. Several times I saw Ascopo, Andacon, or Osocan look up as well. I noticed many other small birds, however, because my eyes sought out movement. A towhee—or *chúwh-weeo*—kicking and scratching in dry leaves on the ground startled me twice, attracting my attention with the flutter of brown leaves. His red eye, striking pattern of black, brown, and white colors, and his sharply accented call—"jor-ee!"—identified him.

A song sparrow sang melodiously from the weedy border of the field, causing me to stop and search for the source of the pretty song. He was perched at the tip of a blueberry shrub, which we left growing along the edge of the field because it produced berries in the summertime, his small chest puffed out so that the central, dark spot on it seemed twice as large as normal.

The striking red body of a redbird, a *meesquouns*, caught my eye as he flicked aside some grass to grab a cricket or other insect from the ground. Among such animated and entertaining creatures, we seemed to finish the third field in no time at all and were soon back at the resting place still talking about the hawk.

While we were chattering with each other, Pooneno suddenly took a quick breath and said, "Look! There she comes again!" He pointed to the tree from which the hawk had sprung to catch the mouse. I looked up just in time to see the hawk land in the tree. Once she settled in and stopped moving, she was difficult to see on her perch.

We boys ran to the fourth field with light steps, scratching a little more vigorously in the hope of scaring out another mouse for the hawk to catch. Even my sister managed to work up close to Ascopo, Kaiauk, and me, and she was poking around with her stick in likely mouse hiding-places rather than concentrating on prying the roots out of the ground. Sure enough, after working through about half of the field, forcing any animals in the grass ahead of us, we saw the hawk leap from her perch, pumping her wings this time as she headed toward us. Instead of darting directly to the ground as she had previously, she pulled up and hovered over the field for several wingbeats, furiously pumping her wings up and down, and then she suddenly dove to the ground. This time, she came up with a colorful snake that we called *tesicqueo*. The snake writhed wildly in her grip, but she had grabbed it behind the head, thereby preventing it from bending around to bite her.

"Look at that!" my sister said in awe as the hawk flew back to its perch and pecked the snake in the head as soon as it landed. The snake twitched and slowly contracted its coils as it lay draped over the limb, and my sister shivered in unease. Noticing her discomfort, Kaiauk stepped up close to her.

"Don't worry," he said. "It's dead, but its muscles still work for a while. I saw that once in a rattlesnake," he added proudly. "It lunged at me even after

I had killed it."

Ascopo sniggered and said, "Well maybe you just didn't do the job right, Kaiauk, and only injured the snake instead of killing it."

Kaiauk turned sharply and stepped up threateningly toward his brother. "It was dead. I know it. You shut up about things you don't know!" They stood facing each other, glaring, while my sister and I paused to watch.

"Get back to work, boys!" Tetszo called from nearby. "Save that energy for the weeds!"

I constantly checked to see what the hawk was doing even as I worked the fourth field, and I bet everyone else in that field did too. The hawk just stood beside the snake as it kept coiling and uncoiling, a little slower each time, until it finally hung limply over the limb. Then the hawk called out with her high shriek and another hawk—her mate— answered back as he came cruising over the village and fields. He landed beside her and immediately began tearing at the snake. I quit working and leaned on my stick to watch, but since the older men and some of the women were also watching the spectacle, I assumed it was okay to do the same. The female hawk must have been full of mouse, because she allowed her mate to eat the entire snake. Her mate was a little smaller than she, noticeable when they were side by side, so we knew that Pooneno was right when he called her female at first sight.

At last we moved to the final field, for sunflowers, and I delighted in nearing the end of the project.

While thinking about the hawk and her hunt, ignoring my hunger was possible, but now that it was late afternoon, my belly was winning the fight with my mind. Ascopo looked rather pitiful as he rubbed his empty stomach. To make matters worse, we smelled the fire that some of the women were already tending. I could imagine the big pot boiling with succotash.

Sweaty and hot, I walked from the field to gather with everyone else at the edge of the river, where we washed the sweat and dirt from our tired bodies. Some of the old women started grumbling when I splashed water up into the face of Ascopo, who responded by jumping on my shoulders and dunking my head under water while he was howling and laughing. As he pushed me down under water, I gave in and was pushed all the way down near his feet, which I grabbed and jerked to tip him over. He came up sputtering and shaking water from his wet hair, and Kaiauk immediately dunked him back under again, laughing all the while. Osocan tried the same trick on his brother.

"How can you boys have so much energy after working all day?" I whirled around at my mother's voice and leapt out of the river to embrace her.

"Mother!" I cried joyfully. "It has been a long time since I have talked with you. I missed you when I stopped by the other day, when Mamankanois told me you were assisting the birth of Cháppacor's child. I have been busy in my training."

"That is how it should be, my son." My mother

smiled at me as she held my shoulders and I saw her glance at my neck.

"The necklace is beautiful. Thank you for making it for me," I said.

"It made me a little nervous to hold the teeth of a shark and know that you were so close to one, but I was proud to prepare such a strong talisman for you. You bear an important responsibility for our tribe, Skyco. Remember that one day you will be chief and you have much to learn before you become as wise as Menatonon." She gave a slight push, directing me up the path to the village. "Come, walk with me, Skyco. Tonight we sit as families during the feasting. You can tell me what you have been learning." I waved goodbye to the other boys, still dunking each other in the river.

Mother stretched her arm out straight from her body and said, "Look how much you have grown since you left my wigwam. Your head is above my shoulder height now." She dropped her arm and glanced down. "Your new loincloth looks very nice on you, as befits a young chief."

I grinned at her, pleased that she noticed my height, which I hoped was continuing to increase, and said, "I think it looks very fine, too, the skin from my first deer. You made a beautiful cloth from it. Thank you again."

When we reached the village, the drummers were already beating drums with a regular, easy rhythm. Mother and I walked up to the common pot and dipped out the aromatic succotash into smaller pot-

tery bowls. We took our places next to chief Menatonon as his oldest sister and his heir. We sat a little behind him and on each side. Next to my mother,
their sister Qvunziuck, and her young children, who
are my cousins, gathered. We all clustered around
Menatonon. Other villagers seated themselves in the
common area, those with some matrimonial ties to
our family closest to us, and those without connections farthest away. Even though Roncommock is a
favored friend of Menatonon, an important shaman,
and my teacher, he was not related to us so he sat at
some distance with the rest of his family.

I ate the food from the bowl with my fingers,
hungrily licking them clean and then wiping them on
my loincloth. My mother and Menatonon were deep
in conversation and I was on my second bowl when
my sister finally showed up.

"Where have you been?" I asked her. "What took
so long? You were with us at the field but then you
disappeared."

Mamankanois leaned over and whispered,
"Mother left me with instructions to gather a root
she needed and I couldn't find it before we were
called to planting. I knew I couldn't harvest any other
plants once the ceremony started tonight, so I went
out to search again."

"So did you get it?" I whispered to her.

"Yes. I finally found it."

"Good thing you did. You know how Mother
always insists that we finish our tasks."

"You don't have any idea! Since I started my

training with her, she has been as tough as a black locust stump. I can't do anything well enough to please her. I was dead tired after planting, but I dared not disappoint her."

"So that's why we are whispering." She didn't want our mother to overhear. "What else have you been doing?" But my sister did not have time to answer.

Menatonon stood up and the buzz of voices quieted, as did the beating drums. He was splendidly outfitted. The tail of a cougar, an animal he had killed as a young man and now wore as a talisman, dangled from his belt. He stripped off his cloak so that we could see the extensive tattoos on his chest, arms, and legs. Three necklaces looped around his neck, each strung with the precious, purple, wampum disks, some of which came from my trip to the banks. He wore a single gorget of copper, which covered his heart. A bracelet of pearls decorated his right wrist. On his left wrist, he wore a leather wrist guard sewn with an intricate design, and he held a fine longbow—Memeo's best work—even though he no longer shot it. The right side of his head was freshly shaven and the left side was decorated with the feathers of several birds, among them the bald eagle, whose great white tail feathers only a chief could wear. From his ears were suspended the largest single pearls our tribe had ever collected. A strand of *minsal*, white beads of bone, rested on his head at the level of his forehead.

"Bring forth the seeds," he commanded, and my

mother, who had unobtrusively gone to her wigwam to fetch them, stood up with several woven baskets, each full of a different type of seed. I looked around, astonished. *How did she get past me so quickly?* She always seemed to anticipate events before they occurred. She wore her necklaces of wampum and a strand of *minsal* on her head to indicate her status as head woman. Some of the shells I gave her decorated her loincloth, and they tinkled together as she walked.

Roncommock moved from his place among the throng, meeting my mother as she joined him at the central fire, directly in front of Menatonon. He wore his special cloak of rabbit skins and carried a bundle of dried leaves, some of which I recognized as those of our crop plants. He cast a little *uppówoc* from the pouch at his waist onto the fire, then picked up a seed from each basket and held them in his hand.

"We sacrifice these seeds in the sacred fire and offer our thanks to their tribes. We hope that they will grow and feed us for the coming year. We will do our best to protect them from harm, to care for the plants that will provide the seeds for the next season. As they are given to us, we give back to them." As he cast each seed into the fire, he called out their names and offered thanks.

"Thank you, *pagatowr*, master of all."

"Thank you, *okindgier*, *wickonzówr*, *macócqwer*, (beans, peas, squash, pumpkins, gourds) and sunflowers."

As he cast in the last seed, rapid, rhythmic drumbeats restarted, resounding throughout the village. At once, I leapt up with the other boys to join the men at the dancing circle, and the best dancers among the men were already whooping and jumping next to one of the seven carved poles evenly spaced around the circumference of the circle. Each pole had a face that represented one of the most important spirits. Tonight, the most important spirits are those of our crops, and our dancing embraced, celebrated, and honored them.

Chaham and Kaiauk already occupied places next to a spirit pole. As they stomped their feet and hopped up and down along with the other dancers, each shook a small *macócqwer* rattle full of pebbles tied to a stick. Kaiauk danced more dramatically than any of the other men, rhythmically pounding his feet as he whooped and jumped. He was really showing off. Chaham, however, only danced briefly before he laid down his rattle, and I quickly grabbed it and took his place in the dance. As I started dancing, I saw my sister pick up the exhausted Kaiauk's relinquished rattle, and the way they passed it from hand to hand caught my attention, but only for a moment.

My mind and body soon resonated with the thumping drums, pounding footfalls, and crackling of the fire, until I was swept into them all. As I danced, lost in this strange unification, my legs weakened as my spirit soared. How long I danced was impossible to judge, but my body asserted itself as my tired legs finally gave way.

Sweat was pouring off me and I was very thirsty. As I stood by the *macócqwers* of water, drinking my fill, I looked back toward the dancing circle to see dust from the dancers swirling in the air, their dark forms backlit by the fire. Chaham, who was with me at the water, said, "It is a good dancing night when the dust rises in the air from all the pounding feet and the soil around the dancing circle is packed smooth as the clay patted by our potters," and I had to agree.

It was completely dark when the drummers beat a final flourish, announcing the end of the dance. The moon was bright and full, the planting moon, and it was easy to see as we walked back to our wigwams even though our eyes were accustomed to the firelight.

Early the next morning, the whole village turned out again at the crop fields. Even though I arrived along with the other villagers before the sun arose, Roncommock was already there. I had not heard him leave the wigwam. He carried a clay pot that contained some embers from the sacred fire.

"I am tired from the work yesterday," Ascopo whispered to me as we stood together.

Somehow Roncommock overheard and said, "Be glad you were preparing an old field for replanting rather than clearing a brand new field. Next year we will shift the fields to a new location."

As Ascopo blushed, Andacon smiled with a rather wolf-like grin at him and said, "What will that entail?"

"We will girdle the trees this winter, before the sap begins to rise and push out the new leaves. Next spring we will burn the fields to get rid of the shrubs, but many grasses and weeds will survive and they will be tough ones. It will take us a day to prepare a single, new field next year instead of working in all four in a single day."

"Does that mean we get to celebrate every night?" Ascopo asked hopefully.

Roncommock laughed quietly as he replied, "Yes, it does. I think it is the anticipation of the evening dance and ceremony that keeps the youth working hard during the day."

Then Roncommock tipped out some of the embers onto the first pile of dry weeds near the edge of the field. It caught fire almost immediately and he carried some of that burning frass to other piles of dry grasses, weeds, and old stalks. As he moved along, transferring the fire to a succession of unburned piles, each previous pile burned quickly to ashes. By the time he reached the end of the field, the first fires burned out and turned cold. In this way he purified and enriched the ground for the next crop.

After purifying the ground, then women arrived to plant the crops. My mother walked out to the center of the field and plunged a sharp stick to poke a hole in the ground. My sister, her apprentice, carried a basket of *pagatowr* seeds and placed four seeds into the hole, then covered them by pushing some soil with her foot. Four other women came out of the crowd of villagers, walked to the field's center and each took a long stride, one to the east, one to the west, one north, and one south. They poked holes at each of these points, and other girls added the seeds and covered them. The men and boys simply watched until the whole field was sown with *pagatowr* and rows ran east-west as well as north-south. These most sacred of seeds would give birth to new plants just as women give birth to children, so only women planted the *pagatowr*.

After women sowed the *pagatowr*, men helped by planting beans—*okindgier*—and peas—*wickonzówr*—in a circle around each corn plant, which allowed these vining plants to run up the corn stalks for support. The *okindgier* also helped the *pagatowr* to grow, for we have noticed that years of poor *okindgier* growth decreased the size of the *pagatowr* and the number of kernels we harvested. Lastly, we planted pumpkins, gourds, and squash, collectively called *macócqwer*, in between to fill in along the ground and shade out weeds.

While the men planted these crops in the first

field, the women had already moved to plant the sunflowers separately, in a different field all to themselves. We left the other three fields bare. We would plant the second field on the new moon, and the third on the next full moon. In this way, we extended our harvest, providing fresh green *pagatowr* and *okindgier* for a long period, and allowing us to divide the harvest into three moderate efforts instead of just one enormous one.

Planting was not as demanding as clearing the fields, but it seemed more difficult because I was still weary from the previous day. Just as Roncommock suggested, I kept thinking about the good food and the fun dancing. Sure enough, soon the sun was low in the sky and we headed to the river to wash before the celebration began anew.

At the river, I could catch up with Ascopo, Andacon, and Osocan. Thankfully, both Kaiauk and Mamankanois were somewhere else and so our older siblings didn't bother us. To immerse ourselves into the cool river water was invigorating and fun, but it was also an important ritual for us—part of the cleansing process that we performed whenever we started or finished an important task. Planting our crops was second only to harvesting our crops in the significance of our rituals. But we could be as silly as we wanted while we were washing in the river, and after two grueling days, hilarity won out. Osocan was sneaky and managed to dunk his bigger brother so unexpectedly that when Andacon came back up he spurted water out of his nose and we all nearly drowned because we were laughing so hard.

The feast on the second night was even better than the first because we added other foods to the meal. In addition to the hearty succotash from the night before, flavorful venison bones added complexity to the stew while strips of tender back muscle browned on skewers over the fire. They popped and steamed as tiny drops of fat fell on red-hot embers, and Ascopo squealed as one strip burnt the roof of his mouth when he ate it straight off the grill. Slender sticks of hickory wood, soaked in water, provided plenty of scented smoke to the fire. Fresh fish gathered from the nearby weirs in the river and grilled over the fire picked up the smoky, hickory flavor as they steamed to moist perfection.

Even though we'd been eating a lot of dried fish since the fishing expedition, the fresh fish flaked delicately into bite-sized pieces and exuded the sweet flavor that only fresh fish from the river carry. I noticed that Osocan never wandered far from the fish grill. A little pot of dried plums, reconstituted with water, bubbled enticingly as it boiled, surrounded by hot coals. I couldn't decide whether I liked it better when its intense sweetness was smeared on the smoky strip of venison or added to the natural sweetness of the fish, so I made several different experimental comparisons. Ascopo was happy to smear it on everything.

While I was sampling the succotash, I realized that someone had even been out gathering plants from the forest, for I noticed an unusual flavor in the stew.

"Hey, Mamankanois, what was that root you were after? Was it one of the seasonings?"

"Good guess, little brother!" my sister teased. "Ginger root provided that flavor."

"Well, I am sure glad you found it. I bet mother would have fumed if you had been unable to provide it."

"You are right about that. I'm just glad I remembered where I gathered it last spring. There was more in the same area." My sister let out a sigh, which ended with a satisfied little burp, as if to say, "Oh, I am pleasantly full now!"

I kept on scooping up succotash while I asked, "So what else have you been doing, Mamankanois? I know you planted the fields, but what else has mother been teaching you?"

"Recently it has been the preparation of skins as well as sewing and decorating them for garments and other uses. For example, I assisted her with the new loincloths. And I continue to learn about plants and their many different uses for food, medicine, rope, and other purposes, too. I doubt that I will ever know all of them. As yet, my weaving of mats and baskets has been rudimentary, but I heard that soon I will apprentice with Poócqueo, who is the most skilled basket weaver in the village. It will be fun to learn from the best."

"You girls have a lot to do even before you have babies to care for. Fishing and hunting seem pretty easy by comparison."

"I thought you had learned that everyone in our

village has important jobs to do and that it takes all of us to make our village prosper. Hasn't Roncommock been teaching you *anything*?" My sister smiled mischievously before she walked over to chat with Kaiauk, and I took the jab with the humor she intended. I liked her much better since we started our training. Both of us now had tasks to focus on and we saw each other less frequently. Perhaps that was for the best when it came to siblings. But why was she always talking with Kaiauk?

The Busk Celebration

It was now the height of summertime, and life was easy. Fish were abundant, and the *pagatowr* grew high in the long, hot days of summer. During the spring, we celebrated the planting of the *pagatowr*, but after its harvest we held the biggest celebration of the year. It was called the busk, and it marked the beginning of the new year for all tribes. It was the greatest celebration and feasting that our tribes held. Once the busk was over, the husquenaugh began, so while I looked forward to more feasting, I dreaded its conclusion.

I was in the field one day, checking the status of the last of the *pagatowr*, when Ascopo came sneaking up behind me. "Do you think it is ready yet?" he asked.

I pulled back the shucks covering one ear, pressed the kernels with my finger, and saw that the kernels were dry and felt hard. The silks were brown and dry, the pollen tassels long since fallen off. We were not supposed to pull back the shucks to see the kernels inside, but we noticed that someone had partially shucked a few other cobs and then wrapped back up again. Someone else was checking too. "Must be close!" I answered.

We'd already picked the early-ripening *pagatowr* at the beginning of the really hot weather. We planted it in the very first field that we sowed. The small ears with their colorful kernels were best while still moist, sweet, and juicy. The late-harvest ripened at the height of the hottest summer period, and its larger ears produced pale kernels that dried and stored better. We planted this late *pagatowr* in separate fields, and its dry kernels kept us fed during the cold winter months. When it was finally dry, ripe, and ready for harvest, we celebrated and thanked the spirits, for as long as we have dry *pagatowr*, we can survive the rigors of the cold season.

Because Chowanook was the main village and Menatonon was chief over all, Chowanook hosted the busk for the whole tribe. Seventeen other villages joined us and swelled our ranks, and to organize such a large ceremony required some planning. Once Roncommock decided when to hold the busk, he sent runners with a bundle of ten sticks to each village. First the runner, and then the village's shaman who received the bundle, removed one stick with each sunrise so that all the villages arrived together on the tenth day and in time for the start of the ceremony.

Just this morning, Roncommock sent out the runners. He picked the fastest runners to go to the most distant villages, and when he selected Chaham for the longest run, Chaham could hardly speak for the pride of it. Ascopo's brother, Kaiauk, and Andacon also ran to distant villages, but Ascopo, Osocan, and I did not. I tried to console Ascopo, who was annoyed that his brother was selected and he was not. The two were so competitive that I knew there would be trouble between them.

"Look, Ascopo, you and I are still pretty small. Kaiauk and Andacon are as big as Chaham, and Kaiauk is older than you anyway. They're bigger and faster than we are. Maybe next year, after we've grown taller, we'll be just as fast as they are." Ascopo grumbled disconsolately, so I continued, "Remember that you and I were among the best guards of the cornfield. Kaiauk has still not lived down the mistake he made during his guard year. Give him some credit for being fast because you have him beat on attention." At this, Ascopo laughed with glee, reflecting on his brother's embarrassment.

Guarding *pagatowr* is paramount. When the tiny plants first emerge from the ground, crows often attempt to pull up the tiny plants and eat the sprouted seed, and once the corn ripens, many animals want to eat it. To keep it safe from these predators, a boy stationed in a little guard shack on the edge of the field keeps his eyes on the crops.

Nearly every harvest season, some animal manages to wreak damage before the guard spots it, but no one will forget the year that Kaiauk was guard. One night a whole family of raccoons—*saquenuckot*—invaded. With their black masks and striped tail, they could be considered attractive animals, but their nimble black feet shuck the corn as well as we can using our hands. They broke down stalks and stripped a whole section bare, leaving footprints that looked like tiny human handprints. The next morning, Roncommock discovered the devastation, and also found Kaiauk asleep in the guard hut. We lost a huge portion of the crop that year, but luckily our earlier harvests were sufficient to maintain us.

Kaiauk probably suffered the most. He was hardly able to contain himself, crying and guilt-ridden that he had allowed such destruction, and when Roncommock assigned his grandmother to join him in the guard hut, he wailed harder still. It was a long time before he lived down the embarrassment of spending the remainder of his guard duty under his grandmother's supervision. Ascopo brightened considerably as he recalled Kaiauk's misfortune.

Unlike his unfortunate brother, Ascopo achieved admiration during his guard duty by capturing an opossum. The strange animals use their naked tail like a hand, sometimes even wrapping the prehensile tail around a tree branch to dangle head-down like ripe fruit. The village awoke one morning to find that Ascopo had caught and penned an opossum behind stakes that he drove into the ground and covered with a heavy branch. The penned opossum was scary looking with its teeth bared, hissing like a snake. They have more teeth than any other animal, and their skulls are easy to identify in the midden. But the animal calmed down after a day or two, and fattened up nicely on some old *pagatowr* until we cooked and ate it. Ascopo was praised by many for his resourcefulness and quick thinking. Now that I considered it, their differing guard experiences may account for the rivalry between Ascopo and Kaiauk.

The most remarkable aspect of opossums is that they nurture their young in a pouch on the mother's belly. When I was the guard, I killed one in the crop field that had twelve petite pink babies inside the pouch. I felt terrible that I had deprived them of their mother, and tried to pull them out of the pouch and raise them myself, but they were stuck fast to the nip-

ples in the pouch and would not turn loose. When I finally dislodged one of them and took it to my mother, she said it would not survive because we could not feed it the mother's milk that it needed. The pitiful thing died the next day. I think that experience may be what discouraged me as a hunter, although I realized that hunting was essential for our survival. I felt such pity for those little creatures.

Those two, the raccoon and opossum, were the most frequent predators in the crop field, but deer sometimes came, especially to eat the leaves of the beans. If, when boys are guarding, they see a deer, they are supposed to get a man so that he can shoot it. In some years, we harvest several deer that visit the fields, but mostly they stay away from the crop fields because they are at the edge of our village and within the sight, sound, and smell of our people. I suppose that now that I have killed my first deer, I might be called upon as the man a guard boy alerts.

After we checked the *pagatowr*, Ascopo and I evaluated the *okindgier* seeds as well. The stalks of the *pagatowr* grew much taller than any man and the vines of the *okindgier* wrapped around the stalks all the way to the top. The flowers of the *okindgier* were usually red in color, and they produced beautiful seeds with swirls of dark purple on a lighter purple background. When the seeds were dry, the whole pod turned brown, so we didn't need to open the pods to check the ripeness of the seeds; instead we just compared the number of brown pods with those that were still green and fleshy. Since harvest of the corn would damage the bean plants entwining the stalks, Roncommock waited until most of the *okindgier* pods were brown and ripe to call the busk. I enjoyed shelling the *okindgier* because each glossy seed, like the colorful coquina shells from the banks, looked slightly different from all the others. The *wickonzówr*—or peas—were similar, but were greenish brown when dry, smaller than the big colorful seeds of *okindgier*, and did not vine up the stalks of the *pagatowr*.

As Ascopo and I stood in the field looking at the *pagatowr* and *okindgier*, I remembered another experience from my guard duty. One day, while I guarded the *pagatowr*, a tiny bird with a straight slender beak buzzed like a bumblebee as it visited the scarlet flowers of the *okindgier*, which were matched by the red throat of the bird. Amazingly, the bird moved forward, backward, up and down while its wings beat so fast that they were just a blur. It moved from flower to flower, hovering in front of each flower and then slipping its bill down inside. On that day, I ran home excitedly to my mother's wigwam even though we were not supposed to leave the field. It was just such an astonishing animal that I had to tell her about it. She called it a hummingbird and I watched for it on subsequent days. I saw the hummingbird regularly, but never heard another boy mention it.

Most other boys focused on the birds they could shoot. Any of the bigger birds that were predators on the ripening seeds were fair game for the small warriors. They shot the birds with blowguns or small bows and arrows, an activity that kept the whole group of boys happily patrolling the edges of the field as the crops ripened. Andacon and Osocan were among the crew who hunted along the edges even when they weren't on guard duty.

Ascopo interrupted my reminiscence. "Do you remember what happened to Keetrauk? His blunder was almost as bad as my brother's. *Almost!*" he chuckled. "Keetrauk allowed a whole flock of red-winged black birds—or *chúwquaréo*—to wreak havoc in the field he was supposed to be guarding. My brother's mistake was far worse because those *saquenuckot* nearly damaged the entire crop instead of just a portion." Apparently, Keetrauk had fallen asleep so soundly in the guard hut that he never awoke to the screeching birds flashing their bright red shoulders, but his brother Tetszo heard them from far away and ran to the field, chasing off the birds while Keetrauk stumbled sleepily from the guard hut. As with Kaiauk, Roncommock reacted by assigning their grandmother to supervise Keetrauk for ten humiliating days. Neither Kaiauk nor Keetrauk lived down the embarrassment. No wonder Keetrauk prefers to fish.

I felt compelled to point out, "Ascopo, it was Keetrauk's *brother* that helped him out and minimized the damage. Don't you feel the least bit sorry for Kaiauk?"

Ascopo shrugged and said, "Tetszo is Keetrauk's older brother. Older brothers are supposed to help out the younger, not vice versa. I'm not responsible for Kaiauk since I am younger than he is."

"Funny," I said, "I thought brothers helped each other, no matter their birth order."

I never had a problem with the flocks of *chúwquar éo* or of grackles, but a noisy group of parakeets surprised me once. They were not afraid of me, and simply flew up as I ran toward them, hovered for a few moments, then descended again as soon as I was past them. They were beautiful birds, bright green with yellow and red faces, but they were destructive in the fields, using their strong beaks and feet to rip open the husks and get to the *pagatowr*, and they were always in flocks of many birds. I swatted and yelled and jumped and screamed, and only after actually striking one did it give the alarm and the whole flock flew away while I stood sweating and panting from the effort. Since there was very little damage, I doubt anyone even knew of it.

A couple of days after the runners left, Roncommock announced the final harvest. We started along one edge of the field and stripped the ears from the stalks, taking care to minimize damage to the other crops in the field, especially the *okindgier* that were using the stalks as support for their vines. Some of their pods were still green, and we left these on the vines still climbing up the corn stalks. But the brown pods we harvested along with the *pagatowr*.

We also collected the different types of *macócqwer*, including big round pumpkins, soft yellow squash, and various types of gourds for water bottles, rattles, and other containers. We used the dry *macóc-*

qwer for making rattles or drinking vessels, but harvested some throughout the summer while it was small, tender, and good to eat. The different *macócqwer* performed different functions, but whether large or small, orange, yellow, or green, all turned brown when they were fully dry and the seeds rattled around inside them. The biggest *macócqwer* formed our water vessels and they had long necks that made it easy to carry them, and through which we filled them with water. The smallest, egg-shaped *macócqwer* made the best rattles, and if the seeds did not make enough noise, we added pebbles or shells through a hole before we attached the *macócqwer* to a stick for a handle.

Like the seeds of *okindgier*, the seeds of *pagatowr* were beautiful, too, and early *pagatowr* was even more colorful than the later variety. Some kernels were blue, some were red, some yellow, and some white. We harvested dry ears of both varieties, rubbed the small round kernels off the cob, and saved their seeds for planting. While we ate most of the early *pagatowr* fresh and only stored its seed for planting, we stored all of the late *pagatowr* as dry seed. We either boiled it whole or ground it dry into a powder. Some, of course, we saved for next year's planting. We burned the cobs in the sacred fire just as we burned the bones of the deer we killed for food.

With everyone pitching in for the harvest, we completed the task quickly. Mother prepared the seeds from late *pagatowr* in a way that made them more nutritious and added an interesting flavor to them. In order to remove the skins from the seeds, she soaked the dry seeds in water that contained ashes from the sacred fire. By vigorously stirring the mixture with a wooden paddle, the seed coats fell off as the seeds themselves swelled up, and then she dried the cleaned seeds again as hominy. She stored the hominy for wintertime.

Once all the runners returned, and with the final harvest gathered, the village was abuzz with anticipation. Other villagers had been arriving for the past two days, and now the final group, from the closest village no less, came straggling in. At last we could begin. At midday of the first day of the ceremony, we held a big feast, with food contributed from all the other villages.

In the center of the village, the central fire grew in size. Several pots with different versions of succotash boiled merrily. Strips of deer meat and whole fish broiled around the fire. Roots of several types roasted for most of the day, buried under coals along the edge of the fire. Some were too hot and spicy for my taste, but the older adults loved them. Although we ate the early *pagatowr*, we did not eat any from the final harvest, saving it for the end of the ceremony.

On this first day of the busk, there was no dancing associated with the great feast as there was for other ceremonies. We just ate and prepared ourselves for the next three days. People were solemn and respectful, considering the importance of the coming few days. Even Ascopo was subdued.

After the feast was over, the cleansing began. The

men tossed all the animal bones and the dregs of left-over food from the bottom of the pots into the sacred fire. Tetszso and Chaham located fish scraps from somewhere and tossed them on the fire. Women brought out any food that was stored from a previous year, and burned it in the fire as well, with my mother presiding over it. We set aside only the new crops, harvested during the current season, to save for the upcoming winter. Roncommock stirred the fire so that all the discarded food burned to ashes while the men observed him. All chanted rhythmically, thanking the spirits and telling them that we were purifying the village.

Meanwhile, the women cleaned everything. They swept all the houses, and even my sister worked hard to help any older women who struggled with the tasks. Every single wigwam was spotless. They threw any broken or damaged wooden utensils into the fire, and I saw Mamankanois tossing on a spoon that I was sure I saw her use yesterday. They burned baskets with holes or tears, and a whole pile of them came out of Poócqueo's wigwam where she must have been storing them. Some just looked a little weird, not really damaged, and I wondered if they were my sister's early attempts at basket weaving. I'd ask her when I got the chance. Under the direction of Roncommock, men cleaned and raked the area around the sacred fire. They burned damaged bows and I thought I recognized a few that Coosine had used with us boys. Men crushed damaged pottery to pieces and the women added the pieces to the fire.

Once the fire consumed all the damaged goods, Roncommock stirred it until the fire burned down to ashes. For the first time in a full year, the fire burned out. Nothing remained except for the broken pottery shards and a few grey ashes. It made me uncomfortable to see the fire pit cold and dark, without the orange flames or glowing coals we relied on to cook our food and keep us warm.

Before the participants left their villages, they too cleaned, burned, and purified their towns. They extinguished their sacred fires. Anyone coming upon their towns would think them deserted. The villages looked dead without their fires, but there was no one left to tend the fires anyway. They were here, with us, at the busk for our tribe.

Roncommock raked up the few ashes and the broken pottery and placed the materials in a basket. Tetszo hauled the basket to the river and tipped it in, pouring it all away. Then Roncommock dug a shallow hole, lined it with leaves of *uppówoc*—our sacred tobacco—and added one of the ears of the late *pagatowr*. He covered the hole with sand. Keetrauk and Chacháquises hauled more sand from the river bank, which they poured on the site of the sacred fire and the ground around the dancing pole, then Roncommock raked both areas clean, leaving a smooth, white surface.

Then all the men who had survived the *husquenaugh* gathered at the site of the sacred fire, but women and children returned to the wigwams. The men fasted for the rest of the day, the entire second day, and into the beginning of the third day, and they did not depart from the site of the extinguished fire, guarding it constantly while the fire was out. While they fasted, they drank the black drink and purged into clay pots that were set around the edges of the site expressly for that purpose. Eracano constantly walked around the site of the fire, mumbling as he conversed with the spirits and asked for their protection. His fasting caused him to lose weight, and we could practically watch him shrink in width and stature from the arduous duty.

While women and children ate food and underwent normal activities, all were expected to be quiet and respectful. There was no running and shouting, no vigorous games. It was difficult, with so many new people in the village, not to play games, but the children waited patiently just like the men. During the men's fast, no one hunted, and mothers put away their boys' small bows and arrows to keep temptation at bay. The four of us who were neither *husquenaughed* men nor small children skulked around together. There was not much for us to do, and it seemed strange to have a few days of forced inactivity, especially since we had trained so hard through the spring and summer.

At last, on the morning of the third day, everyone walked down to the river where we washed and purified ourselves. There was no horseplay this time. We scrubbed clean with sand, soaped up with yucca roots, and made sure we rinsed every inch of our bodies clean, in the same fashion that Roncommock used with me when I first entered training. We reapplied bear grease to our skin and refreshed the stiff grease in our hair. I grinned at the other boys with their fresh, spiky haircuts. We all looked like young warriors now. Soon, we hoped, we would be.

We returned to the village and gathered around the site of the sacred fire, waiting. When the sun was directly overhead, Roncommock started a new fire. He used a piece of dry sycamore wood as a flat base, in which he cut a notch. Using a slender stick from the dried, flowering stalk of a yucca as a spindle, he wrapped a dry deer sinew once around its middle and tied either end of the sinew onto a deer rib bone. The sycamore grew with its roots in the water of the river, and we used yucca in our cleansing ceremonies, making both of these types of wood clean and pure. The deer parts had come from the animal that we boys killed as part of our *husquenaugh* preparation. It was necessary to coax the purifying, sacred fire from wood that was itself pure by using a deer that had given itself to a noble cause.

Stepping down and placing his weight onto the flat piece of sycamore to hold it steady, Roncommock pressed the spindle firmly down into the notch of sycamore with a whelk shell. Then he sawed back and forth with the bow made of bone and deer sinew, which caused the wrapped yucca spindle to rotate in the sycamore block. He began to sweat as he sawed and chanted, sawed and chanted, not very quickly, but in constant, orderly motion. It seemed to take forever until a dark powder from the wood fell into the notch and smoke started to rise, but he did not stop his effort. He continued the sawing and chanting until the smoke grew thicker and a glowing ember became visible, then he finally stopped sawing and carefully poured out the ember into the nest of a bird he had been saving for that purpose. He blew gently, encouraging the newborn fire to take hold. Everyone was tense, wondering whether he would be successful. The fine, dry grasses and fibers in the nest accepted the flame, and he added small twigs and splinters of pine to make the flames grow. Once the tiny fire was clearly burning, the shamans of the other villages took over, adding wood to the fire and gradually increasing the size of the pieces until the fire again roared from its sacred, central location.

Once the new fire was burning strongly, Roncommock added a pinch of *uppówoc* powder and another ear of *pagatowr*. The flames leapt up hungrily and changed color, accepting these offerings. He thanked

the spirits and asked their blessing for the new year, then he turned to the crowd of villagers standing around the fire. He asked that all wrongs be forgiven and that any grudges against the living or the dead be lifted. He called out the names of all the members of the tribe who had died since the last busk and asked that they release their obligations and not walk as ghosts among us. He welcomed new members born, married, or adopted into our tribe since the last ceremony and asked the rest of us to welcome them into the tribe.

All the men then chanted the words of a sacred prayer together. In one voice, they asked for victory over enemies, success in hunting and fishing, and camaraderie for members of the tribe. The women took over as the men finished, and they asked for the safety of their houses and fields, ease in births, and abundant harvests of their crops. The children, which included me, because I had yet to undergo the *husquenaugh,* and my sister, who had yet to start her female courses, all said that we would obey our parents and bring honor to our tribe. Our part was a little less in unison, but we said the important words, the littlest ones just nodding their heads while we four, young, soon-to-be warriors led the group.

With the prayers finished and the fire burning once again, the women cleared us away and began preparing for the great feast, which we held on the fourth day. They brought out new pots and new spoons, which the shamans blessed. All the shamans took part in a dance around the sacred fire, then each of the shamans from the other villages took some of the sacred fire and started another fire, and women from that village built it up and began to cook around it.

By the morning of the fourth day, more food bubbled in pots than could be imagined. Each village had a slightly different version of succotash, with flavors ranging from ginger to mint to sassafras, and I tasted every single one of them. Whole haunches of deer and bear were roasting over the fires, sending up the most delicious aromas of smoky meat. I noticed that Andacon sliced off a piece while it was still cooking and took it away to eat. People from our western-most village even contributed flesh from a bison that one of their hunting parties had killed. It had more fat than a deer, but less than a bear, and it sizzled as the fat dripped out onto the embers. Many different types of fish cooked slowly on high-set grills, and a sturgeon wrapped in wet leaves and buried alongside the fire in the fresh sand baked gently. We ate like we never do at any other time. Everyone ate some of the late *pagatowr*, which was prepared by boiling it in a special, previously unused pot. We added nothing else to the pot so that the *pagatowr* was not contaminated.

We danced around the fires and we danced around the dancing circle. We danced and ate, and ate and danced. We held a great celebration that lasted the entirety of the day. As the sun left the sky, Roncommock announced that the ceremony was concluded and that the new year began with the rising of the sun, but the party wasn't over. In fact, it had just begun. All of the participants gathered around the fires that their shamans set and they kept the fires burning all night long. Children stayed up as late as they wanted, playing with the children from other villages. Adults visited each other late into the night, catching up with relatives and friends who lived in different villages of the tribe. Some people never went to sleep. When the villagers left the next day, shamans carried embers in special clay pots constructed especially for the purpose of carrying the new, shared, tribal fire back to their home villages. Once they started their own fires, they broke the pots and threw the shards into the fire they kindled.

In this way we began a new year. We honored our crops and we asked for help from the spirits. We threw out the old and started again with the new, and this included our food and our promises to other people. All began fresh and pure, uncontaminated by events from the past. It was a chance to start again, with a clean conscience. This year, however, the end of the busk held anxiety for me, because the *husquenaugh* followed hard on the heels of the new year. Was I ready to face this most difficult of trials?

Husquenaugh

AT LAST IT had come to this. I laid in a dark wig-wam, full of smoke. The herbs on the fire made my skin burn and my head ache. The smoke was thick and oily with resins that dulled my mind. I felt hunger, more hungry than I had ever felt before. I lost track of time in the dark hut. We just laid there, in a state close to death.

I remembered happier times. My earliest memory passed before me and I saw both my mother and my father. My mother held me, but turned me gently from her breast and set me down on a warm fur. She pointed to the door and I saw the dark mat drawn aside as someone stepped inside and a momentary beam of brilliant sunlight created an aura of radiant whiteness about him, then just as quickly disappeared as the mat dropped down to close the opening. My father had returned, victorious, from a hunt, for he had a daub of animal blood on his forehead. He smiled, leaned down, and reached for me and I saw my own fat little arms reaching back. I felt warm, happy, and content.

Next, I recalled a moment of fear. I was picking juicy, ripe blackberries with my mother and sister. We worked deep into a patch and I kept stepping forward, going farther and farther inward to reach another. When I tried to turn and get out, the prickles caught in my hair and skin and bound me to the tall canes. I started to struggle, but the thorns grabbed and stuck me. I called out in alarm and did not hear my mother answer. Twisting more and more, I became even more tightly tangled and gashes tore into my arms and legs from the relentless, unforgiving thorns. I twisted and turned, felt pain and fear as ever more thorns pierced and gripped my flesh. At last my mother arrived and began to untangle me from my blackberry bonds, breaking branches and pulling me free with her hands. I sobbed in terror, finding it hard to breathe until she swept me up into her arms. Free at last, held close in mother's arms, I felt her stiffen as she suddenly stopped and stepped backwards. Lying across the path in front of us coiled a large rattlesnake, menacing in its thick body with dark chevron stripes across its brownish back. It climbed out of the blackberry patch just a few feet from us. If the thorns hadn't stopped me, I would probably have blundered into it. The combination of the fear of entrapment and the following encounter with the snake etched deeply into my memory.

Then I recalled the feeling of belonging when I stood on the sand dune. I sensed the spirit world all around me—felt part of a great river of time. I knew the spirits communicated with me there, and I tried to focus on that thought, the likelihood of success, to get me through my current situation.

The *husquenaugh* is a difficult challenge with underlying purpose. It is a ritual meant to train our bodies and wills to withstand hardship, to persevere, and to succeed. The men on the fishing expedition paddled for days, eating little, drinking little, and paddling hard. Hunting expeditions and war parties were no easier. Warriors might jog for days with just a little water to sustain them, sleep one night in a field, and then wake up and fight to the death. We trained our bodies to willfully endure such hardships, which was part of the purpose of the *husquenaugh*.

The *husquenaugh* prepared our minds in other ways, too. Spirits watched us, tested us, determined whether each boy was worthy and which among us might become shamans, medicine men, or chiefs. Although my family line was one of chiefs, the *husquenaugh* tested whether I qualified for that role or failed miserably. By forcing my body to endure privation, I focused my mind on understanding my place in the world and my role as chief.

Instead of concentrating on my body, which hurt, I thought about what I had been taught. From the ant, I understood the importance of village cohesion, cooperation among families and allies, how division of labor and unemotional reliance on deeply tested instincts work together in the effective accomplishment of goals, and how different senses enrich understanding of the world. For fish, living in a world of eat or be eaten, large body size or forming large cooperative schools provided them with some degree of safety. Their ability to detect subtle water movements, another type of sense, enabled them to find food, avoid predators, and school with other fish. The regal nature of the falcon, its acute vision, and the feeling of flight, continued to amaze me, but so did the apparent contradictions inherent in the circle of life. We all take from each other in order to live, but to take too much is unwise, and to give way is sometimes the most prudent course.

I could hear nothing from the other boys. They either were asleep, or, like me, in the strange world of dream and thought that lay between the spirit world and ours. Ascopo, Andacon, Osocan, and I entered the *husquenaugh* together, and our first experience was that of the black drink. After we purged our inner bodies, we cleansed ourselves in the river. Then, before we fully recovered from the black drink, we received our instructions: run to the swamp at the head of a creek and retrieve one of the four strands of wampum left there by Eracano. I could barely make it. Andacon was well ahead of me, Ascopo was just behind, and Osocan was nowhere to be seen. When each of us returned, we handed our strand to Eracano, who counted the beads to ensure it was the same strand he'd left for us to retrieve. No one knew how many beads were on the strands because Eracano changed the number every year. I suspected that Andacon may have picked up two strands, one for himself and one for Osocan so that he would not have to run as far.

After the exhausting run, we leapt into the cool river again and the sudden chill caused my skin to break out in goosebumps and my hair to stand on end. As I gasped for air, I thought my heart had stopped from the shock. After clambering out of the river, we again entered the wigwam and endured the powerful herb smoke and excessive heat from the fire. I could hardly breathe through the thick smoke, yet I was still breathless from the run and compelled to suck in the air. Once we were hot and sweaty from the fire and gagging from the smoke, we jumped into the river yet again, and if I thought that the first two experiences were invigorating, they were nothing like the third one. I shivered uncontrollably from the cold and my forehead felt like it was splitting open from a headache.

Back we went into the wigwam and Eracano arrived to chant and invoke the spirits to accept us. He threw more herbs on the fire until the smoke was nearly too thick to tolerate. I was already lying down, but my head started to swim and my eyes watered so profusely that I could barely see. The coals from the fire glowed orange and the thick smoke rose up and enveloped Eracano as he chanted. He looked like a fiend in the underworld, in *popogusso*.

Clearly, I passed out, because the next thing I knew Eracano was beating the bottoms of my feet with a switch. The sharp pain made me jump up. Night had arrived and it was dark outside. Eracano demanded that we run to the farthest side of the old crop field and return with a shell that he had placed there. We all dashed out of the wigwam together, but could barely see where we were going. I stumbled and fell, cracking my knee against a root, but got back up and kept going. I was the last one to reach the crop field, but the other boys, who wandered about aimlessly, had not yet found the shells.

Streaks of weak silver moonlight shining through the trees illuminated the open field. I tried to think where Eracano might have placed the shells, but my mind was muddled. As I stood there, breathing deeply of the crisp night air, my mind began to clear and I remembered that during planting, some women used shells attached to sticks for hoes; the men used deer bones instead. After planting, we left the hoes and planting sticks in a pile under the big oak tree where we rested. I ran to the tree. Sure enough, four white shells lay in front, and I made some noise to catch the attention of the other boys. When they saw me sprint back toward the wigwam, they knew I had found the shells and they immediately ran to the tree and gathered shells themselves. I finished first and proudly gave the shell to Eracano before entering the wigwam and falling into a deep, dreamless sleep.

The next morning we did it all again, except there was nothing to purge from our empty guts, and there was a new set of wampum strands at the end of the run. This time I was sure that Andacon picked up an extra wampum strand because I was close on his heels, and though I was second among the four boys, there were only two remaining strands of wampum, one for me and one for Ascopo. When I returned to camp, Andacon and Osocan were already there, and then

Ascopo came in behind me. I was pretty sure that it really didn't matter who finished first, just that we finished, but I still wished to do better than third place.

That evening we received a meal of thin gruel to eat and we devoured it. Today's river dunk was easier to endure, perhaps because the cool water was less of a surprise or because our fatigue overwhelmed us. After the river plunge, we shot arrows until my shoulders shook with exhaustion from drawing the bow.

The midnight run again required us to think while our brains jangled from lack of sleep and smoke. Eracno told us to bring back a flame from the sacred fire and use it to light a torch of fibers that he'd stuck in the ground. All of us ran to the fire, but once we arrived, we found the fire banked down to nothing but coals around a huge hunk of smoldering wood. Andacon actually tried lifting the hunk of wood, but it was much too heavy. Then he had an idea, grabbed four of the kindling sticks piled nearby to start up a blaze in the morning, and held them against the glowing coals. He gave one to Ascopo and one to Osocan and motioned to me, but I shook my head in refusal. Something wasn't right. As soon as the kindling burst into flame, the boys made a beeline for Eracano's unignited torch.

I had a sneaking suspicion that it wouldn't be quite that easy. I dug through the pile of kindling and noticed that the sticks were damp; the flame would never hold until the boys reached the torch. I found a flat piece of bark in the pile, teased out a glowing coal with a stick, and pushed the coal up onto the bark. I put another piece of bark on top so that I could carry it pressed between my fingers, but air could still circulate in from around the sides. When I arrived at the wigwam, three dejected faces greeted me, along with three blackened sticks and a torch that was not aflame. I removed the top piece of bark and rolled the ember onto the torch, blew gently, and it lit. I went into the wigwam, but the other boys had to run back to the fire and bring back an ember before Eracano permitted them to enter the wigwam.

The next day on our morning run, I was astonished to see that Cossine was waiting at the swamp and he gave us each a wampum strand and directed us to a different site that extended our run considerably. Apparently, I was not the only one who knew about Andacon's and Osocan's trickery from the day before. This run on the third morning was at least twice the length of the first two and it was exhausting. I could barely finish, collapsing as I entered the clearing where the *husquenaugh* wigwam stood.

Each day was like the next, black drink followed by a thorough wash in the river, death run, river dunk, smoky wigwam, river dunk, shooting trial, then some unexpected event in the middle of the night. I began to look forward to the thin, tasteless gruel because afterwards I could drop off into the oblivion of sleep. Finally, after days and days of absolute effort from my body, on one morning run I lost track of the other boys. I don't know what happened to them, but they were no longer near me, and I could simply go no farther. I stopped and sat down, nearly crying from exhaustion. I felt I was a failure, unable to keep up with the other boys in the physical tests. I thought that I would never become chief, probably not even complete the *husquenaugh*.

I lay back on the ground and closed my eyes, and I felt a sense of well-being. It was just like the time that Roncommock first introduced me to the spirit world. My mind and my body were empty, and I felt the spirits' pity.

My bear spirit entered my mind and I recognized him at once. He told me to get up and go on. "Just walk back to the wigwam," he said, "but get there. Your trials are nearly over. I will come to you again when you need me. Call me the way that Roncommock showed you."

Following the bear-spirit's advice, I somehow clawed my way back to the wigwam. The other boys were already there. I lay exhausted, starving, and nearly mad from the overpowering herbs. But I could wait. The bear spirit had promised that the trials were nearly over. So here I lay, longing for death or enlightenment, whichever arrived first.

The door-flap of the wigwam opened, emitting a stark, white light that hurt my eyes. I lifted my head up slightly and saw Eracano enter. He moved among us, leaning down over each of us and lifting our heads in his hands. I dropped my head back down, too drained and exhausted to hold it up on my own. When he came to me, he touched my cheek and called my name. I looked up at him and he nodded. He moved back to Osocan and lifted his arm, holding his wrist. He put his ear on Osocan's chest and listened, then he stepped outside, the brilliant white light blinded me again, and he returned with someone else. They lifted up Osocan and took him away. I was too tired to wonder whether he was dead.

When we next awakened, instead of a black drink, Eracano gave the three of us who remained a thin gruel. He allowed us to rest instead of making us run, and he changed the herbs on the fire to something much more pleasant. I definitely detected the sweet, spicy fragrance of sassafras—*winauk*—in the fire. Andacon asked about his brother, but Eracano did not answer. Instead, he said it was time to contact our animal spirits. Although we had completed the difficult tasks of the *husquenaugh,* an animal spirit had to accept each of us as a worthy tribal member before we could be called men.

Eracano added the sacred mixture of *uppówoc* and herbs to the fire and told us to concentrate and to call our animal spirits, to ask them to find us and claim us. I relaxed my body, just as I had done with Roncommock, and once I felt calm and relaxed, I opened my mind and called to the bear spirit. He answered me at once and I sensed that Eracano was nearby.

"This boy has completed the tasks of the *husquenaugh.* He has withstood the deprivation and difficult tasks. Do you accept this boy as a man?" I heard Eracano ask.

The bear replied, "I accept Skyco. I sensed him when he was just a boy. I will guard and protect him, and I will send him visions from the spirit world. His future is bright because he is honest and thoughtful.

His listens to those who would teach him. He learns and grows in wisdom. He will become a shaman as well as a chief."

A shaman as well as a chief! I was proud of myself, but humbled, too. I felt honored. The responsibility I was given was entrusted to me by my tribe and by the spirits who guarded us. I bowed until my head touched the ground and I thanked the spirits with all my heart. When I raised my head, Eracano was looking at me.

"We must wait on the others," he said. Ascopo appeared to be in a trance, eyes closed and posture stiff, but Andacon was fidgeting. Something wasn't right with him. Ascopo exhaled, opened his eyes, and Eracano nodded at him.

"The spirits said they would accept me. Like the other carvers, the woodpecker spirit accepted me. I will carve, but my guardian spirit told me that I will still have time to hunt and to fish. I am thankful." Ascopo actually smiled, the first I had seen in days.

Then Eracano said to Andacon, whose eyes were still screwed closed and who was clearly uncomfortable, "Andacon, you have not been accepted by the spirits. Do you know why?"

Andacon opened his eyes. "Where is my brother? Where did you take him? Is he dead?"

"Osocan offended the spirits because he did not complete one of the runs. He cheated by receiving the wampum beads from you before he reached the swamp. He did not run the entire distance." The boy's eyes opened wide in terror and he said, "But I didn't mean to get him into trouble! I was just trying to help him. We always help each other. I stole them and threw them at his feet. He just picked them up."

"Andacon, you tempted Osocan, but he should have resisted the temptation."

"But is he alive? I can't tell! I always feel his presence, but now it is not there," Andacon said in a strangled cry.

The room was deathly silent for a few very long moments, and then Eracano sighed and said, "He is not dead. We removed him before contacting the spirits and did not allow him to attempt it. You failed to contact the spirits. Both of you must undergo the *husquenaugh* again next year. In the meantime, the tribe will shun you both for the entire year. It will be as if you are dead to us. No one will speak to you. No one will acknowledge your presence. You will leave our territory. Perhaps you have now learned the value of honesty."

Andacon hung his head and looked as if he might cry. I felt sorry for him, and for Osocan, too, having to undergo the *husquenaugh* for a second time. They could have stopped after the second day since that was when each faltered. Now both he and his brother would be shamed for the whole year. I wished there was something I could do. Maybe there was.

"Andacon and Osocan have a strong bond because they are twins," I heard the bear spirit say, in my mind. "Take the boys together to the spirits. Neither boy alone even made the attempt today—their *husquenaugh* is not complete. They may attempt to contact the spirits once more, after waiting for another sunrise. Perhaps each has gained some respect for the spirits, for the ritual, and most of all, for himself."

Eracano looked sharply at me, and I realized that I had been speaking as the bear spoke to me. The other boys looked at me with their mouths agape.

"Is everything okay?" I asked.

"Oh, yes," said Eracano, but he seemed stunned by my pronouncement. He left the wigwam and soon returned with Osocan stumbling behind him. "You two will stay here," and pointed to Andacon and Osocan. "You two may sit outside," and he pointed to Ascopo and me. "The *husquenaugh* will last one more day, which, I presume, means that no one is released until tomorrow. Is that right?" Eracano directed the last question at me, somewhat hesitantly.

"What do you mean, Eracano? You are in charge. I just reported what my bear guardian spirit said."

"No. You spoke *as* the bear. Your spirit guides you now, speaks through you, and commands the fate of others. You are a shaman now, Skyco. You have the spirits' favor and can interpret their will. You are now my equal." He bowed toward me and I was stunned. The other boys looked up, their faces betraying similar emotion.

"You got a bear?" Ascopo whispered in awe. "That is a powerful totem. Maybe you really will be chief, and a shaman too?" he continued, with a look of respect on his face.

"Outside with you two, now," Eracano said to us with a look of mild reproach, but when he turned back toward the brothers, his face became stony. "These two boys have some more thinking to do."

Ascopo and I walked outside and lay down in the sun. It felt good to lay there, resting, as we talked about our experiences.

Ascopo said, "I've never felt the spirits before, Skyco. Is this what you have meant all along? This deep feeling of understanding and direction and belonging? Now, like you, I have the guidance of the woodpecker to help me and to lead the way. She will show me how to ask the trees for their favor. Now I understand why you kept talking about the importance of the spirits. I just didn't understand until I contacted them myself. But you, a shaman. How is that even possible?"

Ascopo and I spent the whole afternoon resting and talking in the fresh open air next to the wigwam, and thankfully not inside its smoky interior. When the sun reached its zenith, Andacon and Osocan emerged from the wigwam to begin the regular run to the swamp and back again, but both Ascopo and I noticed that they repeated the run a second and then a third time. They ran until it was dark. Sweat poured off their backs and chests, their hair plastered down, dripping sweat into their eyes, and their bodies sagged from exhaustion.

That night, Ascopo and I slept outdoors under some skins that Eracano brought for us. I awakened once when the brothers passed us in the night, running again, off on another mission. They redoubled their efforts for the last day of the *husquenaugh*. I couldn't believe they had anything in reserve, but they were clearly demonstrating their resolve.

We reentered the wigwam at dawn, when the

brothers were to make their attempt to contact the spirits. All five of us sat around the sacred fire, Eracano between the two brothers. The brothers looked exhausted: faces pale, hair disheveled, eyes with black bags underneath them. They had hardly stopped running since the previous morning. Eracano began the chants again, adding *uppówoc* to the fire and asking the spirits to accept the brothers. I closed my eyes and immediately felt the bear spirit again. I was able to see through his eyes as the wolf spirit stepped up to claim the two boys. The boys were there, too, watching anxiously in anticipation.

"These boys erred in their ways, but because they demonstrated their remorse by voluntarily running both day and night, it is clear to us that they understood the enormity of their error. Because they chose to run even though they were exhausted, because they truly repented, and because the bear spirit asked us to consider them, I accept Andacon and Osocan and will be their guardian." The wolf spirit nodded his head to me—the bear spirit—clearly asking my permission.

Once again, I returned to myself, sitting before the fire. Andacon bowed to me and poked his brother in the ribs so that he bowed too. "Thank you, Skyco, for interceding on our behalf. I know that you asked the spirits to give us an opportunity to prove ourselves. They told us so."

"I am glad they accepted you. I asked the spirits to consider that your case was complicated by the close tie between twins."

"We will never forget what you did for us. We are

your men now, Skyco."

"Nevertheless," Eracano interrupted, "it is time to conclude the *husquenaugh*." He added herbs to the fire and began a long chant. At his instruction, we each added a pinch of *uppówoc* powder to the fire and we danced three times around it. We all thanked the spirits for their guidance, and I felt the answering reply from my bear. I thanked him again for guiding me and he replied, "Remember the dream I gave you, Skyco. I shall give you what you need if you will follow me."

Eracano presented each of us with a medicine pouch, which was a small bag made from soft deerskin. We tied it around our waists with a strip of leather. He added a pinch of *uppówoc* powder to each pouch and we closed them again.

"During your lifetime as tribal members, you will find important objects that will identify you to the spirits. You will know what to add to your medicine pouch. Each man is different and adds different items. Tonight, after the feast, go to your mothers to receive the object that identifies your clan. It should be the first item in your bag."

All of us exited the *husquenaugh* and stood nearby while Eracano burned down the small wigwam that sheltered us for so many days, purifying the space and putting an end to the ritual. That night, for the first time since the last new moon, we celebrated our success with the rest of our village and feasted. Our childhoods were behind us.

We had been reborn as men.

Author's Note

Skyco was an actual Algonquin boy who played a role in the earliest English explorations of America. He lived in the town of Chowanook on the Chowan River in present day North Carolina. During his boyhood, English explorers first arrived in America, combing the coastline for a defensible location with a port to harbor ships, which would provide an English foothold in the new world. The initial scouting expedition in 1584 was followed one year later by the first English colonists. They built a fort on Roanoke Island, strategically located between the Outer Banks and the mainland, as well as between the Pamlico and Albemarle Sounds.

The party of men sent by Sir Walter Raleigh included the scientist Thomas Harriot, the artist and mapmaker John White, and the military commander Ralph Lane as Governor. Together, they explored the region for one year, from the summer of 1585 until the summer of 1586. During this time, they encountered many Native Americans, including the Roanoac tribe on Roanoke Island and the Chowanoacs, a powerful Algonquin tribe ruled by Chief Menatonon and centered on the Chowan River in western Albemarle Sound. Lane said that Menatonon ruled 18 towns with 700 fighting men, but most historians think that the tribe was about 2000 total people.

Menatonon told the English about the Chesapeake Bay to the north, and about a land to the interior, called

Chaunis Temoatan, which produced copper, or as the English hoped, gold. Once settled, Lane kidnapped Menatonon's son or heir, Skyco, and held him for several months to force Menatonon's support of the English by providing them with food, guides, and protection from warring tribes. During the period of his captivity, the Englishmen befriended Skyco, and Skyco, in turn, aided the English by telling Lane of a plot among the Roanoacs to kill Lane and his party. As a result, Lane struck first, killing the chief of the Roanoac tribe and thus, not only heightening the animosity between the English and the Roanoacs, but increasing the tension among all the Algonquin tribes in the region.

Faced with rising native hostility, dwindling food supplies, and the delay of resupply ships, Lane's group of colonists welcomed the appearance of Francis Drake's flotilla of English ships, full of booty acquired from his lucrative raids against the Spanish in the Caribbean and Florida. Although Drake delivered hardware and trade items, he did not carry enough surplus food to sustain the fledgling colony, and rather than face the uncertainty of resupply by Raleigh's ships, the colonists abandoned America and returned home to England aboard Drake's ships. Skyco's fate was not recorded, although it was noted that three Englishmen were left behind in America. It is probable that Skyco was freed to return to his own people when the colonists left.

A larger group of English colonists arrived one year later, in 1587, and this time included women and children. They planned to settle on the shores of Chesapeake Bay, but disembarked on Roanoke Island instead. There, the first English-American child, named Virginia Dare, was born, but her grandfather, John White, the artist who by then was Governor, was compelled to return to England to secure additional supplies. Unfortunately for the Roanoke colonists, his return was delayed for three years because England

and English ships were fully engaged in a war with Spain. Ironically, it was the privateering raids of Drake against the Spanish that aggravated the English-Spanish conflict and led to the battle of the Spanish Armada. When White finally returned to Roanoke in 1590, the colonists had disappeared, but left the word "Croatoan" carved on a tree near the abandoned fort. The fate of those First Colonists remains a mystery.

Some historians think that the colonists went to the island of Croatoan on the Outer Banks, which has since been separated into Ocracoke and Hatteras Islands by the breach of Hatteras Inlet. Other historians argue that the colonists abandoned Roanoke for the Chesapeake, their original intended destination, and left only a small contingent of men to await John White's return. Sometime during White's long, three-year absence, these men went to Croatoan, and it was they who left the carved message. According to this view, the bulk of the "lost colonists" migrated to the Chesapeake while a remnant later moved to Croatoan. Twenty years later, in 1607, the first Jamestown settlers heard reports from Powhatan, the chief of the Chesapeake tribal confederacy, that he had killed the first English colonists who had settled on the Chesapeake and intermarried with members of a local tribe.

Manteo, from the Croatoan tribe, and Wanchese, from the Roanoke tribe, were taken to England from North Carolina by the first English explorers in 1584. They returned the next year, with the 1585 English expedition. Manteo continued to work with the English as interpreter and guardian, and may have suggested Croatoan as a place of refuge. Wanchese, however, returned to his tribe, turned against the English, and was implicated in an attack on the 1587 colonists.

With Manteo's assistance, the polymath Thomas Harriot learned and preserved the Carolina Algonquin language, but only a brief report, which he wrote for Raleigh back in England, exists today. Harriot also labeled some of John White's beautiful and accurate watercolors depicting the Algonquin villages, people, animals, and plants. Many of the drawings of animals are identified in Algonquian (the language of the Algonquin), which can be correlated with the English (and Latin) names used today. Ralph Lane recorded some Algonquin words, most of which were the names of important people and villages, in his report to Raleigh.

Many of the documents from these first settlements have been preserved, though Harriot's extensive notes on language were not. Countless historians, David Quinn foremost among them, have pored over early records, annotated them, and mapped the area of English exploration during the Roanoke voyages. Another source of information comes from John Lawson, who traveled through what is now North and South Carolina in 1701, and published detailed information on the animals, plants, and native people he encountered.

While this story is one of fiction, I have adhered to the factual information that is available about the Carolinian Algonquins. The names of the characters are all Algonquin words, listed in the vocabulary included as an appendix. The Algonquin culture and customs presented came either directly from historical records, or suggested by what is known of other natives of the Southeast. In this story, Skyco is Menatonon's heir, which is not the same as his son in the matrilineal society of Native Americans. Because children remain part of their mother's clan or family line, the children of a man's sister are more closely related to him than the children of his wife. Thus, a man's nephew is in his same family clan and would be his heir whereas his biological son is part of a different clan, that of his mother. It is unlikely that Lane understood this distinction, leaving Skyco's designation as son or heir questionable.

In addition to presenting to historical and cultural information factually, biological detail is also accurate. Medicinal uses of plants as well as the behavior and distribution of animals are realistic. In some places, I specifically chose to highlight animals and plants that are rare today but were common historically and important to native peoples.

Most of the early Carolina Algonquin died from disease and other effects of English arrival, and those who survived largely assimilated into the growing European population. The Chowanoke Indian Nation, however, persists today near its historical location and is currently striving for legal federal recognition. The Algonquin people stretch all the way into Canada, and although they belong to the same ethnic and language group, linguists suggest Canadian Algonquin dialects are probably rather different from those of early Carolina Algonquin.

Today, Algonquian history is being preserved by those who are genealogically descended from the original historic Roanoke-Hatteras Indians of Dare County, and Mattamuskeet Indians of Hyde County, North Carolina. They aim to keep the heritage and culture of their ancestors alive for the benefit of their tribe members and the rest of their community. You can learn more about their mission at http://www.ncalgonquians.com.

The Chowanoke Indian Nation of Gates County, North Carolina, is currently seeking formal recognition from the federal government. You can learn more about their mission and history at http://meherrin-chowanoke.com.

VOCABULARY

THESE CAROLINA ALGONQUIAN words were recorded by the first English visitors to America in 1585-1587. Their spellings are variable because each person who heard them may have spelled them slightly differently and even our English letters and spellings have changed somewhat in the intervening 425 or so years. (For example, White writes f for s; Raleigh is sometimes spelled Ralegh and Harriot is sometimes spelled Hariot). However, I used the words as Harriot and White spelled and recorded them on their documents; these are collected into *The Vocabulary of Roanoke*. I used Geary's "The Language of the Carolina Algonkian Tribes" from Quinn's *The Roanoke Voyages* to provide the meanings of words. His text describes sometimes extensive possible interpretations, and I picked what seemed to be the most logical one. I also used some of his words. Geary suggests that Harriot's accent marks indicate stress or higher pitch on that syllable.

Governor Lane in 1586 recorded various human names, some of which I used, but I also selected from general vocabulary to create other names of characters. In 1701, John Lawson recorded a list of words in Pampticough, Woccon, and Tuscarora languages, but not in Chowan Algonquian, and the only word I have used from his book is the name Roncommock, a Chowan conjurer. Instead of "conjurer" or "priest," the terms used by Lawson and Harriot, I use the terms "shaman" and "medicine man" because they are more associated with Native Americans of today.

While the recorded dialect was that of the Roanoac, and my characters are primarily Chowanoac, these tribes undoubtedly shared overlap in language. Manteo, who was of the Croatoan tribe, could converse with members of the Roanoac, Weapemeoc, and Chowanoac tribes and probably other Algonquin tribes as well. The Mangoaks, later known as the Tuscarora, spoke another language that was very different from the Algonquins, for they were derived from Iroquois rather than Algonquin.

JW indicates John White's labeled drawings; TH indicates Thomas Harriot's *Brief and True Report*; GQ indicates Geary from Quinn. Quotation marks are placed around possible meanings of the words as suggested by Geary.

Amakwa = general name of fish, GQ

Andacon = actual name of Roanoke warrior with Pemisapan, Lane; used as one of the twin boy's name

Anshaham = Crayfish or Lobster "he swims backward," GQ

Arasémec = Needlefish or Houndfish, 5-6 feet in length, JW

Artamóckes = Blue Jay, "bird that flies and eats certain things," JW

Asanamáwqueo = Common Loon, "has on a head-dress," JW

Ascopo = Sweet Bay Tree, "sharp taste," TH, used as the name of Skyco's friend

Black Drink = A tea brewed from yaupon holly leaves shown to have high levels of caffeine

Chacháquises = Downy Woodpecker, "small bird that cries out," JW; used as name of assistant woodcarver

Chaham = Shad or Alewife, 2 feet in length, "great swimmer," JW; used as name of young fisherman

Cháppacor = plant root, perhaps New Jersey Tea or Dogwood, TH; used as woman's name

Chawanoac/Chowanoac = tribe on the Chowan River with Menatonon chief, Quinn

Chesepian = tribe on Chesapeake Bay, Quinn

Chigwusso = Red Drum, Channel Bass, Spot-tailed Bass, 5-6 feet in length, JW

Chúwhweeo = Towhee JW

Chúwquaro = Red winged blackbird, "little flame," JW

Coppáuseo = Sturgeon, 10-13 feet in length, "he swallows shellfish or close-mouthed," JW

Coscúshaw = plant root, likely Arrow-alum or Golden-club, "enclosing ear," TH

Cossine = actual name of one of Manteo's friends, Lane, used as the name of teacher of bow

Crenepos = Women, "she hinders death," Lane

Ensenor = actual name of elder in Roanoke tribe who supported English, Lane

Eracano = actual name of one of Manteo's friends, Lane, used as the name of medicine man

Granganimo = actual name of chief's brother in Roanoke tribe, Lane

Habascon = plant root that is hot in taste, TH

Hockepúweo = Lamprey, 1 foot in length, "hides with effort," JW

Jackáwanjes = Bluebird, "bird that eats from time to time," JW, used as name of Roncommock's wife

Jawéepuwes = Surf Scoter, JW

Kaiauk = Gull, JW, used as name of Ascopo's older brother

Kaishúcpenauk = plant root, TH

Keetrauk = Catfish, 2 ½ feet in length, "they dart around," JW, used as name of young fisherman, Tetszo's brother

Kewás = Image of a god, TH

Kowabetteo = Gar, 5-6 feet in length, "he has rough teeth," JW

Machicómuck = Temple where kewás is kept, TH

Macócqwer = Squash and gourds, "container," TH

Mamankanois = Tiger Swallowtail Butterfly, "flying creature with big holes in wings," JW, used as Skyco's sister's name

Manchauemec = Croaker, 1 foot in length, "wonderful fish," JW, used a name of fisherman

Mangoak = tribal name, later Tuscarora, Iroquois federation, "rattlesnakes" GQ

Mangúmmenauk = Oak Acorn, "big nuts," TH

Manteo = actual name of Croatoan prince and English supporter, traveled to England, Lane

Mantóac = Gods, TH

Maquówoc = perhaps Muskrat or Beaver (small mammal), "carves or burrows in ground," TH

Marangahockes = Bowfin, 3-4 feet in length, "fish that burrows in mud," JW

Maraseequo = Red headed Woodpecker, "gets his food by pecking," JW

Masunnehockeo = Sheepshead, 2 feet in length, "he is painted on his body," JW

Meemz = probably a Blue-grey Gnatcatcher, JW, used as a name of a warrior

Meesquouns = Cardinal, "he calls loudly from a distance," JW

Memeo = Pileated Woodpecker, JW, used as name of master canoe carver

Meméskson = Skink, 1 foot in length, "he conceals himself well," JW

Menatoan = actual name, Lane

Menatonon = actual Chief of Chowanoac tribe, Lane

Mesíckek = Striped Bass, 5-6 feet in length, "big fish," JW

Metaquesúnnauk = Prickly Pear Cactus, TH

Minsal = Small Beads of Bone, TH

Moratuc = tribe at mouth of Roanoke River, Quinn

Nahyápuw = Bald Eagle, "he frequents the river," JW

Okeepenauk = edible plant roots found in dry ground, TH

Okindgíer = Beans, TH

Okisco = actual name of Weapemeoc chief, Lane

Openauk = edible plant roots found in moist ground, TH

Opossum = derived from the tribe of Opossians

Osámener = Acorn, TH

Osocan = actual name of Roanoke warrior with Pemisapan, Lane; used a twin boy's name

Pagatowr = Corn, "put in a kettle to boil," TH

Pashockshin = Flounder, JW

Peeáwkoo = probably female or juvenile Common Loon, "he is covered in down," JW

Pemisapan = actual name of Roanoke chief Wingina after his brother is killed, Lane

Piemacum = actual name, Lane

Pocosin = swamp on a hill

Poócqueo = Brown Thrasher, "he makes a hole by pecking," JW

Pooneno = actual name, Lane; used as name of warrior with red hawk

Popogusso = Hell, TH

Pummuckóner = perhaps Hickory nuts, TH

Quurúcquaneo = Flicker, JW

Qvúnziuck = Merganser, JW

Rakíock = perhaps Tulip Tree, "soft wood," TH

Renapoaks = Generic name for all Indians, Lane

Ribuckon = White Perch, 1 foot in length, JW; used as name of chief of Ricahokene

Roanoac = tribe on Roanoke Island and mainland, Quinn

Roncommock = Chowan conjurer, Lawson

Sacquenúmmener = Berries on a plant in shallow water, TH; used as name of Skyco's grandmother

Sagatémener = Acorns, perhaps Chestnuts, TH

Sapúmmener = Nut like Chestnuts, perhaps Chinquapin nuts, TH

Saquenuckot = perhaps Raccoon (small mammal), TH "black footed or foot like a bear"

Seékanauk = Horseshoe Crab TH

Skyco/Skiko = actual name of Chowan boy, son of Menatonon, Lane

Tanaquiny = actual name of Roanoke warrior with Pemisapan, Lane

Tangomóckonomindge = tree whose bark is used for red dye TH

Taráwkow = Sandhill Crane JW

Tesicqueo = a colorful snake, perhaps Milksnake, JW

Tetszo = Mullet, 2 feet in length JW; used as name of fisherman, Keetrauk's brother

Tetepano = actual name of warrior with Manteo, Lane; used as name of atlatl warrior

Towaye = actual name of warrior with Manteo who traveled to England, Lane

Tsinaw = Smilax root, "china root," TH

Tummaihumenes = Grackle, "bird that gets a big meal of seeds," JW

Uppówoc = Tobacco, TH

Wanchese = actual name of Roanoke warrior, traveled to England, abandoned English, Lane

Wapeih = Medicinal Clay, "white earth," TH

Wasewówr = perhaps Pokeweed, used for red dye, TH

Wassador = Copper, Lane

Weapemeoc = tribe on north side of Albemarle Sound, Quinn

Weeheépens = Barn Swallow, JW

Weewraamánqueo = Bufflehead Duck, JW

Werowans = chiefs or head men of village, Lane

Wickonzówr = Peas, TH

Wingina = actual name of Roanoke chief, Lane

Winauk = Sassafras, TH

Wisakon = Milkweed, "it is bitter," JW

Woanagusso = Swan, JW

Wundúnaham = Shad or Alewife, "he swims fast," JW

Wysauke = Milkweed, antidote to poison arrows, JW

"Indians Fishing" by John White (created 1585-1586)

This watercolor shows various fishing techniques, including a fish weir with a pen.

"Indian Village of Secoton" by John White (created 1585-1586).

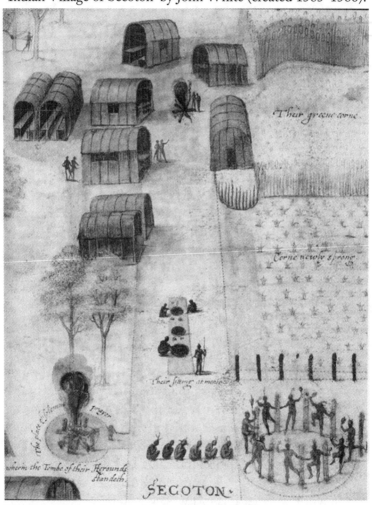

This watercolor shows the sacred fire, dancing circle, wigwams, and crop fields of the village of Secoton.

REAL PLACES TO VISIT

IT IS HARD to get a sense of what North Carolina looked like before Europeans arrived, but natural areas preserved by our state and national parks provide perhaps the closest approximations.

1. Merchants Millpond State Park, on Bennett's Creek that flows into the Chowan River, is in the region occupied by the Chowanoacs, Skyco's tribe. John White's maps locate Chowanook (Chawanoac) on the west of the Chowan River near a creek mouth. Quinn's overlay onto current maps places Chowanook near the mouth of Wiccacon Creek; Bennett's Creek flows in on the east side very near that point.

2. The area around the bay of Edenton is marked in White's map as the region occupied by the Weapemeoc, with four villages indicated on both the east and western sides of the bay. Quinn singles out one town, Warowtani, as located on the west side of Edenton's bay, with the other Weapemeoc towns at other locations. White's map also indicates an English fort on the land between the Chowan and Roanoke rivers, but it is unclear whether this fort was ever built.

3. Cypress dugout canoes were discovered in Phelps Lake in Pettigrew State Park. While there does not appear to be a town site there, or at least White didn't record

one, there were certainly natives who left behind their canoes. Perhaps the canoe Skyco worked on was one of them.

4. Roanoke Island, with its two primary towns of Manteo and Wanchese, has several locations worth visiting. The Fort Raleigh National Historic Site, part of the National Park Service, has a museum with recovered artifacts and a reconstructed earthen fort base. The Lost Colony Play is located nearby. The Roanoke Island Festival Park houses the Elizabeth II vessel, a wooden ship that represents the type of ship the colonists arrived in. There are also reconstructions of both Native American and colonial village life that provide good approximations of how both groups of people lived in America as well as museums and other attractions.

5. Jockey's Ridge State Park is fabulous for its sand dunes and provides an idea of how Skyco may have viewed the area. During Skyco's time, some of the sand dunes were so big that they were called Kendricks Mount. These dunes have eroded down and are now offshore shoals called Wimble Shoals.

6. Town Creek Indian Mound, a North Carolina historic site, is a little farther afield, located near Mount Gilead in the piedmont of North Carolina. Archaeologists have spent many years working to uncover artifacts and information regarding these natives of the piedmont region, belonging to the Pee Dee culture. They were mound-builders who constructed a temple on top of a built mound along the banks of the Little River. They lived inside a palisade and their houses were built of wattle and daub. Parts of their village have been reconstructed. These Native Americans were probably incorporated into the Catawba and were not closely related

to the coastal Algonquins.

7. The Cherokee in western North Carolina are not closely related to the Algonquins, but they are the only (currently) federally recognized tribe, and their towns and land in western North Carolina can be visited today. The Cherokee belong to the Iroquois language family. The Tuscarora, who lived in close proximity to the coastal Algonquins, are close relatives of the Cherokee and are likely the same as the Mangoaks described in this book and others. When the Tuscarora lost the Tuscarora War of 1711, they migrated far to the north, where they joined the Iroquois Confederacy and became the sixth nation.

About the Author

Dr. Jennifer Frick-Ruppert is the Dalton Professor of Biology and Environmental Science at Brevard College in western North Carolina, where she has taught since 1997. She earned her Ph.D. in Zoology from Clemson University. She teaches courses in environmental perspectives, biodiversity, biology, and natural history and was awarded the 2003-2004 Award for Exemplary Teaching at Brevard College. She is a frequent presenter for naturalist groups, including the Roan Mountain Naturalist Rally, NC Native Plant Society, and The Wilderness Society.

Originally from South Carolina, she grew up with a love of nature and the outdoors that was fostered by her close-knit family. She listened to story after story around campfires, barbeque pits, and fishing ponds and is now telling her own stories to other listeners. Her writings all have a strong sense of the natural world, and she explores how people interact with nature. Since she is a professional biologist as well as an award-winning teacher, her writings can be trusted for their accuracy in addition to their engaging portrayals.

She authored websites for South Carolina Educational Television and wrote a regular column for The Transylvania Times, Brevard's local newspaper. She has written several scientific articles, the most recent co-authored with her undergraduate students; one of these compared the caloric values of native fruits, another examined diet of coyotes in the Southern Appalachians, and a third focused on the biology of the Blue Ghost Firefly.

In 2010, she published *Mountain Nature: A Seasonal Natural History of the Southern Appalachians.* Illustrated with both color and black-and-white images, it conveys the seasonal change in animals and plants of the region, emphasizing their interactions and unique characteristics. It received several notable reviews for its quality and lively writing style and was a finalist in the Philip Reed Memorial Award for Outstanding Writing about the Southern Environment.

In 2015, she published *Waterways: Sailing the Southeastern Coast.* Like Mountain Nature, it centers on natural history, but it is a story of a single cruise that she made with her husband aboard their sailboat Velella when they sailed from Charleston, SC to Lake Worth, FL across to the Bahamas and back to Beaufort, SC. It relates their joy in seeing the natural world while learning to sail, it reflects on environmental changes and concerns, and it discusses the value of understanding the interrelationships of humans and nature.

ABOUT THE ILLUSTRATOR

Lorna Murphy is an author/illustrator of children's books based in Suffolk, UK. She grew up on the coast but has been landlocked for 20 years. She still misses the sea.

After 16 years working in the public sector, she decided enough was enough and signed up to study illustration, at the Cambridge School of Art in the UK. It was here that she discovered the world of illustrated books and has been hooked ever since. Since graduating with an MA in Children's Book Illustration, she has worked as a freelance illustrator of children's books for clients such as MacMillan and Burroughs Wellcome as well as many independent publishers.

She feels very privileged to be living and working in a world of books and the children who love them. When not working as a freelance illustrator, she spends her time creating her own books, writing, critiquing, and attending any event with the words: "book" or "illustration" in the title. She can often be found wandering around the East Anglia with a sketchbook or camera in search of inspiration.

If you would like to see more of her work, please visit: www.lornamurphyillustration.com.